ACCLAIM FOR SHARYN McCRUMB AND ZOMBIES OF THE GENE POOL

Please turn the page
more critical acclaim. . . .

D1007216

"Sharyn McCrumb's painstaking research of the traditional routes of the science fiction field has given this book even more depth and power than *Bimbos of the Death Sun*. Wonderfully amusing and thought-provoking, and a terrific mystery in its own right."

—A. C. CRISPIN

"McCrumb adds plenty of zing to her plot with a bevy of well-drawn, eccentric characters, witty dialogue, lots of science fiction trivia and some merciless swipes at academia and publishing."

—*The Orlando Sentinel*

"Sharyn McCrumb is definitely a star in the New Golden Age of mystery fiction."

—ELIZABETH PETERS

"A good read . . . and the conclusion is a real surprise."

—*The Denver Post*

"The cast is well-drawn, the whodunit puzzle deftly accomplished, and the writing has McCrumb's customary charm and humor."

—*Ellery Queen's Mystery Magazine*

"Highly recommended."

—*Library Journal*

"[McCrumb] handles drama and comedy with equal ease."
—*The San Diego Union*

"Sharyn McCrumb's knowledge of the world of S-F fandom is extraordinary, and never before have I read such an *affectionate* spoof of the phenomenon. The fact that it comes wrapped up in a crackerjack murder mystery is an added bonus."
—Barbara Paul

"*Zombies of the Gene Pool* shows McCrumb to be a veritable wizard with an oddball plot. . . . The novel crackles with insider S-F lore (McCrumb has a wellspring of weird trivia at her disposal) and with amusing sideswipes at academia."
—*Booklist*

"Sharyn McCrumb strikes again! *Zombies of the Gene Pool* is even better than *Bimbos of the Death Sun.*"
—DANIEL STASHTOWER

"Very bright and clever, a marvelous, well-done book."
—Marion Zimmer Bradley

"It's fun for all."
—*The Grand Rapids Press*

By Sharyn McCrumb:

The Elizabeth MacPherson Novels
SICK OF SHADOWS*
LOVELY IN HER BONES*
HIGHLAND LADDIE GONE*
PAYING THE PIPER*
THE WINDSOR KNOT*
MISSING SUSAN*
MACPHERSON'S LAMENT*
IF I'D KILLED HIM WHEN I MET HIM . . .*

IF EVER I RETURN, PRETTY PEGGY-O*
THE HANGMAN'S BEAUTIFUL DAUGHTER
SHE WALKS THESE HILLS
BIMBOS OF THE DEATH SUN
ZOMBIES OF THE GENE POOL*

Published by The Ballantine Publishing Group

ZOMBIES OF THE GENE POOL

Sharyn McCrumb

BALLANTINE BOOKS • NEW YORK

Poems by Don Johnson are reprinted with the permission of the author, from *Watauga Drawdown* by Don Johnson, Overmountain Press, Johnson City, Tennessee, 1990.
Fannish definitions from FANCYCLOPEDIA II, compiled by Richard H. Eney, 1959.
Quotes from Francis Towner Laney from *Ah, Sweet Idiocy*, Fan Amateur Press Association, 1948.

Library of Congress Catalog Card Number: 91-43889

ISBN 0-345-37914-4

This edition published by arrangement with Simon & Schuster Inc.

Manufactured in the United States of America

First Ballantine Books Edition: March 1993

10   9   8   7

To Michael Dobson,
the State of Franklin Science Fiction Society,
and Francis Towner Laney

With thanks to Don Johnson, for the
use of *Watauga Drawdown*.

Even death will not release you.

An expression of the
Los Angeles Science
Fiction Society, ca. 1949

CHAPTER 1

JAY OMEGA DECIDED to wait until the shouting
stopped before he knocked. Against his better judgment he had left the happy anarchy of the Electrical
Engineering building and ventured into the English
department to see if Marion wanted to go to dinner,
but the sounds coming from her office indicated that
Dr. Marion Farley was otherwise engaged. The typed
index card on the door announced that she had office
hours from four to five P.M., so Jay assumed that she
was in conference with a student. He had put his
ear to her office door to see if she was nearly finished and had heard the following exchange.

"This is a world literature class, not a science fiction class!"

"But—"

"And I can't believe that you actually wrote a paper
comparing Joseph Conrad to Robert Silverberg!"

"But, Dr. Farley, when I read *Heart of Darkness*,
I recognized *Downward to the Earth* almost exac—"

"And you accused Joseph Conrad of plagiarism!"

Jay Omega sighed and walked away. Marion was
going to be a while. He wondered how late their
dinner date was likely to be. Jay Omega and Marion

Farley had little in common besides the fact that they were both carbon-based life forms, but despite the differences in temperament, interests, and income, they had been a couple for two years now. The relationship began when Jay ventured into the English department with the manuscript of his first book, and Marion asked if he had a note from his adviser. He still looked young for a Ph.D., and his jeans from the tenth grade did still fit, though Marion had made him throw them away. He supposed he had changed for the better since then. Marion had once seen his high school yearbook photo and said, "You looked like a mosquito." Now he had contact lenses instead of Coke-bottle glasses, and his brown hair was cut in a longer, more flattering style. They had both blossomed after adolescence. Marion had endured high school as a fat and friendless intellectual; now she was a slender, dark-haired Ph.D. who ran in the local marathons and sparred with the women's fencing team. It was no coincidence that the poster above her desk featured *The Avengers'* Emma Peel, Marion's role model in adolescence.

Jay looked down at his khaki work pants and plaid shirt. He still didn't dress like the dapper young professors in English, but Marion had given up on him in that department. He didn't wear power ties, but he kept her decrepit car running, which more than made up for it. Jay and Marion were in a romantic holding pattern, waiting to see if they would both get tenure so that neither would have to leave the university and start over elsewhere.

Jay ventured back to the office door. She was still at it. He sighed. If things dragged on for too long, he could always go in search of a snack machine, but since most of the English professors seemed to be on a health and fitness kick, he wasn't even sure that they *had* a snack machine, and if they did, it might offer such arcane items as wheat germ and carob candy bars. Long ago he decided that the English department was about as alien as anything Robert Silverberg could come up with. Even after several years' association with one of their assistant professors, he didn't understand their tribal customs. Or their bulletin boards. Every now and then he would come in and read the notices while he was waiting for Marion, just to see if any literary culture had worn off on him. Apparently, it hadn't.

WARREN WRITES BETTER THAN ANNE.

Now what did *that* mean? Jay Omega turned to a pink-haired young woman in overalls who was pinning a Literary Lions notice over the campus newspaper clipping announcing that Professor Byron Snipes had just been published in the avant-garde (which Marion said was pronounced "mimeographed") literary magazine, *The Maggots Digest.*

Jay knew about the Literary Lions. They were a group of English instructors and other town writers who gave readings every Sunday afternoon in the New Age Café. Marion had dragged him there once when her office mate Toni Richardson was reading from her stream-of-consciousness novel about a Labrador retriever who thought it was Virginia Woolf. Every time the dog had to go into the water to retrieve a duck, there would be pages and pages of inner dialogue over whether or not it would get back out. Jay didn't understand it at all, but everyone else had told Toni that it was very experimental and definitely not accessible. (Marion said that "experimental" meant writing in the present tense, and "not accessible" meant that they didn't understand it either.)

Jay Omega's opinion was not solicited. He was the only nationally published author in town, but since he had written a science fiction novel called *Bimbos of the Death Sun*, he was not invited to read with the mineral water and tofu crowd at the New Age Café. Not even for their four-dollar beans and rice fund raisers in support of El Salvador. (Or was it *against* support in El Salvador?) Anyway, Jay didn't remember any Literary Lions called Warren or Anne. So what was that about?

"Excuse me," he said, pointing to the hand-lettered graffiti. "Could you tell me what that means?"

The pink lady glanced at the sign. "Warren Writes Better Than Anne." She nodded, with a frosty smile. "Beatty, of course. Only they spell it differently." Seeing that he still looked blank, she explained kindly, "Warren Beatty is Shirley Mac-Laine's little brother."

Before he could explain that it was Anne he had never heard of, she had walked away with her sheaf of notices, and another student was tugging at his sleeve. "Dr. Mega, I'm glad I ran into you!"

The tall red-headed guy with a Starfleet patch on his jacket looked familiar. What was that kid's name? Second row, first seat in engineering fundamentals. Jay managed a feeble grin, hoping he wasn't about to be asked for a reference.

The young man set his books on top of the covered trash can and chattered on, happily unaware of his anonymity. "When I was home on spring break, I tried to buy a copy of your book for my high school physics teacher, but our local bookstore said it wasn't on their order list."

Dr. James Owens Mega—aka science fiction author Jay Omega—heaved a mighty sigh of resignation. "Did you look under G?"

"No. Is that a new one? I wanted your first book— *Bimbos of the Death Sun.*"

"I know. It's listed under G. For *Galactic Wonders #2: Bimbos of the Death Sun.* The first part is the series title. Alien Books lists all their titles that way. The first one in the series is *Galactic Wonders #1: Betrayal at Byzantium* by Susan Shwartz." She's not happy about it either, he finished silently.

Several months earlier, when they found out about this nationwide blunder, Marion had re- marked, "This is the only book in history that re- quires a password in order to purchase it!"

The student was looking at him as if he were crazy. "Under G," he repeated carefully. "Uhh—I've taken some marketing courses, Dr. Mega, and I have to tell you, that doesn't sound like a good idea."

Jay Omega nodded sadly. "So my royalty state- ments would indicate."

It seemed to Jay Omega that he had the worst of both worlds—another reason that the English de- partment made him uneasy. The way he figured it, an author could either go for respect in the literary world—critical reviews in prestigious journals, scholarly articles on one's works, small print runs at respected university presses—or he could write popular fiction and receive fan mail and big bucks. The lurid bikini-clad girl on the cover of Jay Omega's paperback original left no doubt in the English department as to which category *his* work fell into. They assumed that he was making a fortune, and that it was easy money.

Every time Marion talked him into attending a faculty party, one of her colleagues would sidle up to him, margarita in hand, and say, "You know, maybe during spring break I'll dash off a science fiction novel. I could use the extra cash."

Apparently they didn't intend to be insulting. They all thought that he was rich and lazy. Jay suspected that if he admitted to them how hard he worked and how little he made, they would simply replace their envy with contempt, so he left well enough alone.

The professorial misconception was that genre writing was easy and high-paying, and that anyone with scholarly training could do it in a matter of hours. Occasionally one of them tried. Jay Omega had been forced to read some of these dashed-off manuscripts, and he found them to be plodding exercises in obscurity. They sounded like dissertations. Finding excuses not to give out the name of his agent or his editor was beginning to require more creativity than his latest book. He was losing patience. Sooner or later one of them was going to sneer at him once too often, and he was going to say,

"Look—if you really want a surefire scheme for cash from trash, forget genre fiction. Just write a long convoluted novel in the present tense with no quotation marks and sell it to a university press. Get your friends to write reviews of it in the *MLA Journal*, get tenure on your literary reputation, and then sit back for the rest of your life collecting a fat salary and teaching two classes a week."

Marion would kill him.

He decided that he'd better stop loitering in the halls of the English department, before one of them accosted him with a new plot summary. Perhaps he could write Marion a note asking her to meet him at his office.

"Ah, Dr. Mega! I've been meaning to speak to you."

Too late!

Jay Omega looked up, hoping that he wasn't about to be presented with another manuscript. To his relief he saw Erik Giles, empty-handed, beckoning from the door of his office. Professor Giles taught nineteenth- and early twentieth-century British literature, and as far as Jay knew, he wrote only for scholarly publications.

"I take it that Marion is busy," Giles was saying. "Why don't you come in for a cup of coffee, and you can keep an eye on her door." He raised one eyebrow. "Or at least monitor the noise level."

With a grin of considerable relief, Jay Omega hurried into Professor Giles' shabby, book-strewn office. Compared to the engineering offices, it was a Victorian parlor. (Marion once said that *his* office looked like the inside of a pinball machine.) He removed a stack of papers from the Goodwill armchair and sat down. Despite the clutter, it was a comfortable room, well suited to Giles himself. It had the same air of *old, but still serviceable*, and its genial mix of well-worn books and prints of English landscapes suggested an old-fashioned gentility indicative of an aging scholar. This, of course, was a carefully cultivated pose on the part of Erik Giles, and it served him very well. His Dickensian office, his rimless glasses, and his baggy cardigan sweaters tallied with everyone's expectations of a kindly but dull middle-aged professor of English; few people bothered to look beneath the facade.

Marion had found out the secret quite by accident, on her way to her science fiction class to lecture on the history of the genre. Four minutes late as usual, she had scurried around the corner, balancing a chin-high stack of paperbacks, and crashed into Professor Giles, who was just leaving his lit class on Kipling. The collision sent the books flying. Ever the gentleman, Erik Giles had stooped to help his colleague gather up her belongings.

"So frightfully clumsy of me," he murmured, although it had clearly been her fault.

Marion claimed all of the blame for the mishap and tottered on to her classroom. She hadn't given the incident another thought until midway through her lecture when she was discussing the writers of the early fifties. ". . . And one of the most visionary and lyrical of the new generation of S-F writers wrote as C. A. Stormcock, which, as I'm sure you've guessed, was a pseudonym. His major work was *The Golden Gain*. . . ." She began to rummage through the stack of books in search of her copy. She found that she had acquired an edition of Kipling's poems during her collision with Professor Giles. Idly, she opened the volume at a place marked with a paper-clip, half intending to save herself further embarrassment by pretending that this was the volume she sought. She looked down at a well-marked passage of "The Mine Sweepers," intrigued by a phrase in the poem.

She looked up to find thirty pairs of eyes staring at her expectantly. She resumed her search for the real book. "This landmark work, totally ignored when it was first published . . . it's here somewhere . . . illustrates the theory that . . . no, that's not it."

It wasn't there.

In the end, Marion bluffed her way through that part of her talk, dispensing with the reading of the death scene of Selig in chapter nine, but for the rest of the lecture, Dr. Farley was on automatic pilot. As she recited the particulars of genre history, her mind was analyzing the problem of the missing volume. She had taken it off the bookshelf in her office, and she remembered placing it in the stack. . . .

"It is only in recent years that S-F scholars have taken any notice of Stormcock. His paperback originals were virtually ignored by the critics of the time. C. A. Stormcock was, as I said, a pen name. Many writers—especially in science fiction—used pseudonyms in those days."

"Like Jay Omega," said an engineering major.

Marion reddened, almost losing her train of

thought. "Oh, yes. Our own Dr. James Owens Mega, of the electrical engineering department, writes as Jay Omega, which is a physics term—"

"Frequency times the square root of negative one," said the engineer.

Marion scowled. "I knew that."

"So what was Stormcock's real name?" someone called out.

"There are several theories. One is that he did not exist, and that Curtis Phillips and the notorious Pat Malone actually wrote his works in collaboration. Others think that—"

"Is this going to be on the test?" asked a serious-faced little blonde.

Marion sighed. "No," she said. "Because, after all, we really don't know who he was."

But suddenly she did.

When the chimes sounded the hour, Marion got out of the room faster than the football players. She ran down the hall and into Professor Giles' turn-of-the-century lair without bothering to knock. "Why did you take my copy of *The Golden Gain*?" she demanded.

He looked up from a stack of term papers, genial but apparently puzzled. "Did I?" he said mildly. "It must have got mixed with my own papers."

Marion almost wavered, but then she remembered. "You weren't carrying any papers when I ran into you."

He sighed. "Oh dear. Well, I'm afraid it isn't a very good book. Reverse alchemy, in fact—turning gold into lead. Must you include it?"

Marion looked stern. "May I have my copy back, please?"

With a sheepish smile, Professor Giles reached under the stack of term papers and brought out the tattered paperback.

Marion made no move to retrieve it. "May I have it autographed, please?"

He blinked in confusion. "I beg your pardon?"

Marion sat down on the arm of the easy chair. "Look," she said, holding up the volume of Kipling. "You're a Kipling scholar. God knows why, but you are. And on the frontispiece of this book, someone has written 'Stormy.' And I think I know where the name C. A. Stormcock came from. Listen to this." She turned to the page on which "The Mine Sweepers" was printed and read aloud: " 'Mines reported in the fairway,/Warn all traffic and detain./Sent up *Unity*, *Claribel*, *Assyrian*, *Stormcock* and *Golden Gain*.' "

Marion snapped the book shut with an air of triumph. "I can't imagine why no one picked up on that before."

"The Stormcock and *Golden Gain* connection?" said Giles. "Science fiction people wouldn't catch that. They don't do much out-of-field reading. Why, the great Irish fan Walt Willis had a column once called 'The Harp That Once or Twice,' and for years fans asked each other where the title came from."

Marion allowed herself to be diverted from her prey. "It's vaguely familiar. *The harp that once through Tara's halls. . .*"

"Exactly. Thomas Moore. An Irish poet. And *no one* got it!" Professor Giles smiled sadly. "Of course, this isn't literary scholarship, because neither

Willis nor Stormcock matters. It's a form of Trivial
Pursuit. All the same, it was well noted on your
part. But it does not give you the identity of the
author."

"Oh, no?" said Marion sweetly. "How about this?
The main character is Selig Stone. Selig is Giles
spelled backwards, and that comment you just
made about 'reverse alchemy' is the punchline from
the review of the novel in a fifties fanzine called
Grue. Now don't try to tell me all that is a coincidence, or you'll find yourself in *Locus* so fast it'll
make your head spin!"

He groaned. "Oh, please! Not that!"

"We thought you were dead," said Marion. "We
weren't even sure you *existed*. Why all the secrecy?"

Erik Giles smiled sadly. "I grew up."

CHAPTER 2

"I'M VERY GLAD you're here, Jay," Erik Giles was saying. "Actually, I need your help."

Jay Omega immediately looked around for a broken radio or a new-looking computer. That's what people usually meant when they said they needed his help, but he saw no evidence of electronic disasters in the English professor's office.

"Your help *and* Marion's, actually," the professor amended.

Then it definitely wasn't auto repair. Jay waited for enlightenment.

"There's a journey I need to make, and I'd like the two of you to go with me. You may have heard about my heart attack last year." He smiled at Jay's expression of concern, but signaled him not to interrupt. "No, I'm fine. I've lost a few pounds since last spring, and my blood pressure has improved somewhat. I'm not going to keel over on you. Anyway, I've received an interesting invitation, and because of my health and for other reasons, I don't particularly want to go alone. Actually, I don't want to go at *all*, but I believe I should, and I thought it was something that the two of you might be interested in."

13

Jay sighed. "Where *is* Worldcon this year?"

Professor Giles smiled. "It isn't that. And it isn't the MLA, either, which is just Worldcon hosted by Chaucer scholars." He looked intently at Jay Omega. "You *do* know who I am?"

Jay understood at once that Erik Giles was referring to his literary past as C. A. Stormcock, and since he seemed to expect an affirmative response, Jay decided to admit that he did. "Marion mentioned it to me a while back," he said.

"Yes, I thought so. Restraint is not one of Marion's virtues." Giles grinned at his colleague's unease. "And what was your reaction?"

"To the fact that you passed up fame? Well, I suppose I thought that it was a little strange. I mean, so many people seem to want to be famous writers, and science fiction is such a cult anyway, that it seemed odd for anybody who got mixed up in it in the first place to just walk away from an achievement like yours."

Professor Giles smiled sadly. "In a kingdom of the blind, the one-eyed man is king. When Marion found out who I was, she asked me the same thing, and I told her *I grew up*. It wasn't much of an explanation, but it was true. As time went on, I began to be less enchanted with my accomplishments. To give you one small example—I learned that almost any reasonably clever person can make puns. The truly intelligent person refrains from doing so."

Jay couldn't for the life of him make puns, but he decided not to argue the point. He was still wondering about the mysterious invitation, but Erik Giles had launched into a one-sided discussion of philosophy—probably a holdover from his days in science fiction.

"I am one of those unfortunate people who cannot appreciate a compliment unless I respect the person giving it," he said, with the air of someone who has given the subject much thought. "A great many people liked my book—but what else had they read? I felt hampered by their opinions and their expectations. There are a good many six-book critics in the genre."

"Six-book—?"

"People who have read six books and think that it entitles them to be critics. The sort of person who doesn't recognize a pastiche of *Lysistrata* because he's unfamiliar with the original."

Jay nodded. He had heard Marion say much the same thing, although at greater length and with considerably more venom.

"Anyhow, I got tired of being Gulliver. What I really wanted to do was to explore my potential as a writer."

"And what are you writing now?" asked Jay uneasily, thinking of the New Age Café readings. He wondered if Erik Giles was churning out slices of monotony in the present tense.

"I'm not. I discovered I couldn't do literary fiction. I'd got out of the habit of being tedious. So I said the hell with it, and now I teach undergraduate courses and do a bit of scholarly research to keep the department happy. How about you? Burned out yet?"

Jay was saved from having to reply by the appearance of Marion, who still glittered from her recent bout of intellectual combat. Her dark hair was tucked behind her ears, and her reading glasses were balanced precariously on the top of her head. Clearly she was still in office mode. "Somebody told me they'd seen you come in here," she said, scowling.

"Good afternoon," said Jay tentatively, in case she hadn't got all the rage out of her system.

Erik Giles was chuckling. "Finished your conference?"

"It is a fortunate thing that electric pencil sharpeners are too small to accommodate the heads of sophomores," Marion growled. "Well, at least I set him straight on his chronology."

"We heard," said Jay.

Marion sighed. "I know that tone of voice. You sound like someone making small talk with a hand grenade. I'm fine, really!" She managed a smile. "What have you two been up to?"

"Erik was just telling me that he wants us to go somewhere with him."

"Oh?" Marion looked interested. "And where is that?"

"To dinner," said Professor Giles quickly. "This is going to be a long story, and I feel that I owe you both a steak just for listening to it."

Marion sighed. "I wish more authors felt that way."

The Wolfe Creek Inn was an eighteenth-century farmhouse that had been converted into an elegant restaurant. When the pasture lands adjoining the university were sold off one by one for apartment complexes and gas stations, most of the large old houses were torn down as detriments to the land value, or perhaps because they clashed with the current ambience of neon and asphalt. The Wolfe family farmstead was salvaged by a resourceful couple of Peace Corps veterans, who had not managed to make much of a dent on the problems in Bolivia during their years there, but who had learned carpentry themselves, a skill infinitely more useful than their majors in political science. They figured the Wolfe house would be easier to tackle than the Bolivian rural economy, so they bought the eighteenth-century house with its graceful wraparound porches, its oak floors buried under fifties linoleum, its huge stone fireplaces, its field mouse population, and its dry rot. The house was priced at only fifty-one thousand dollars, a price roughly equal to the cost of restoring it. With loans from their long-suffering parents, the Peace Corps veterans rewired, refinished, and rehabilitated every square inch of the old mansion and turned the result into a cozy, antique-filled restaurant much favored by faculty members and visiting parents. The meals were priced at roughly the average monthly income in Bolivia. Undergrads eager to impress their dates confined their visits to Friday and Saturday nights, particularly during football season, but tonight—a Tuesday in late May—the place was nearly empty.

Giles-Party-of-Three, as the waitress called them, was tucked into a pine-paneled alcove decorated with Bob Timberlake prints in rough wood frames. They were trying to read the hand-lettered menus by the light of the candle in a red jar, which doubled as a centerpiece on the oilskin tablecloth.

"This looks like a séance," said Marion, watching their shadows flicker against the pine wall.

"It is," said Erik Giles. "I'm about to raise a number of ghosts."

He waited until the waitress had taken their order and had gone to fetch the drinks before he began. "You want to know where it is that I have to go, but in order to explain that I'll have to backtrack." He began to trace patterns on the tablecloth with his knife. "Do you know much about science fiction fandom?"

"I read science fiction," said Jay. "Does that count?"

"No," said Marion. "Erik means the organized subculture that grew up around the genre. It began in New York in the thirties when the people who had been writing to the letters columns of the pulp science fiction magazines began writing to each other instead. Then clubs sprang up, and people began to publish amateur fanzines, reviewing books and arguing about topics of science or technology. By the fifties, it had become an end in itself."

Professor Giles smiled. "By then, there were people who scarcely bothered to read the genre, because they were so busy with the social aspects of fandom."

"I missed all that," said Jay. "I was into crystal radio sets as a kid, and after that computers. So you two were fans?"

Marion blushed. "If you grow up as a social misfit in a small town, it can be a very attractive option. I was smart when girls were supposed to be bubble-brains, and I wasn't very pretty in high school, which is a real burden for the teenage ego. Fandom is good about accepting people for being kind and clever, without caring about age, sex, race, or appearance."

Erik Giles looked thoughtful. "Why was I in fandom? I wanted to be a writer, I guess, and these people encouraged me. It's easy to get 'published' in fanzines. Of course, later I realized—" He shook his head sadly. "Well, it doesn't matter. I was explaining the reunion, wasn't I? Have you ever heard of the Lanthanides?"

"Sure," said Jay, reaching for a bread stick. "The lanthanide series is a group of fourteen elements on the periodic chart, consisting of lanthanum, cerium, samarium—"

"Hush! We're discussing literature, not chemistry!" said Marion. "I think that Erik is referring to a group of writers back in the Golden Age of Science Fiction."

Erik smiled. "I'd put the Golden Age a little farther back than that group of chowderheads. The early forties, maybe. Whereas, the Lanthanides began publishing in—"

"1957?" asked Jay Omega.

"About then," Giles agreed.

Marion stared at him. "How did you know, Jay? You never read that stuff!"

Erik Giles laughed. " 'What do they know of literature who only literature know?' " he said, misquoting his beloved Kipling. "Jay guessed correctly the date of the Lanthanides' fiction debut because he was right about the origin of the term. The group's name was chosen from a chemistry book, and the lanthanide series begins with element number 57, which is the year the members thought they'd all be published authors." He sighed. "It took a bit longer than that, of course, even for the luckiest members, and some of them never even got published."

"Pretty good name for a science fiction group, though," said Jay with a glint of mischief in his eyes. "The lanthanides are the rare-earth series of elements."

The older man nodded. "Yes, that was the real reason we chose it. We thought rare earth described our visions rather well. And, of course, the name itself—Lanthanides—is from the Greek *lanthanein*, meaning to be concealed, which is perfect for a secret society of adolescent crackpots."

"Now, wait a minute, Erik. Those writers were—" Marion gasped. *"We?"*

He smiled modestly. "Yes, I was a member of the Lanthanides. Of course, back in 1954 we were just a bunch of redneck beatniks in Wall Hollow, Tennessee."

"Tennessee?" echoed Marion. "Wasn't Brendan Surn one of the Lanthanides? I thought he was from Pittsburgh."

"He was. And Curtis was from Baltimore, Mistral was a Brooklynite, and Peter Deddingfield and I grew up in Richmond. But the year that the group was formed, most of us were in our early twenties, and our job prospects were middling. It was 1954. We didn't want to become the men in the gray flannel suits, and nothing else was paying too well. Anyway, we weren't ready to settle down.

"Dale Dugger and George Woodard were just back from Korea and Fort Dix, New Jersey, respectively. A couple of us were just out of college—with or without degrees—and a few were tired of the jobs they did have. We all knew each other the way science fiction fans do—through correspondence and a mimeographed fanzine—and we decided to get together. Nobody had anything better to do."

Marion frowned. "This is not an era I've done much reading about. It's the beginning of Sixth Fandom according to S-F fannish history. I'm familiar with Walt Willis and the *Wheels of IF* . . . Lee Hoffman and *Quandry*. . . . Wasn't there a fanzine associated with the group?"

"*Alluvial.* George Woodard still publishes it. Or at least something called that. Of course, none of the rest of us have contributed to it in years."

"I never knew Stormcock was a member of the Lanthanides."

Erik Giles smiled modestly. "I wrote *The Golden Gain* while I was there." His fingers trembled a bit on the hilt of the table knife, and he suddenly looked old.

"So you formed a commune?" Jay prompted.

"Slanshack!" murmured Marion, correcting him.

"Back then, with Joseph McCarthy's witch hunters hiding under every bed, I don't think we would have called it a commune, but by your generation's standards I guess it was. We called it the Fan Farm. Actually, Dale Dugger's daddy had died while Dale was overseas, leaving him a hardscrabble farm in the east Tennessee hills, and we decided that life didn't get any cheaper than that, so we all packed our belongings and typewriters, and descended on Dugger's farm. We planned to live on beans and hot dogs while we each wrote the science fiction equivalent of the Great American Novel, and then we figured we'd all drive away in Cadillacs and live on steaks for the rest of our lives." He smiled, remembering their youthful naïveté.

The waitress appeared just then, balancing three plate-sized skillets on a tray. "I have two prime ribs and a broiled-flounder-no-butter."

"The fish is mine," said Erik Giles. "Doctor's orders."

Marion attended to her dinner for a few minutes, but her thoughtful expression indicated that she was more interested in the conversation than the food. "So you actually lived with Surn and Deddingfield in—what did you say the name of the place was?"

"Wall Hollow, Tennessee. That's where the post office was, anyhow. Dugger's Farm was seven miles up a hollow. It was beautiful country. Green-forested mountains that looked like haze against the sky."

The Green Hills of Earth, murmured Marion.

"No," said Giles, catching the reference. "He wasn't there. I didn't meet him until the late sixties."

"Well, your crowd didn't do too badly," said Marion, thinking it over. "Maybe you didn't leave the farm in Cadillacs, but you certainly produced some giants in the field of science fiction."

"Peter Deddingfield," nodded Jay. "Even *I've* heard of him. I loved the *Time Traveler Trilogy*."

"He writes in a very *literary* style," said Marion, offering her highest praise. "Critics have compared him to Herman Melville."

"Well, I like him anyway," said Jay.

Marion frowned. "And Brendan Surn is the greatest theorist in the genre. I think he's required reading in NASA. I always think that he looks like a snow lion with that white mane of hair and his white beard. Who else was in the group?"

"That you would have heard of? Pat Malone, of course."

"He's a *legend*. What was he really like?"

"You mustn't rely on my judgment," said Erik Giles. "I didn't know at the time which of my friends to be impressed by."

Jay Omega, who had no memory for authors' names and was thus at a dead loss at Trivial Pursuit, was trying to place Pat Malone. "Should I have heard of him?"

"Yes!" said Marion. "He wrote *River of Neptune*, which wasn't a classic or anything, but it was a very promising work for a young writer, but then Pat Malone did another book that will be remembered forever in fandom—*The Last Fandango*. It wasn't officially published—just mimeographed and distributed by FAPA, the Fantasy Amateur Press Association—but it was so caustic and critical of certain fans that it became an underground classic. He revealed their sexual preferences, their lapses in hygiene, and their petty machinations in

fan politics. I hear that it was really hot stuff in
its day."

Erik Giles nodded. "It was an unpleasant duty
that Pat positively reveled in doing. The glee in his
tone is at times unmistakable."

"I imagine that publication cost him a few
friends," said Jay. "I have friends in engineering
who dream of doing that on a faculty level, but they
dare not."

"I would strongly discourage it," said Marion,
with a repressive glare suggesting that she suspected *which* engineer harbored such a fantasy.
"Because a professor who did that would have to
live with the consequences, while Pat Malone did
not. He simply dropped out of sight. Apparently he
became very embittered with science fiction because
of his disillusionment with all his old associates and
he gafiated."

Jay stared. "I beg your pardon?" He was picturing
Japanese rituals of disembowelment.

Marion blushed at having been caught speaking
fanslang. "GAFIA. It's an acronym for getting away
from it all. It means dropping out of the world of science fiction."

"And lived happily ever after?"

"Apparently not. My source materials say that he
died in mysterious circumstances. The word is that
he was found dead on a mountaintop in Mississippi."

"There *are* no mountaintops in Mississippi," Jay
pointed out.

Erik Giles laughed. "A grasp of material facts has
never been a strong point in fandom. That was the

story that went around the grapevine back then, and I never heard otherwise."

"Those are all the Lanthanides I know about," said Marion. "I confess I've never heard of Dale Dugger or George— What was his name?"

"Woodard. He's still around. He never published much of anything, but he lives in Libertytown, Maryland, now; and, as I told you, he puts out a fanzine called *Alluvial*. That and his incessant correspondence seem to take most of his energy. Aside from that, he teaches algebra."

"And Dale Dugger?"

A spasm of pain crossed Erik Giles' face. "He died some years ago. He became an alcoholic, and finally at the end, a street person. I heard about it later. Wish there was something I could have done."

"There aren't many of you left then," said Marion, doing a mental tally.

"No. There's Surn, but he's quite feeble now, I hear. And Woodard. Angela Arbroath. Jim and Barbara Conyers, and Ruben Mistral."

"Mistral," murmured Jay. "That name sounds familiar. He's a screenwriter, isn't he?"

"Yes. When I knew him his name was Reuben J. Bundschaft. We called him Bunzie. He's probably got more money than Surn and Deddingfield by now, with all those movie deals. Still, I hear he's coming to this little show."

"What show is that?"

Erik Giles sighed. "The Lanthanides are having a reunion."

Noticing the lack of enthusiasm in his announcement, Marion said gently, "Don't you want to go?"

"There's more to it than that. I have to tell you *why* there's a reunion, and why we didn't have it in 1984 like we'd planned."

"Why didn't you?"

"Because Wall Hollow, Tennessee, is at the bottom of a lake."

It was late. After cheesecake and several cups of coffee, the three professors had finally called it a night and said their good-byes on the porch of the Wolfe Creek Inn. Jay was driving Marion home. She leaned back in the passenger seat of Jay's temporarily functional MG, clutching her headscarf against the wind that whipped through a crack between the canvas roof and the windscreen. "I was just thinking about Erik Giles and his extraordinary reunion," she called above the roar of the wind and the 1600 engine.

"Quite a story!" Jay agreed.

"After he told us about it, I remembered hearing bits of it before. The underwater slanshack. It's a legend in science fiction circles, of course. But before my time," she added hastily.

"I can see why it's a legend," said Jay. "It's the Atlantis of fandom."

"And they held their own substitute convention! Wouldn't that be a wonderful story to write for a volume of fan history?" mused Marion, whose brain was never quite out of gear.

"Surely someone has already written that tale," said Jay.

"Knowing the Lanthanides, they probably fictionalized it. I'll bet that if we read all of Deddingfield, all of Surn, all of Mistral, and so on, *somewhere* we'd find the story of the unfinished journey and the time capsule. Writers always cannibalize their own lives for fiction."

"Oh, so you recognized yourself as the green lizard woman in *Bimbos*?"

Marion made a face at him and went back to contemplating the moon. "I can just see them in 1954, can't you? A bunch of postadolescents with plenty of idealism and ambition, but no money or common sense. And because the Twelfth Worldcon is being held in San Francisco, six of them decide to pile into a disintegrating Studebaker and off they go!"

Jay Omega shrugged. "Why not? Gas was about eighteen cents a gallon then."

"But they were still broke. How much cash did he say they took with them? Twenty-five bucks? For a cross-country trip!"

"I guess it wasn't much money even for that era, because Giles said that when the car broke down in Seymour, Indiana, they couldn't afford to get it fixed. Apparently mechanics were expensive even then."

"Thank goodness it was only a radiator leak, so that they were able to limp back to the farm. I can't imagine Brendan Surn having to hitchhike."

"They must have been pretty game, though," said Jay. "If I had been unable to make a trip I'd had my heart set on, I don't think I'd have taken it as well as they did."

"No, you'd sulk for days. But, then, why should they have cared about missing that convention? As far as future generations are concerned, the great literary minds of the era were all in Wall Hollow, Tennessee, that weekend. Except for Friday night when they went to Elizabethton to see the movie. Wherever *they* were, there was science fiction." Marion sighed. "That's the con I would like to have attended: all the great minds of the genre in an old farmhouse miles from anywhere, swapping story ideas."

"It should be easy to arrange. Erik Giles told us what they did that weekend. So we rent a copy of *War of the Worlds*, buy a couple of cases of beer—"

"It wouldn't be the same. I'd like to know what Peter Deddingfield said to Pat Malone about the movie. I'd like to have heard them talk about their work!"

"Well, at least you may have a chance to see what they were writing at the time. If they can find the pickle jar," said Jay. "To me that is the most amazing part of all. An anthology of unpublished works by the greatest minds in science fiction, and it has yet to be recovered. It must be worth a fortune."

"I expect so. When Giles said that all the Lanthanides were coming back to this reunion, I realized that there must be quite a lot of money in it somewhere. Sentiment seldom guarantees perfect attendance, but money usually does."

"I don't know, Marion. Maybe—and this is far-fetched—this reunion could be helpful to my career as an S-F writer, but you don't stand to gain anything by going, and it isn't just out of kindness to Erik Giles that you're going either. You wouldn't miss it."

Marion sighed. "But I, my dear, am a recovering fan."

Erik Giles studied his reflection in the bathroom mirror. There was a colorless look to his lined face, as if he were gradually fading to black and white. Even his eyes were gray. He glanced at the assortment of pills on the rim of the basin and wondered if he ought to go back to his doctor for a new prescription. How many formulas are there to stave off death? Can you switch from one nostrum to another and stay one jump ahead of it?

Not forever.

His mouth looked thin and sunken, and the muscles in his neck stood out like cords. Worse than any monster in Curtis Phillips' horror stories, he thought. This specter of death was much more invincible than the puny demons of *Weird Tales*. No magic words or pentagrams would drive it away. He must live with that mirrored reminder of his own mortality for whatever time he had left. He didn't think it would be long. The doctor tended to address him in patient, gentle tones that were more terrifying than any rudeness.

Was that why he wanted to see them all again? A moment's consideration told him that he did not particularly want to renew the acquaintance with his old companions, but at least the immediacy of his fate would ensure that the encounter would be mercifully brief. And he was curious after all these years to see how they had turned out. And what they looked like now. How much youth can you buy with Hollywood money? Perhaps they would still be

fit and youthful looking. After all, he was just past
sixty. He should have quit smoking years ago. The
heart condition had devastated his health. Was he
the only one who was old? Then he remembered
that some of the Lanthanides hadn't even made it to
sixty. Giles supposed that he could consider himself
lucky that cancer or heart disease hadn't carried
him off sooner. But he didn't feel fortunate. Not
compared to the boys of summer out there in the
Land of the Lotus Eaters. He suddenly realized that
he was picturing them as men in their early twenties. Except for Brendan Surn. His white-maned
features had become so famous that everybody pictured him as he looked in that one godlike publicity
shot, clutching his malacca cane and staring out
with what seemed to be infinite wisdom and pity.

Funny . . . In his mind, the others had not aged at
all. He always imagined them as they had been
thirty-five years before. He had to admit that most
of them hadn't looked young even then. Dugger was
pudgy and bespectacled; Phillips' hairline was beginning to recede; and Woodard had looked middle-
aged since puberty. The Lanthanides had never
been prize physical specimens, but he supposed that
their interest in science fiction may have stemmed
in part from that. Shunned by their classmates for
being "eggheads," they retreated into a world of
books and pulp magazines. They found their peers
in the magazines' letters columns, and formed
friendships by mail.

He could see them now, owlish young men in
jeans and white T-shirts, loading up that old '47
Studebaker with cans of pork and beans and moon

pies. It was a hot morning in mid-August, and the sky blazed blue and cloudless above the encircling mountains of Wall Hollow. The house was a weathered one-story structure nestled in a grove of oaks, in an acre of scrub grass and lilac bushes fenced in from the surrounding pasture land. No other human habitation was visible from the farm; it might have been an outpost on a genesis planet.

The car was parked in the patch of red dust by the front porch, and the six departing members of the group were standing on the porch bickering about what to take along. George Woodard wanted to take two boxes of books to be autographed and a carton full of copies of *Alluvial* to give away to prospective contributors. Dugger insisted on packing food instead. While the debate raged on, Jim Conyers opened the Studebaker's trunk and began to hoist boxes into it, without a word to the quarrelers. Conyers wasn't even going on the expedition—he had opted to stay behind with Curtis Phillips to feed the three cows and fourteen chickens—but he was the only member of the group who could do anything without analyzing it for two hours beforehand. What ever happened to Jim?

Bunzie was going to drive. The pilgrimage to the San Francisco science fiction convention had been his idea to begin with. Even then—years before he became the celebrated screenwriter Ruben Mistral—Bunzie had been fascinated by California.

The others were less enthusiastic.

"San Francisco?" said George Woodard with his customary worried frown. "Isn't that where they had the earthquake fifty years ago?"

"I don't care if they're having regular afternoon tidal waves!" yelled Bunzie. "They're hosting the Worldcon! Everybody in the world will be there! Slan Francisco!"

Since this was the tenth time Bunzie had made that particular joke, no one bothered to laugh. Finally Woodard called out, "Fans are slans!" but it was more out of politeness than conviction. The phrase would be chanted often in the days to come. Slan: a type of superior being described in the 1940 novel by A. E. Van Vogt. The Lanthanides had almost believed it in those days. They thought that they were the superbeings who had evolved one step beyond the mundanes of the planet. They would be the titans of the next century (and maybe the one after that; they all agreed that aging ought to be curable).

Erik Giles sighed wearily, remembering the mole-faced Dugger, the pedantic pettiness of Woodard, and the '54 version of himself: a bantam intellectual full of youthful arrogance. Slans, indeed. Because they understood the in-jokes in the magazines; because they knew who had written which pulp novella; because they were clever—too clever to really work hard at anything (low threshold of boredom) but endlessly capable of memorizing the facts that interested them. (What year did Asimov first publish? Who was the cover artist for the December 1947 issue of *Astounding*?) Might as well call a ghetto kid a genius because he knew the batting averages of every one of the Dodgers. So the Slan/Fans wrote to each other, and argued with each other, and created endless feuds by gossiping about absent friends, secure in the knowledge of their slandom, and all the while, the world trickled right on past them. Now Giles could look back and see that *they* didn't break the sound barrier; *they* didn't walk on the moon; *they* didn't invent the transistor. The mundanes did that . . . while *they* were busy arguing over the ethical considerations of time travel, or writing exhaustive accounts of the last science fiction convention they attended.

It wasn't fair, though, to filter the memory of that summer through the glare of his later understanding. They had been so innocently pleased with themselves back then, and so sure that merit was the only determinant of success. They might as well have believed in fairy godmothers.

He smiled ruefully. They had certainly believed that Dugger's dilapidated green Studebaker, the Tin Lizard, would make it across country. Fortunately it had died in Indiana instead of stranding them in the desert farther west.

It had been a glorious beginning, though. They set off from Wall Hollow for a three-hundred-mile straight shot to Nashville before heading north on Highway 31, which went through Kentucky on its way to Indianapolis. They had got a late start because most of them were night people anyway, so the first day's drive only got them as far as south Kentucky, just past Bowling Green. They spent the first night camping near Mammoth Cave, swapping stories about John Carter, Edgar Rice Burroughs' Virginia gentleman who was chased into a cave by Apaches and ended up on Mars. As they sat around

their campfire, Dale Dugger told them a true story
about the Kentucky caver Floyd Collins, who was
trapped in the Mammoth cave system twenty years
back and died of exposure while rescuers bickered
about the best way to rescue him. "Who does that
remind you of?" said Pat Malone.

The others ignored his comment, preferring to discuss the existence of deros, and debating whether
they ought to go looking for them in Mammoth Cave.

"What are deros?" George Woodard wanted to
know. He had got so caught up in his fan correspondence and in *Alluvial* that he had very little time
anymore for reading science fiction.

"Didn't you read that stuff in *Amazing*?" asked
Surn. "About ten years ago, Richard Shaver published a short story called 'I Remember Lemuria.'
Shaver claimed that a race of insane beings lived
beneath the surface of the earth."

"Deros," said Bunzie. "That's short for disente-
grant energy robot. Someone whose mind has been
destroyed by the Dis rays given off by the sun.
Wouldn't that make a great movie?"

"It would," Surn agreed. "But Shaver claimed
that it was all true."

Bunzie shrugged. "Curtis believes it, too. He told
me so."

The conversation had ended there.

The next morning the Stalwart Six, as they
called themselves, climbed back into the car and
headed north toward the Indiana border. The direct
route from east Tennessee to California would not
have led through Indiana, but Surn, the navigator,
decided that since it was August and since Dugger's

car was decrepit, they had better avoid the southern desert country. Besides, like most fans they had a nationwide network of friends and practically no cash, so the logical route would be the one that led from one fan hostel to another. Another bonus of the expedition was the chance to see famous fan landmarks along the way. Before they reached the second night's stopover with an unsuspecting fan host in Bloomington (showers optional, but highly encouraged), they wanted to drive through New Castle, Indiana, which was famous for being home to one of fandom's famous eccentrics, Claude Degler. Degler had formed a newsletter staffed by a whole society of fellow enthusiasts, who, upon investigation, proved not to exist. People still talked about Degler and his grape jelly—his only form of sustenance when traveling. He mixed it with water, an economy that provoked sneers even among the impoverished denizens of fandom. Degler didn't live in New Castle anymore, but that didn't matter. The traveling Lanthanides wouldn't have wanted to stay with him anyway. They just wanted to look at where he lived, and maybe ask a few townspeople for anecdotes about Degler so that they could report their findings to the rest of fandom at the convention.

Bunzie drove at whatever speed he felt like, and Brendan Surn played navigator, while Dale Dugger read the Burma-Shave signs aloud and made comments on the landscape in general. He kept trying to convince the others that there was more than one kind of cow, but was hooted into silence. In the back seat, Erik was crammed between Woodard and Pat

Malone, who were keeping a running travel diary of their great adventure for publication in the next issue of *Alluvial*.

They sang "Shrimp Boats" for hours on end, trying various harmonies, and they took turns reading aloud from Poul Anderson's latest book, *Brainwave*, amid Dugger's bitter complaints that Ballantine Books had the nerve to charge thirty-five cents for it instead of the usual quarter.

The trip ended in a puff of smoke outside Seymour, Indiana. The Stalwart Six stood at a safe distance from the Tin Lizard's radiator, watching their dreams of Worldcon evaporate in clouds of steam.

"Well," said Woodard at last. "It could have been worse. At least we didn't hit a train."

"Can we fix it?" asked Bunzie, close to tears. He clutched his Esso road map as if it were a talisman.

"Can't afford a new radiator," Dale Dugger told him. "That would cost at least twenty bucks. We can stop every half hour or so and fill this one up as it leaks. That will get us home. But the Lizard would never make it across the prairie like that. It's too far between water holes."

"We have to turn back," Brendan Surn announced, and nobody argued. With a last look westward, they climbed back in the car, and for a full half hour no one's voice dispelled the gloom.

The ailing Tin Lizard headed for home, with her six Gunga Dins running for water at every streambed. By the time they reached Nashville, their spirits had revived, and Giles and Surn had immortalized the journey in a parody of Kipling's poem:

You may talk o' Blog and Bheer
When your fellow fen are near,
But Tin Lizard doesn't give a damn for boozing;
Studebaker's bastard daughter
Runs on Indiana water,
And about six quarts an hour she was losing.

It went on from there, with dwindling coherence and many forced rhymes, for some fourteen verses. Long before the composition was complete, Malone had retreated into the pages of *Brainwave*, and he kept ordering the revelers to shut up so that he could read.

They reached home just after nine, trailing ribbons of steam in the lingering twilight of a summer evening. The dark mountains closed behind them, walling out California and all the rest of the inaccessible world. Fireflies flashed like tiny meteors among the clumps of tiger lilies, and from the cow pond, the rhythmic chirrup of frogs welcomed the travelers home.

"How ya gonna keep 'em down on the farm?" said Bunzie. As he climbed out of the Tin Lizard, he kicked a tire in disgust. "So much for the goddamned Worldcon."

"What do we do now?" asked George Woodard.

Pat Malone, who was helping to unload the trunk, looked thoughtfully at the box of supplies he was holding. "We've got the makings for a hell of a party."

"We could have our own convention," said Bunzie. "We have everything but the Worldcon guest of honor. John W. Campbell Jr.—hell, I'll be him!"

"We have no femmefans," Pat Malone pointed out. "Jazzy is at the con, and Earlene has to work Saturdays."

"We can call Angela Arbroath. She couldn't make it to 'Frisco, but I'll bet she could drive up from Mississippi. Maybe she could bring a girlfriend."

"We still have most of our travel money," said Brendan Surn. He was tall and lean in those days, with a hawklike face that seldom smiled. He was smiling now. "Twenty-two dollars will buy a hell of a lot of beer."

Dale Dugger took a running leap at the pasture fence and disappeared into the darkness.

"Where are you going?" Woodard called after him.

"To get some more water for Tin Lizard's radiator!" Dugger yelled back. "The closest beer joint is eight miles up the road!"

Professor Erik Giles closed his bedroom window, shutting out the night air and the sound of chirruping frogs. He didn't want to think about the Lanthanides anymore. The years in Wall Hollow had been enjoyable but useless blocks of time out of his life. Not long after the Worldcon expedition, they had gone their separate ways. Shortly after the dissolution of the group, the Tennessee Valley Authority had condemned the entire valley, paying its residents nominal value for their land. Then, in order to keep the Watauga River from flooding farther downstream, the TVA built a dam, creating a vast artificial lake in the sprawling valley. He had never been back to see it. There had been a letter from Dugger at the time it happened, but he had waited too long to answer it, and his reply came back marked "No forwarding address." Dugger was gone by then, drinking up his settlement money in the honky-tonks of Nashville, giving up fandom for different and more dangerous obsessions. Giles wondered if the government's seizure of the Dugger land had caused Dale's downward slide into alcoholism and poverty. It was too late now for Dale Dugger, but for the rest of them, there was a chance to get together again and to recapture at least some of the past. In his last letter, Dugger had written: "I didn't dig up the time capsule. I got no future to take it to."

*For three months gravity feeds the main sluice
pulled nightly at the dam. The reservoir
drains. Each afternoon he stops on the bluff
to watch the valley fill with air, light
wrapping the fine branches of trees rising
from the surface full-grown but leafless, though
no wind has blown for thirty-seven years.*

—DON JOHNSON
Watauga Drawdown

CHAPTER 3

THEY MIGHT AS well be exhuming a corpse.

Jim Conyers stood on at the edge of the grass line—the spot where he usually fished—and stared at the dead landscape stretching out below. Where once the opaque green water of Breedlove Lake lapped at the hillside, there was now red mud, a no man's land of bare trees and asphalt roads leading back into the mire. This patch of grass used to be the edge of the lake, but now if Conyers wanted to he could walk farther down, into the valley of . . . *the shadow of death* . . . Wall Hollow, into the remnants of the drowned village. He could revisit the farm and the other places he remembered from long ago. If he would just go down, he could go back.

He stood as still as the black trees that had appeared from beneath the receding waters of the man-made lake. Conyers could imagine the body of a drowned swimmer caught by the hair in the skeletal branches of those trees, like some modern

40

Absalom condemned for his trespasses. He did not want to go back.

In early May, the Tennessee Valley Authority had decided that after nearly four decades under water the foundation of the Gene C. Breedlove Dam needed inspection, and the only way to examine the structure and to effect any necessary repairs would be to create a drawdown. They were going to drain the lake.

A drawdown was a slow process, a matter of opening the sluices to let the lake water bleed into the Watauga River, so that gradually, over a period of three months, the green shroud would diminish, exposing the valley for the first time in thirty-five years. There wasn't going to be any big ceremony, though, to mark the event. Even people who never got over losing their homes in Wall Hollow didn't feel called upon to celebrate its temporary resurrection. Everyone seemed to feel a little embarrassed at the prospect of having to look at the decayed remains and then having to say good-bye again. The drawdown was not a permanent reprieve, merely an incident in a bureaucratic summer. For approximately three weeks the valley would have a horizon of sun and sky instead of mud clouds in a sheet of green water. And then the floodgates would close again, and the water would come stealing back.

All summer long the people came quietly, in groups of twos or threes, to stare at the ebbing lake, straining for a glimpse of the ruins. Jim Conyers always went alone. A couple of afternoons a week he would leave Barbara to mind the shop, and he would drive the fifteen miles or so from Elizabethton to his fishing spot to watch the progress of the drawdown. It shamed him to come, though. He felt like a man at a peepshow, or, worse, like a spectator at the scene of an accident.

In one more week, the drawdown would be complete, and what was left of Wall Hollow would be visible to all comers. Perhaps by then he would be so busy with the reunion that he would not mind about the lake anymore. He tried to imagine meeting the guys again, but no clear image would form in his mind. He was somebody else now, and that somebody didn't have much in common with the Hollywood types like Mistral, or with Woodard, who had just turned eighteen for the forty-fifth time.

Jim Conyers reckoned that he had never been one of them, really. He was just Dugger's buddy from home. He and Dale had gone to high school together, and they were probably kin somewhere on their mothers' sides of the family, if you went to the trouble to trace all the Millers and the Byrds in that end of the county. They had never bothered. Everybody in east Tennessee had a passel of cousins; friends were even more special. He and Dale had pooled their dimes to send away for copies of *Astounding Stories* and the other magazines that were the staples of adolescent reading back then. They'd swapped tattered Zane Grey novels for dog-eared copies of H. Rider Haggard, and they'd sat side by side in the dark watching Flash Gordon battle the moon men. But Dale had been the one who took everything a step further.

When the army sent them their separate ways,

their approaches to the hobby began to change. While Jim went on reading Damon Knight and Jack Finney in blissful solitude, Dale began to answer the "Pen Friends" ads in the science fiction magazines, and he became involved in all the fan publications. All this was detailed in Dale's carefully typed letters to him, but Jim, who was stationed in Korea, was too caught up in events there to notice when Dale's hobby turned into a way of life. When they got home to Wall Hollow, fandom didn't particularly interest Jim, but he was glad to see Dale again, and it seemed as good a pastime as anything else in east Tennessee, so he put up with it.

Maybe it would have been different if he had moved away. As it was, he enrolled in Milligan College on the GI bill, and took a job at the Esso station in Wall Hollow to cover his other expenses. In order to save money on rent, Jim moved in with Dugger and the collection of fan friends he had accumulated on the Fan Farm. The new guys were intelligent—certainly more interesting to converse with than anyone down at the gas station—and although he found them a bit silly at times, they were good people who shared his interests. He was the only practical one of the bunch, though. Take the great expedition to San Francisco, for example. The Lanthanides had talked about going to Worldcon for months. They had written to their entire network of pen friends announcing the journey, but not one of them had saved a penny toward expenses for the trip. In the end, they had borrowed five dollars from him—his gas station paycheck—so that they could go.

He remembered the bustle of activity as they

prepared to leave . . . *on that bright and cloudless morning*. That phrase from the old hymn had fit both the morning and the mood of the Lanthanides on the day of their departure. "When the Roll Is Called Up Yonder I'll Be There." Dugger had been singing it all morning, but he was probably referring to the Golden Gate of San Francisco rather than to the Pearly Gates of Heaven. They reminded him of pilgrims headed for Mecca in their mixture of ecstasy and zeal.

But for all their enthusiasm, they were very inefficient pilgrims. They announced that they were going to leave at seven, but it was well past ten before they even got around to loading the car. In the end, Jim had to load it for them, because they had no more idea of utilizing space than a bluejay. Then, when he'd offered to check over the car for them, Bunzie had protested that they were in a hurry, and off they went, promising him postcards and autographed paperbacks upon their return.

He smiled at the memory of their return the next night. He and Curtis had been sitting on the dark front porch, smoking Camels and watching the lightning bugs flash in the fields, when they heard the sound of an engine and a discordant version of "Shrimp Boats" carried on the wind from the direction of the highway. A few minutes later, a gleam of headlights along the gravel drive signaled the return of the Lanthanides. He had expected them to be despondent or enraged over the ruin of their plans, but they were all in good spirits, already bubbling with an alternate scheme. He would always remember the courage and good humor they had showed in the face of disaster.

Without a word of regret for their ill-fated journey, the Lanthanides had plunged into their preparations for their own convention. Erik, who fancied himself a ladies' man, got on the phone and persuaded femmefan Angela Arbroath to borrow her mother's car for the weekend and drive up to join the festivities; Dugger had gone off to spend their travel money for beer and party snacks; and Surn, as usual the serious one, had proposed that they commemorate the event with a time capsule.

"A time capsule?" snorted Deddingfield. "In Wall Hollow, Tennessee?"

"Sure," said Woodard, eager to ingratiate himself with Surn. "When the Russians bomb Washington, the Smoky Mountains will protect us from the clouds of radiation. It's one of the logical places for civilization to be reestablished."

If Dugger had been there, he would have pointed out that the prime target of nuclear attack, Oak Ridge, lay just to the west of them. Jim said nothing; bickering was his least favorite of the Lanthanides' attributes. Besides, since they were stranded on the farm with a crippled car, there seemed no point in debating where to place a time capsule. It seemed to him to be a fine and solemn gesture. Leave logic out of it.

The others spent an hour discussing the properties that a time capsule should have, with Dugger, who had returned by this time with "refreshments," arguing that what they really needed was a deactivated torpedo. That being pronounced generally unavailable, they were about to agree on using an old carpetbag that had belonged to Dugger's grandmother. At that point, Jim decided that it was time to put logic back into the discussion.

"You need something waterproof," he said. "There's a lot of groundwater here in the valley, especially in the spring. What if we got another flood like the one they had in 1903?"

Surn agreed with him. "We need something airtight and waterproof. Preferably something that won't rust, too. Remember that a lot of what we're putting into the time capsule is paper. You want your short story to be readable in 1984, don't you?"

The others nodded. "How about a milk can?" asked Dugger.

The suggestion was thoroughly discussed but finally vetoed on the grounds that milk cans might be susceptible to rust. By then they had reached the two-hour mark in the discussion, always a danger point in Lanthanide planning sessions, as it was the time at which things either dissolved into a shouting match or were postponed indefinitely for lack of sustained interest. To keep the previous two hours from having been a total waste, Jim Conyers spoke up. "How about a pickle jar?"

"Too small," said Deddingfield. "It wouldn't even hold *one* story."

"Not the pickle jar in the refrigerator," Jim explained patiently. "I mean one of those ten-gallon jobs that they keep on the counter at McInturf's store. It's made of glass so it won't rust, and it's watertight, and it's big enough to hold just about anything you'd care to save."

"We don't have a ten-gallon pickle jar, though," said Woodard.

"True, but I was in McInturf's this morning, and there were only five or six pickles left in the jar. I say we buy whatever ones are left and offer Xenia McInturf a dime for the jar. All in favor?"

The motion carried, after Bunzie added a rider that the pickle jar expedition be extended to include a trip to Elizabethton to see *War of the Worlds* at the Bonnie Kate Theatre. After that, another two-hour discussion began over what was to be put into the time capsule, but Jim went to bed and left them wrangling. Knowing the Lanthanides, he was sure that they wouldn't actually get around to burying the time capsule for a couple of weeks, and that whatever went in would depend upon their moods on the day of the burial. He had been right on both counts.

For another ten days they had worked on their short stories for the time capsule, and Bunzie had written to John W. Campbell Jr., asking him for "a letter to the future" to be included. When the reply came a few days later, it was placed unopened in the pickle jar along with the *War of the Worlds* poster that Pat Malone had swiped from the theatre in Elizabethton and the rest of the Lanthanides' treasures.

The burial ceremony took place at sunset one Tuesday evening. The Lanthanides had marched up the hill behind the house to a spot chosen by Jim and Dale Dugger, and pronounced by them "easy to locate again." It was midway between the stone fence and an old sycamore tree that grew about ten feet south of the fence line. After the first ceremonial spadeful of earth had been dug by each of the Lanthanides, accompanied by speeches in varying degrees of pomposity, Jim and Dale took turns digging the three-foot hole. After that, the pickle jar/time capsule was wrapped in a burlap feed sack and buried, while the group sang "Off We Go into the Wild Blue Yonder," referring not to the Air Force but to the future of space travel. Jim Conyers' last memory of them all together was on that September day, standing in the shade of the sycamore before a tiny mound of freshly turned clay, gazing skyward and singing.

That had been the last perfect day, and when he felt twinges of nostalgia it was always that scene that he pictured. He wasn't really sorry when it ended, though, as it had a few months after that September day. Pat Malone had taken off a short time later, after what was reported to be a huge fight with Surn. Jim wasn't there at the time; he had been spending more and more time with Barbara since the fall term began. After that breach in the Lanthanides' solidarity, more factions began to form, so that there was nearly always a feud going with somebody at the Fan Farm. Jim took to studying late at the library with Barbara. He had already begun to be tired of the slanshack by early 1955, when Stormy got that teaching job in Virginia, and Bunzie finally took off for California. Jim had just become officially engaged to Barbara, which meant that he had less time to spend at Dugger's. Finally he found a roommate at Milligan and moved on campus to be closer to his bride-to-be.

By March they were all gone except Dugger. When the TVA announced that it was constructing a man-made lake in the Wall Hollow valley, there was no one left to care except Dugger, who couldn't afford to hire a lawyer to fight it. Not that it would have done any good. Poor people never did seem to stand much of a chance against the government, as far as Jim could see.

He remembered Dugger's last day on the farm. The TVA had spent most of the spring months preparing its new lake bed. It had hauled farm-houses away to higher ground, lumbered the oaks and poplar trees from the yards of the former residents, and relocated some—but not all—of the family cemeteries. The day the floodgates closed, Jim had driven out to Dugger's farm, partly out of curiosity and partly on a hunch that Dugger would be there alone and in need of a friend.

He had found Dugger sitting on the rocks that had once been the foundation of his farmhouse. The house was long gone, and the empty cellar looked like a bomb site. Together they looked out at the bulldozed desolation, and Dale had said, "Kind of puts you in mind of Korea, don't it, Jim?"

They walked on past the house site then, into what had been the backyard, and they sat for a long time on the stone fence, talking about the rest of the guys, and about books—about anything except the water that was spilling over the banks of the Watauga and coursing into the valley. Conyers thought of asking about the time capsule then, but he decided that it would have been rude, a denial that there would even be a future. So he tried to

keep Dugger's spirits up by talking about his forthcoming wedding. Dugger must come, of course. He
didn't remember what plans, if any, Dugger had
been making for his own future. He wasn't going to
live in the new Wall Hollow. A lot of the old residents chose not to.

When the sun was low in the sky, they could see
the shine of water from the old cow pasture, and in
order to get Dugger out of there Conyers offered to
buy him a fifty-cent dinner at the college cafeteria.
Absently, Dugger agreed. His eyes kept straying
back to the valley, as if he were trying to take a picture of it in his mind.

They got out by going straight up the wooded hill
past the stone fence and coming out on the paved
roadway that skirted the mountainside. Jim had
parked his motorcycle there, knowing that vehicles
weren't allowed down in the valley anymore. With
Dugger riding astraddle behind him, he gunned the
bike and took off for town, too fast for Dugger to
look back.

It was on this same road that Jim Conyers was
standing now, looking down into muddy water that
receded day by day. He was twice a grandfather
now, and Dale Dugger had been dead for thirty
years. He couldn't get over the feeling that somewhere down in that lake bed was his youth, waiting
for him to come back and dredge it up. Conyers
smiled at this bit of fancy, wondering if the other
Lanthanides felt that way or if the reunion was a
colorful way to make a buck. Impossible to tell.
They had long been strangers to him. He wasn't
sure he wanted to get reacquainted with these

successful old men who had once been his friends, but he supposed that he would have to try. Barbara was very excited about the prospect of the reunion, and about meeting famous people from Hollywood. It was only a few days, after all.

He kept looking at the lake, trying to get his bearings. Was this the spot where the farm had been, or the cliff overlooking the town? Near the bottom of the slope a skeletal tree had risen out of the depths. Was it the Dugger sycamore? The blackened trunk might have been any species of tree, and the other landmarks were still submerged. He would have to wait. Soon the lake would diminish even more. Then perhaps he would be able to distinguish the ruins of Dugger's house and the road that had led to McInturf's store. Perhaps when the drawdown was complete, they could locate the time capsule which now seemed so valuable. But that was not what brought him week after week to the fading shore. Jim Conyers knew that whatever he was looking for in the dead waters of Breedlove Lake, it was not that.

*Fans are always at their best in letters, and
I took them at their self-stated value.*

—FRANCIS TOWNER LANEY
"Ah, Sweet Idiocy"

CHAPTER 4

FORTY YEARS AGO, when the Lanthanides were
reading comic books instead of selling serial rights
to them, there was a comic series called "The Little
King," featuring a diminutive cone-shaped monarch
with a red robe and a perpetual scowl of ill-humor.
People of a certain age invariably remembered that
cartoon character when they encountered the less
regal but equally peevish George Woodard.

The resemblance at the moment was great.
Wearing a tatty red bathrobe over his clothes to
combat the chill of the basement, the stout and
shortsighted George Woodard paced the damp concrete floor, back and forth between the clothes drier
and the mimeograph machine, in search of literary
inspiration.

The next issue of George Woodard's fanzine *Alluvial* was due out in a week, and he had to begin the
page layouts tonight. There were many articles to
be typed up, and many estimates of column inches
to be calculated to make sure that everything fit in
the correct number of pages, which is to say: the
most that could be mailed for a single first-class
postage stamp. George believed in getting his

money's worth from the post offal (or *post orifice* or *post awful*—the puns varied per issue), but since his three dozen subscribers were of mostly straitened means, he could not expect them to pony up more money for a bigger *ish*.

He knew that some of the younger "publishers"— indeed, most of them—used word processors these days, and some even had software packages like *Pagemaker* which could produce very professional-looking 'zines, but George would not be converted by the lure of technological ease. The mimeograph machine was within his ability to operate, and it was paid for. The prospect of a complex and expensive computer strained both his self-esteem and the uneasy peace within the family on the subject of his hobby.

It was late. His wife had long since gone to bed, advising him to do the same since he had "school" tomorrow. It was the same phrase and tone of voice she had employed when the children were young. She said "school" as if he were a pupil rather than a professional educator. Indeed, there was much in Earlene's manner toward him lately that suggested she had abandoned the role of wife for the more authoritative one of mother. The mousy little girl of the fifties was now tart and forthright, bossing him about with contempt masked as concern. Her attitude implied that it was he who forced this change in her behavior. *What but a mother can one be to someone who refuses to grow up?* But all of this had taken place without the utterance of one cross word, without one syllable of reproof from her. Gradually, the shy waif had given way to the Valkyrie, and one of the chief illusions lost in the process had been her image of George.

He sighed. Women were too mired down in the here and now to really be idealists, he told himself. They were always ready to turn practical at the first phone call from a creditor, or when the baby got sick, or when someone they knew saw them using food stamps. No devotion to causes. He had long ago stopped asking her to help him address issues of *Alluvial*.

He yawned. He should go to bed, of course. Those hellions in Algebra I would require every ounce of patience and stamina in him tomorrow, but his self-imposed deadline for *Alluvial* forced him to keep working. After all, this was a special issue, containing actual *news*: the announcement of the Lanthanides' reunion in Tennessee. He picked up the article, which he had composed on stencil, and read through it again.

LANTHANIDES REUNITE
TO RETRIEVE TIME CAPSULE

Has it really been thirty-six solar years since we left the Fan Farm?

Indubitably it has. The Lanthanides, as an organization, is but a golden memory in the minds of those of us who were a part of it, but its effect on SF springs eternal. From this group of devoted fans, living in idyllic squalor in Wall Hollow, Tennessee, came many of the names in the genre's (illusory, because we can't afford to build one) Hall of Fame: Angela Arbroath, Dale Dugger the original co-editor of *Alluvial*, and of course your faithful correspondent: myself.

The group spawned a few dirty old pros, too: Surn, Deddingfield, Phillips, Mistral. (Just kidding, guys!) In the last ish of *Alluvial*, I recounted our adventures on the Great 1954 Tennfan Expedition to Slan Francisco, and how it came to grief in the Indiana outback due to an excess of hot air. (Always a problem with some of the Lanthanides, most notably P. Malone.) Your humble chronicler went on to recount how he managed to at least partially repair the auto (much to the admiration of Surn, who only knew theoretical rocket mechanics), so that the Stalwart Six were able to make it back to the Fan Farm. He then suggested that they use their remaining funds to have a Con of their own.

It was during that weekend that the Lanthanides Time Capsule was planned, and subsequently buried. In the last ish (back issues of *Alluvial* available for $1/postage), I told how we came to bury that amazing cache (after much bheer had been consumed) which included a short story by each member of the group. Since we had no copy machines and nobody typed on stencils, all these stories are unpublished! No one has ever seen them! (A pity. Curtis Phillips said that Yours Truly's story was the best he'd ever read.) For a list of the rest of the contents of the time capsule, see page 4.

In the last issue's article, we lamented the fact that no one ever would see those unpublished yarns of ours. As all Trufandom knows, in the mid-Fifties, after the Lanthanides had gone their separate ways, the TVA turned the whole valley into a lake, and the famous Wall Hollow Fan Farm was hundreds of feet under water. For the past thirty-five years the *time capsule* has been at the bottom of the Gene C. Breedlove Lake. (Known to fandom as the Gene Pool.) (Gene C. Breedlove was some mundane Tennessee politician. *Not* important.)

Be that as it may (and I'm not sure that it was), after I printed this tale in the last *Alluvial*, I had a letter from a Tennfan, who enclosed a newspaper clipping from the *Bristol Herald-Courier*, saying that THEY'RE GOING TO DRAIN THE LAKE. The dam needs repairing (no noun omitted here, folks), so the TVA is going to drain the Gene Pool, and after a few phone calls from Ye Editor, it was all settled. It turns out that Jim Conyers and his lovely femmefan Barbara (would you believe she's a grandmother now?) still live in the area, and they were receptive to the idea of a reunion. Jim's going to make the lodging arrangements for this micro-mini con. Many of the Lanthanides are going back to Tennessee to attempt the recovery of the Lanthanides' Time Capsule. Surn! Mistral! Angela Arbroath! And Moi. What a reunion! Fan history in the making. And a new chapter in the annals of Science Fiction. Yours truly will be on the scene, and the next ish will carry a full report!

#30

TO THE FUTURE WITH LOVE:
The Contents of the Lanthanides' Time Capsule*
(*To the best of my recollection and that
of Jim Conyers)

- One WAR OF THE WORLDS poster, wheedled from the manager of the Bonnie Kate Theatre in Elizabethton.
- Deddingfield's treasured copy of the August 1928

issue of AMAZING, signed by E. E. "Doc" Smith and Philip Francis Nowlan.

- One jar of grape jelly (in case Claude Degler should survive the Nuclear Holocaust).
- One typewritten manuscript of a short story or novella from each member of the Lanthanides.
- John W. Campbell's Letter to the Twenty-First Century.
- Curtis Phillips' copy of THE OUTSIDERS by Lovecraft, annotated by Lovecraft expert Francis Towner Laney.
- Letters from various people now famous, or infamous for being nonexistent (e.g.—Sgt. Joan Carr).
- Copies of all the issues of *Alluvial* up to that time.
- Copies of ASTOUNDING and WEIRD TALES, including a dummy issue of the last, never published issue of WEIRD TALES, containing a story by Peter Deddingfield.
- Some Ray Bradbury fanzines.
- A picture of a dog (To confuse the Aliens).
- One propeller-beanie.
- Other stuff that we have forgotten over the years.

EDITOR'S NOTE: All you Trufan collectors out there know that this stuff is worth a lot of money in today's market, but of course the greatest treasure of all is the manuscript collection of the Lanthanides themselves. (Little did we know!) (But we had a hunch!)—Anyway, I foresee all kinds of excitement over this resurrection of the Holy Grail of Fandom. Look for news about a forthcoming anthology in future issues of ALLUVIAL! (Sure LOCUS will report it, but WE'LL KNOW FIRST.)

George read the articles, inserted a few open parentheses, and pronounced them up to his usual standard, despite his fatigue. He thought he'd better make himself a pot of coffee before he tackled the article on the future of NATO. He would have to pull an all-nighter to finish the issue. It would be better to get it in the mail to his subscribers before Earlene read it and found out he was going to raid their Christmas club account to fund a trip to Wall Hollow, Tennessee. At least the phone bill wasn't too bad this month. Woodard didn't have telephone numbers for most of the Lanthanides, even if he could have afforded to call them. He did manage to reach Ruben Mistral, and Bunzie had put one of his secretaries to work arranging the rest. George clutched the lapels of his bathrobe, trying to keep out the basement chill. It was good to know that somebody still treasured the old days, even if he had become rich and famous. Ye Editor resolved not to use the term "Dirty Old Pro" quite so often in the next few issues.

Brendan Surn, the legendary lion of science fiction, no longer lived on earth. For some time now, his mind had been elsewhere; it returned from time to time for increasingly shorter intervals, but the ties between the author and his life and work were nearly severed. Soon he would be gone for good.

Surn sat in his monogrammed deck chair, staring out at the placid sea. He wore a cowled beach robe of natural fibers and leather sandals, and his white mane of hair reflected the sunlight in a halo around his serene face. He looked like a monk in holy contemplation. Even the architecture of the house fitted the conceit: its exposed-beam cathedral ceiling formed a nave above Surn's head, and the setting sun turned the window to stained glass. With his classic features and that expression of sorrowful contemplation, he could have posed for a portrait of a medieval saint. He might have been Thomas à Becket, saying his last mass at Canterbury.

Lorien Williams wondered what Brendan Surn did think about these days. He spent most of his waking hours gazing out at the ocean, saying little and writing nothing. She liked to think that he still lived in the dreaming spires of Antaeus, the world featured in his greatest works, but he never mentioned his books to her. She hoped that he had not forgotten them. The sound of the ringing telephone a few moments before had pierced the silent house, but it had not reached his still point. He sat as calmly as ever, studying the endless motions of the green waves.

Lorien stood with her finger poised on the hold bar of the phone, wondering what she ought to do about the call. There wasn't anyone to ask. When she had first arrived on her fan pilgrimage to Dry Salvages, Surn's futuristic aerie on a cliff in Carmel, she had been afraid that no one would let her in to meet the great man. His reputation for solitude was legendary, and few people dared to test it. But Lorien had read all of Surn's works, and she felt that she had to express her admiration for him in person. She hoped for an autograph; maybe even a picture of herself standing beside him.

Surn himself had answered her knock, shambling

to the door in his robe and slippers and admitting
her without question. A few moments' conversation,
and the litter of spoiled food and unopened mail told
Lorien what she had stumbled into. Her grandmother had been much the same in the last years of
her life. Lorien didn't remember being affected
much by that, but Brendan Surn was her idol, and
she could see that he needed her. So she cleaned up
the mess and fixed him a hot meal, and then she
decided to stay until someone else turned up. Surely
he had a housekeeper?

As the weeks passed, Lorien became used to her
new surroundings. Her fast-food job in Clarkston,
Washington, was not something she had wanted in
the first place, but it supported her science fiction
activities and placated her parents. She wrote to
them and said that she'd found a better job in
Carmel, which, in a way, was true. She noted that
Surn had good days and bad days. Sometimes he
was almost normal. He could still carry on a conversation, write checks, and decide what he wanted to
eat, but he seemed very much like a little boy. The
depth of adult emotions was missing, and he com-
pensated for it by becoming more pleasant, and by
agreeing with almost anything she suggested.
Lorien thought it was lucky that it had been she
who found him, rather than some gold-digging
blonde or some unscrupulous businessperson. She
wondered if Surn ought to see a doctor, but when
she suggested it, he would become agitated, making
her afraid that he might tell her to leave. That
would be bad for both of them. It would mean that
she would have to go back to a dead-end job some-

where, and he would be thrown to the mundanes. He might even end up in an institution. It was better this way; at least, until he was much farther gone.

At first she was afraid that someone would turn up and tell her to go away. Now she thought she would view eviction as a rescue; but that possibility grew more remote with each passing day. Months passed and no one came, so gradually she began to belong here. She learned the routine at Dry Salvages, and she picked up the skills to take over the business side of Surn's life. The editors and other business people who telephoned for Surn accepted her without question. If anything, they seemed relieved to have someone capable and courteous to talk to, and no one seemed to care who she was or why she was there. Least of all Brendan Surn.

She identified herself now as Surn's assistant. Perhaps some of them thought she was his daughter. She looked quite young, with her sexless body and her dark hair worn flower-child long. She had sad brown eyes in a dreaming face, and no one would ever mistake her for a bimbo, the human furniture for the rich man's beach house. She was not that. Surn seemed to take her presence for granted, but sex did not appear to be one of his physical needs anymore. Even when she bathed him, he gave no sign of arousal. He had never even asked her name.

She looked again at the telephone, wondering what she should say. Most of the decisions were easy: *Yes, you can reprint that,* or *please add a jar of coffee to the grocery order.* But this was different.

Would Surn want to go to Tennessee to see his old friends? Could he handle it?

It wasn't a decision that Lorien Williams wanted to make. She thought she'd better try to make him understand about the call. She knelt down beside his deck chair and touched his arm to rouse him from his reverie. "Brendan?" she said softly. At first she had called him Mr. Surn, but it seemed silly to be so formal with someone who could not even fry an egg. Now she thought of him as two people. There was Mr. Surn the great writer, and Brendan, the sweet, childlike man who needed her so much.

He blinked once or twice, as if he had been asleep. "Yes, Lori?"

"There's a man on the telephone who says to tell you that his name is Bunzie." A note of awe crept into her voice. "It's really Ruben Mistral, from the movies."

Surn nodded. "I know Bunzie," he said softly.

"He's calling about the Lanthanides." Lorien had read the biography of Surn, so she knew about his early years on the Fan Farm. "They're having a reunion back in Wall Hollow, and he wants to know if you would like to go. It's in Tennessee," she added, in case he had forgotten.

"Yes," said Surn in his mild, dreaming voice. "I know Bunzie. I'd like to see him again. Will Erik be there?"

"I don't know," said Lorien. She had not asked for details. "I can find out more about it now. I just wanted to see if you were interested in going."

"And Pat. Will he be there? Pat Malone?"

"I don't think so, Brendan," she said, patting his

arm. Pat Malone had been dead for a long time.
Everybody knew that.

On one side of Ruben Mistral's weekly engage-
ment calendar there was an astronomer's photo of
the Horseshoe Nebula, a billion pinpoints of light
making a haze in the blackness of space. Under the
picture, Mistral had written: "This scene represents
the number of meetings I attend per year!"

"Damn it!" he thought. "It's almost true." The
many components of his film and publishing empire
required considerable maintenance. He could delegate the day-to-day chores, but he supervised his
underlings closely. After all, it was *his* money and
his reputation on the line. The next few weeks of his
datebook looked like a timetable for the Normandy
invasion; nearly every damned hour was filled.
When did they expect him to write? They didn't, of
course. These days he had rewrite men and assistant screenwriters and a host of other flunkies to
see that his barest idea was transformed into a two-
hour movie. But Bunzie missed the old days, and
the seat-of-the-pants style of production: the days
when he was "Bunzie" instead of "Ruben Mistral."
Being a Hollywood mogul had seemed like a wonderful dream in those far-off days; too bad reality
never lived up to one's expectations.

Bunzie, clad in a red designer sweatsuit and
matching Reeboks, was pedaling away on the exercise bike in the corner of his office. He hated it,
but it kept his doctor happy. He was supposed to be
able to think "creative thoughts" while he exercised,
but his brain wouldn't stay in gear. Instead of

considering his current project, he looked appraisingly at his chrome and glass office, decorated with posters from his hit movies. He had probably spent more to furnish that office than poor old Woodard had spent for his house in Maryland. So, he told himself, life wasn't perfect, but he shouldn't kvetch. He was successful. The money was certainly okay; he still had his hair and his teeth; and his health was good thanks to the diet and exercise, every minute of which he hated. But, he thought, at his age, who had any fun anyhow? Better he should be rich and fit and miserable than poor and fat and miserable.

He looked up at the large framed photograph above his desk, as he usually did when the word "poor" entered his head. Most people thought that the picture of the blue mountain lake, nestled among green hills was a soothing landscape, a device to relax him like the crystals on his desk, but for Ruben Mistral the lake picture was a memorial to the days when he *could* relax. It was the only picture he had of Wall Hollow, Tennessee. It had been taken years after the guys left the Fan Farm, but he knew that somewhere under that expanse of green water lay his youth.

Bunzie forced himself to keep pedaling the damned exercise bike. That was the story of his life, wasn't it? Keep pedaling. Maybe everybody else was willing to give up, willing to take no for an answer, and willing to settle for less, but not Ruben Mistral. Mistral would have the best for himself, and he would demand the best from himself and from everyone he worked with.

After all these years, Bunzie still felt schizo-
phrenic about his two identities. In the Wall Hollow
days, he had dreamed of becoming Ruben Mistral—
rich and famous—and several decades later, that
person certainly did exist in all the imagined glory
of Bunzie's daydreams. But inside that tanned and
calorie-controlled body, the old Bunzie still existed,
too. Science fiction legend Ruben Mistral bought
two-thousand-dollar suits; Bunzie the fan from
Brooklyn saved paper clips from the business letters
he received. Mistral had discreet affairs with starlets whose year of birth coincided with his age;
Bunzie secretly preferred Alma Louise, his wife of
thirty years. Mistral was a tiger shark who could
smell blood in a business deal a mile away; Bunzie
missed his old pals from Dugger's farm.

Most of the time, Bunzie felt that he was a flunky
who worked for Ruben Mistral; the great man never
did the actual scutwork of writing, or editing
scripts. That was Bunzie. Mistral was the glad-
hander in Beverly Hills; the maven of the talk
shows; the one with a thousand associates, contacts,
and employees, but no friends. Bunzie had once had
friends. Mistral had his business cronies and, now
that the movie versions of his books had made him a
celebrity, he had "people," those who were paid to
like him, and paid to keep anyone else from ever
getting close to him. Mistral was cold company for a
nice guy like Bunzie. He was necessary, though;
Bunzie had to admit that. The cold and brilliant
Ruben Mistral made merciless deals, paid all the
bills, and he enabled Bunzie and Alma to live in a
beautiful house in Topanga Canyon. He even tossed

a few scraps to worthy charities from time to time. Not a bad guy by the local lights. He made so much money that he could *afford* to endow a hospital ward. What could goodhearted Bunzie have done without the ruthless Mistral ambition: give quarters to panhandlers? Bunzie knew that if there ever came a time when irreconcilable differences forced one of them to depart from the body for good, it would be Bunzie, not Mistral, who would have to go.

Still, in the brief periods of solitude when Mistral's presence was not required, Bunzie thought back on the old days with nostalgia and regret. If you were a true pal, he told himself, you'd have taken your buddies with you to the Promised Land.

"But I tried," said Bunzie to himself—or rather, to Ruben Mistral, who was sneering as usual. "Didn't I try to get Woodard to go to that Worldcon in the sixties and meet some people? Editors buy stuff from people they know, I told him. But he couldn't take the time off work, he said. And didn't I tell Stormy everything he needed to know about promotion, so that he could make a name for himself with his book? But, oh no, he wanted to be a college professor, and college professors are above that sort of merchandising." On the exercise bike, Bunzie kept pedaling. He *had* tried to help the old gang; not that some of them needed it. Surn was a legend, and Deddingfield had been the richest required-reading author he knew. As for the others, he figured that there were some people who could not even have greatness thrust upon them. But he had tried. And sometimes, when Mistral was too busy to sneer at what a bunch of woolly-headed losers they were, Bunzie missed them.

He remembered the pizza. Years ago, when he had just moved out to California to pursue his dream of a screenwriting career, he was living on beans and buying old scripts at the Goodwill, trying to teach himself how to write one, but his letters to the gang scattered up and down the East Coast were always cheerful, full of hope. Bunzie agreed with Churchill that one should be an optimist; there wasn't much point in being anything else. Still, some glimpse of his dire straits must have shown through in the letters, because in the mail one day Bunzie found a check for fifteen dollars and a note saying: "You sound really down. Go buy yourself a pizza." And it was from Dale Dugger! Fifteen dollars must have been hard to spare for Dale back then, but he'd sent it anyhow, not even making it a loan. Just a gift from a pal. Bunzie never forgot that, and even these days, when Alma paid fifteen dollars for a cake of soap, Bunzie was still touched by the memory of that gesture. They had been his *friends*, not like this new bunch with their little axes to grind, their deals to make.

That was why Bunzie, ignoring the protests of Ruben Mistral, had agreed to organize the Lanthanides' reunion. George Woodard had called him about it, bubbling over with enthusiasm, but short of money as usual, and completely hopeless when it came to organization. If George handled it, it would end up being a three-man get-together in a cheap motel, and nothing would come of the book. Bunzie saw the potential, and he was pleased at George's

eager display of gratitude when he volunteered to
take over. Sometimes it helped to be famous. "Leave
it to me," he had told George. Poor old humbug,
thought Bunzie with a sigh; this reunion will be the
thrill of a lifetime for George. Who could I bring
along as a treat for him? Nimoy? Bob Silverberg?
But he dismissed the idea of bringing other celebrities. That would mean that Ruben Mistral would
have to come, too, and he'd insist on bringing some
bimbo starlet to impress his pals. Bunzie didn't
want that to happen. He wanted this weekend trip
to yesteryear to belong just to him. But he wanted it
well organized, and he wanted its potential mined
to the fullest.

Wall Hollow, Tennessee?, one of his "people" had
sneered. Is that anywhere near Hooterville?

But for once Bunzie had overruled the snobbery of
Ruben Mistral and his minions. This time he wasn't
going to take no for an answer. Dale Dugger had
been dead for thirty years, but still there was a debt
there that Bunzie wanted to pay. And a debt of
friendship to poor old hopeless George Woodard, and
to Conyers and Erik, and to the memory of that silly
ass Pat Malone, who might have made it if he'd lived.

So Ruben Mistral would call in favors from a few
influential people in the media, and he'd start the
publicity ball rolling about the proposed anthology
in the time capsule. He couldn't even remember
what he'd written for it anymore. But he did
remember doing one, handwritten with a cartridge
pen in peacock-blue ink. Maybe he could revise it a
little before publication. There are limits to the
charm of nostalgia. He'd get a couple of his editor

friends and his New York agent, and some movie people to film the event, and he'd fly the whole caboodle of them first class to the Tri-Cities Airport outside Blountville, Tennessee.

Then what? God only knew what accommodations there'd be. He had people working on it, though. They would charter the nearest acceptable motel. Maybe two motels. No point in having the press and the editors underfoot all the time. They were all a bunch of kids, anyway.

The thing was a natural from a publicity standpoint. A sunken city, a buried time capsule full of priceless manuscripts, a reunion of the giants—hell, the thing could be a movie in itself. (The Mistral part of his mind delegated somebody to work on that.) With all the hype he could arrange (Steve King to write the introduction to the anthology, maybe?), the collection of stories in that time capsule could be worth a pot of money. They could easily get a million at a literary auction. Not that Ruben Mistral needed the money—Bunzie hastily told himself that he was doing it for old times' sake—but the prospect of a big literary kill would make things more interesting. Why shouldn't they capitalize on it? And he'd split it with the gang. *They* certainly needed the cash. Say, ten percent for each of them, the rest to him . . .

The wall phone by the exercise bike buzzed once, and, still pedaling rhythmically, he picked it up. "Ruben Mistral here," said a cold, smooth voice.

And he was.

Real Soon Now—When the MSFS/DSFL was going to have: a convention, a decent fanzine, an active membership, a properly run meeting, and many other fine things that didn't quite happen.

—*Fancyclopedia II*

CHAPTER 5

"I AM LOOKING," said Marion Farley. "It isn't on the map, I tell you!"

It was a blazing day in late July, and the reunion journey to Tennessee had begun. Jay Omega was driving his *other* car (the gray Oldsmobile he used for trips and for times that his MG was in the shop; i.e. the car he used), and Marion had been assigned to the front passenger seat on the condition that she act as navigator and that she use her reading glasses when consulting the map. She was dressed for the expedition in khaki shorts, an Earth Day T-shirt, and several layers of sun block. Jay had suggested that the outfit needed chukka boots and a riding crop to really complete the look, but Marion was not amused.

Erik Giles, in a white suit and straw hat, looking like a cleanshaven version of Mark Twain, was settled into the backseat, reading the current issue of *Atlantic*.

"I thought they saved Wall Hollow," said Marion, running her finger over the area south of Johnson City. "I mean, I thought that a new town bearing that name still existed. Didn't the TVA move the church and several of the town buildings to higher ground? I thought that some of the residents moved there."

"They did," said Jay Omega. "I asked Wulff in civil engineering about it. Dams are his specialty. According to him, the present village of Wall Hollow is one street, with half a dozen buildings, one general store, and a scattering of houses. It's smaller than it was in the old days before the lake. Rand-McNally didn't think it worth mentioning."

Erik Giles leaned forward and peered between the seats for a closer look at the map of Tennessee. "Never mind," he said. "I know how to get there. See if you can find Hampton on the map."

With her nose almost touching the map, Marion finally announced, "Hampton. Got it. Highway 321. It doesn't look very large, either."

"I don't suppose it is. It wasn't much more than a crossroads in the early fifties. Back when we lived on the farm, the little diner and service station there kept a black bear in a cage as a tourist attraction. Tourists used to buy bottles of chocolate soda to feed it, and the bear would hold the bottle in its forepaws and chug it down in one gulp."

Marion looked stern. "If that is an example of the good old days, I'm thankful to have missed them."

"Look at the map again," said Jay Omega, hoping to forestall another of Marion's lectures. "We're not going to Wall Hollow, are we? I thought the reunion was being held somewhere nearby."

Marion consulted the reunion brochure, a three-paneled flier on baronial ivory paper. It had been printed in considerable style by MistralWorld, Inc.

and mailed to everyone connected with the science
fiction genre. On the front was a blue computer-
designed graphic of Atlantis sinking beneath the
waves, and above it in gold-foil avant garde script
were the words: Return of the Lanthanides. The first
panel gave a brief history of the Lanthanides and
the fate of Dugger's farm, probably taken from a reference work on science fiction, since several of the
less important members were omitted altogether
(Woodard, Giles, Conyers). The center panel gave a
schedule of events, culminating with the Saturday
trek to the newly drained Fan Farm to recover the
time capsule (proceedings to be filmed by the television program *A Current Affair*). The literary auction
would take place on Sunday morning, followed by a
press conference with the surviving Lanthanides
and their newly acquired publisher, the high bidder
of the auction. The last panel, authorship credited to
George Woodard of *Alluvial*, listed the contents
of the time capsule and a brief description of the
mini-con weekend that led to its creation. One of the
two back panels provided a map of the Gene C.
Breedlove Lake area of east Tennessee, with instructions on how to get there by air or car, and the last
panel said "MistralWorld Productions" in the customary and instantly recognizable flourish.

"There is a map on the back of the folder," Marion
announced. "According to this, we are staying at a
state park motel on the shores of Breedlove Lake."

Jay Omega snickered. "Not the Breedlove Inn?"

"Alas, no," grinned Marion. "It's called the Mountaineer Lodge. It's beside the dam, on the western

side of the lake, a few miles from the present Wall Hollow."

"The best local motel by a dam site," chuckled Erik Giles.

Marion turned to stare at him. "I thought you didn't make puns anymore."

He sighed. "It's the reunion. God knows what I shall be saying and doing after a few hours of their collective presence. Singing 'Shrimp Boats,' I expect. I hope we don't shock the editors."

Marion consulted the brochure. "Not much chance of that. I believe they will be lodging at the Holiday Inn in Johnson City so as not to cramp your style."

"I suppose Bunzie will have them bused in for the auction."

"You wouldn't shock the editors, anyway," said Jay Omega. "Writers are supposed to be eccentric. Besides, they're filming this reunion, aren't they? If you all clown around, the media will love it. It will be good for the auction."

"They're having a literary auction in Wall Hollow, Tennessee?" said Marion. "That doesn't sound like publishing as *we* know it, Jay, because your editor wouldn't cross the street . . ."

"I know," said Jay, "but this is a publicity deal. Remember that the whole thing is going to be filmed for national television, and Mistral is connected with the movies. Even New York is impressed by the presence of movie people."

"It's Bunzie's doing, I am certain," said Erik Giles. "He had an instinctive grasp of publicity. He faxed press releases to *Publishers Weekly* and to all the major newspapers, announcing the reunion. A couple of reporters are actually being sent down to cover it. To me it all sounds like a scheme to get an outrageous sum for the anthology. I confess that I am not averse to such a plan."

"It will probably work, too," said Marion after a moment's consideration. "People don't buy books unless they've heard of them. All of this star-studded publicity could turn this into a best-seller."

"That would be a pleasant surprise after all these years."

"Aren't you worried about what the English department will say when they find out who you really are?" asked Jay Omega.

Erik Giles looked startled. "What do you mean?"

"C. A. Stormcock."

The professor smiled. "I imagine that the department will forgive that youthful indiscretion if I promise not to lapse again."

"Don't you think you might like to write science fiction again?"

He shook his head. "Definitely not. To quote Mr. Woody Allen, I plan to take the money and run."

"Well, the auction should provide you with plenty of that," said Jay Omega.

"Do you think Alien Books will be there to bid?" asked Giles.

"No," said Jay, reddening a little at the mention of his neglectful publishers. "They only do paper-backs. I don't think they could afford a deal of this magnitude."

"They're probably all in summer school, anyhow," giggled Marion, who contended that Alien Books filled its editorial vacancies by calling the Runaway Hotline.

"Well, it should be a very profitable venture for you, Erik," said Jay. "Imagine getting thousands of dollars for a short story thirty-five years later. What was your story about, anyhow?"

Erik Giles smiled ruefully. "I've been trying to remember. I believe that all our stories were very much in the style we later became known for. Surn did a story on colonialism set on a distant planet; my old friend—er—Pete—Deddingfield, I mean, wrote a poetic alien encounter thing that reminded me of *Moby Dick*. Or maybe *I* wrote that one. We lived in each other's pockets in those days, and some of us dabbled in each other's styles. Well, if Pete wrote that one, then I think I wrote one about a man dying of radiation poisoning."

Marion shuddered. "In 1954?"

"Oh, yes. The Fan Farm library had a paperback copy of *Hiroshima* by John Hersey, and I remember being very struck by his account of the aftermath of the bombing."

"It will be an interesting story to read in today's world," Jay remarked.

Giles blushed. "I hope I got my details right. We didn't do much research in our Fan Farm days. Too far from a library."

"Do you remember anyone else's story?"

"Dugger wrote a high-tech yarn from the point of view of an alien PFC. He was drawing on his army experiences. I remember laughing a lot when he read it. Dugger had a keen sense of irony." He paused for a moment, remembering his friend.

"Let's see, who have I forgotten? Woodard. I can't remember Woodard's story. I never could. Not even five minutes after I'd read one of them. And, of course, poor old Curtis wrote about demons."

Marion nodded. "Curtis Phillips. I don't suppose any of you realized back then?"

"No, of course not. We thought he was a fine storyteller with a gifted imagination and a genius for description. We had no idea."

"Such a pity," sighed Marion. "He was a gifted writer."

"I'm not following this," said Jay Omega. "What didn't they realize? What was a pity?"

"About Curtis Phillips," said Marion. "The great fantasy author who wrote *Demon in My View.* He was considered the successor to Lovecraft, and he wrote a whole series of novels and stories relating his characters' lives and even world events to the intercessions of demons."

"I haven't read any of Phillips's books, but I've heard of him. He's supposed to have been a brilliant fantasy writer. What is so tragic about him?"

"He was writing nonfiction," said Marion softly.

The four-lane highway that led from southwest Virginia into east Tennessee was built to run through the flattest and widest of the valleys so that it missed most of the beautiful mountain scenery of the Blue Ridge, but it was the fastest and most efficient route. On this trip, no one bothered to look at the scenery. When the three professors ran out of conversation, Jay Omega turned the car radio to the local National Public Radio station and lost himself

in a program of classical music, while Erik Giles
dozed in the backseat.

Marion soon lost interest in the novel she had
brought along. The bulletin board was right about
Warren, she thought. Deprived of other distrac-
tions, she thought about the weekend ahead, and
the phrase *there but for the grace of God go I* came
to mind and would not be dispelled.

The prospect of attending a reunion of old fans of
science fiction reminded Marion of the days when
she had been a member of fandom herself, and her
memories were not altogether pleasant ones. I
wonder why Erik asked us to come along with him,
she thought. They had never asked him to explain
the invitation, which, after all, could be considered
an honor, but after the initial excitement wore off,
Marion found herself questioning her colleague's
motives. Erik Giles had hinted that he was worried
about his health and that he did not want to travel
alone, but he seemed completely recovered from his
heart attack of the year before, and she wondered if
that was the real reason for his asking them or just
a convenient excuse. Of course, meeting the famous
Lanthanides, and all the agents and movie people
who attended them, might be good for Jay's career,
but she doubted if he had the drive to pursue it.
Although Jay Omega was a nationally published
novelist, he was essentially a hobby writer, quite
content to be an electrical engineer. He had no
reason—financial or otherwise—to put forth the
time and effort to become a successful full-time
writer. He was happy in engineering, and in that
profession he was considerably better paid than

most writers. If Jay had wanted to try for a serious career as a novelist, Marion would have helped him, but she knew better than to push him. You couldn't change people. She had learned that finally, after ten years and half that many relationships.

That was one thing fandom had taught her. Within its ranks she had met many talented people who could have made a fortune illustrating comic books, designing dresses, developing computer games . . . but. She sighed, remembering the frustration she had felt in her relationships with her fan friends. After years of stymied friendships and bitter romances, she had learned that you cannot give people ambition as if it were a virus. It is not. It is a genetic trait, and either it is waiting deep inside you to evolve, or else it is entirely absent, and it cannot be imparted to someone full of talent but lacking the drive to succeed. Nothing that anyone can do—not praise, or scolding, or work on one's behalf—can make them try.

Marion had watched her brilliant acquaintances fritter away talent that she would have killed for. The comic book creators answered endless pages of correspondence on their computers, ignoring their own deadlines, while their artistic creations died of neglect. Another gifted friend scrapped her dream of becoming a costume designer in favor of a new boyfriend who wanted to go and live in the wilds of Oregon. The computer whiz *went home one night and put a bullet through his head.*

Edward Arlington Robinson, thought Marion, mentally acknowledging the quote. When life became painful she always turned to literature. That was how she had become an English professor; it had been the ultimate escape from a marriage that she later compared to two years in an opium den. Only Jeremy hadn't done drugs; he had done dragons. To a sober outsider the addictions had seemed similar and equally incomprehensible.

Marion had met Jeremy when they were undergrads. He had been a computer science major, and she was a smart girl with enough personal problems to keep the psych department busy for years. She was overweight; she had no idea how to manage her thick, curly hair; and she came from a cold and repressive family. Batting a thousand, thought Marion in retrospect. Hello, Middle Earth! She had possessed all the qualities necessary for psychological emigration: she had been rejected by the world, and she was perceptive enough to know it. So she left. She still went to her classes—well, most of the time—and her parents received dutiful letters that discussed the weather and asked after the cats, but Marion was gone. She had found the *real people*, and joined their ranks.

The real people. Another literary reference. She wondered if Fredric Brown had ever realized the enormous impression his short story made on young egos. It was a simple fantasy story, probably suggested by the coincidence that began the tale: you are humming a song, and suddenly that very song comes on the car radio. The story's hero discovers that most of the people in the world are not real, they are like walk-on players in a film. Just there to set the stage, to create an illusion of reality. But a few people are *real*, the characters for whom the drama exists. Those people think and feel and care about things; everyone else is an automaton who ceases to function as soon as a real person leaves the scene. The reason the song came on the car radio was that the driver humming the tune was a *real* person, and he was able to will things to happen.

It was an excellent fantasy story; Fredric Brown was one of the best. But to the troubled adolescent Marion that story was not just an entertaining tale, it was a serious philosophy that explained her feelings of alienation.

When Marion read that story, she knew at once that she was one of *them*. She knew that she could think and feel, that she was more alive somehow than most of the bubblebrains in her dorm. So *that* was it. They weren't real. She didn't exactly believe that they were robots, or hallucinations, but on some deeper spiritual level she felt that she possessed something that *they* lacked. In medieval times, she might have termed it a soul.

Armed with her new understanding of the world, Marion neglected her classes and her correspondence in favor of the search for more *real* people. Every now and then she would find one—someone with whom she got along especially well from the moment they met—and she'd catch herself thinking, Ah. He's *real*, too.

Jeremy had been the realest of the real. They had shared the same ecological politics, the same yearning for things medieval, and the same bewilderment over contemporary society. For two years they had a wonderful relationship, exasperating their parents and their respective university departments, before Marion grew tired of the game and of Jeremy's endless defiant failures. "I couldn't take mid-terms," he would explain earnestly. "Because I had to go to Maryland for a meeting of the Shire that week. After all, I am a baron." Such priorities had seemed logical when they were dating, but when Marion was a student wife, working low-wage jobs to pay his tuition, the logic in his actions escaped her entirely. She began to feel like the sober guest at a beer blast. Finally, deciding to bet her money on her own abilities instead of his, Marion enrolled in graduate school, moved out, and never looked back.

Still, she wasn't sure she had ever got the old philosophy out of her system. She had consciously renounced it a few years later when she discovered that most of her *real* friends bickered endlessly and accomplished very little. Later she came to the uneasy realization that her concept of *real* and *unreal* people was very similar to the chauvinistic male's idea of women, the bigot's perception of other races, and, most troubling of all, similar to the way in which serial killers view their victims: *they're not real, but I am. They don't matter, but I do.* That was when the philosophy of exclusion had begun to frighten her.

Now, of course, she told herself that everyone had a soul and feelings, and that *mundanes* were very worthwhile people, but sometimes the old attitude came back anyhow. Just last week, Marion had been in line at the Chinese restaurant's lunch buffet, and the pixy-faced young woman in front of her had taken forever, staring at the rice and bean curd as if she couldn't remember what they were. Marion had caught herself thinking, Well, *she's* not real! The realization that she had thought that about someone even for an instant was an unsettling feeling. It gave her kinship with people she would rather not think of at all, and it made her wonder where such arrogance might have led. Did any of the Lanthanides share this view of reality? Now that she thought of it, it was just the opposite of Curtis Phillips's problem: Marion thought that most people weren't real and didn't matter; Curtis Phillips had fervently believed that demons were, and did.

"So tell me about Curtis Phillips," said Jay Omega, as if on cue. (Marion could never decide if Jay was *real* or not, but he was utterly unlike Jeremy, and that was enough.)

"Poor Curt," said Erik Giles, who had suddenly awakened. "He had such talent."

"When someone mentions Curtis Phillips, I always think of Richard Dadd," said Marion. She glanced at Jay to see if he recognized the name. It was obvious that he did not. Dadd was one of the things Marion had learned about in her "Middle Earth" period. "Richard Dadd was a mid-nineteenth-century English artist who became famous for his wonderfully complex paintings of fairy life. His paintings—surrealistic in style and much ahead of their time—were much admired, right up until the night that the artist cut his father's throat."

"Another practitioner of nonfiction?" asked Jay.

"Apparently so. He seemed to be having delusions about demons, and hearing voices ordering him to kill, so perhaps he was painting what he saw. He was tried and found insane, and they put him in Broadmoor, where he spent the remainder of his life painting increasingly bizarre landscapes peopled by demons." In lecture mode, Marion prattled happily on. "The asylum kept his paintings, and many of them are still on display there. They're worth a fortune."

"It sounds very like poor Curtis," Erik Giles agreed. "He didn't kill anyone, of course, but after the early success of his horror novels, his behavior became more and more erratic, and I believe there were a few episodes of violence with various editors."

"What sort of episodes?" asked Jay, possibly in search of inspiration.

"I believe he mailed a dead opossum to one of them. And he threatened another one with a razor. He confounded the local police a few times by confessing to murders."

"Murders?"

"Yes. President Kennedy, Janis Joplin, and, I believe, Joan of Arc. I'm told that every police department has cranks whose hobby is confessing. He once wrote to me saying that he had killed George Woodard and Pat Malone, but since Pat had been dead for a couple of years and I had a letter from George that same day, I dismissed it as wishful thinking."

"It sounds as if he needed psychiatric treatment," said Jay.

"He got it. That was when it was decided that he

had to be institutionalized. I am told that he continued to write his fantasy stories even while he was in Butner, and in fact two of his short story collections were written there. In the end, of course, his personality became too fragmented for the discipline of composition, and he degenerated into—well, I didn't go and visit him in those final years. I did go once in the mid-sixties, and he seemed lucid enough then."

"Did he seem well enough to be released?" asked Marion.

"Oh, no. He asked about Brendan and Peter, and I told him what they were doing, and then he told me about his demons and what *they* were doing. I never went back."

"Do you suppose the asylum owns the copyright to Curtis Phillips' later work?" asked Marion. "You know, the way Broadmoor owns the Dadd collection?"

"I don't know. I doubt it, though. Curtis was so well known before he was committed that I would have expected his family to take legal steps to administer his estate."

"It will be interesting to see if anyone turns up to represent his interests at the auction."

"Bunzie will know about all that. His people contacted us, because we all had to agree to let Bunzie's agent represent us in the book deal. He thought negotiations would be much simpler if we had only one representative working for the entire group."

"He has put a lot of work into this reunion," said Marion, taking another look at the brochure.

Erik Giles grinned. "He hates to see other people

screw up. Besides, he can delegate most of the arrangements to his staff."

"I suppose he can," said Marion, but she made a mental note to observe Bunzie carefully. She tended to distrust altruistic people.

Jay Omega slowed the car. "Look! A 'Welcome to Tennessee' sign. Shall we go in search of the Mountaineer Lodge, stop for dinner, or go and look at the lake?"

Marion shivered. "I don't think I want to look at the lake just yet."

"Nor do I," said Erik Giles.

In the town's open grave he lies under star spillage, bone cold and sore, thinking his way home.

—DON JOHNSON
Watauga Drawdown

CHAPTER 6

THE MOUNTAINEER LODGE had been designed to be picturesque. In the early eighties an architect for the Tennessee State Park Service had designed a rustic-looking hotel of timber-framed oak and glass, intended to make out-of-state visitors think of Davy Crockett and to satisfy environmentalists that the new building harmonized with its pastoral surroundings. The Mountaineer Lodge was an imposing fretwork of rafters, joists, beams, and purlins slotted together with hand-tooled joints: a modern version of the pioneer cabin, expanded to accommodate fifty guests in neo-rustic splendor, i.e., with central heating and air conditioning, multilevel decks encircling the building, and floor-to-ceiling vistas of the Gene C. Breedlove Lake. Nestled into a hillside of oaks and mountain laurel, the lodge was known for its simple elegance and for its breathtaking views of the lake.

At present, one of these attributes was missing.

Gone was the shining green lake that had formerly stretched out from beneath the lodge's decks to meet the green hills on the far side of the valley.

In its place was a mud hole two miles wide, dotted with rubble and dead trees. In the center of this moonscape, the Watauga River coursed along in its accustomed banks, carrying the lake water on downstream in daily increments.

Erik Giles stood at the glass wall of the hotel lobby and stared out at the desolation. His suitcase sat forgotten beneath the ledge of the check-in booth.

"Do you think we ought to go and talk to him?" whispered Marion to Jay, who was filling out a reservation card.

"I don't know," said Jay. " 'What company are you with?' Should I put the university?"

"No. This isn't an academic conference." Marion looked at Giles's unmoving figure in the fading light. "It's a wake." Without waiting for Jay's reply, she hurried to Giles's side, touching him lightly on the arm. "Are you all right?"

He turned to look at her. "Yes, of course. I was just a bit surprised by the look of it. I'm trying to get my bearings, but this bears no resemblance to the valley I remember, so I've no idea where we are in relation to the farm. Still it's fascinating to see what engineers can do in such a short time. I wonder what they did with all the water."

"I expect Jay would know," said Marion, still trying to gauge Giles's mood. She pointed to the dead landscape of rocks and red mud. "You don't find this depressing?"

Giles seemed puzzled by her concern. "Why? They're going to put it back, aren't they? It isn't as if it were strip mining. Three weeks from now this will be a lovely lake again." He started back toward the registration desk. "Well, that's enough sight-seeing for now. I suppose I'd better go and check in. Are any of the others here yet?"

"I didn't ask. Of course, the reunion actually begins tomorrow, but you could ask if anyone else has arrived early. Someone may have left you a message. Jay and I thought that we would wait to see if any of your old friends had turned up, and then we'll go to dinner. Unless you need us to stay around. Or you're welcome to join us if you like."

He smiled at her. "Let me see what my options are."

"Good idea," said Marion. "While you check in, I think I'll help Jay take the bags up to our room. We'll meet you here in the lobby in ten minutes."

She found Jay Omega hauling suitcases out of the trunk of the Oldsmobile and loading them onto a rolling cart that he had borrowed from the hotel lobby.

"That was organized of you," said Marion approvingly. "I came out to volunteer my services as a bearer, but I see that you don't need my help after all."

"I'm an engineer," Jay reminded her. "We are trained to be efficient and organized. That's what we do."

"And English professors are trained to be sensitive, but I don't see much of that in Erik."

Jay Omega finished loading the luggage cart and began to maneuver it toward the glass doors of the lobby. "What do you mean? How is Erik being insensitive?"

She shrugged. "I thought that he would be more

upset by the destruction of the valley he used to live in, but he seemed to think it was exciting. As far as he was concerned, the whole process was an engineering conjuring trick." She looked suspiciously at the self-confessed engineer. "I suppose *you* agree with him?"

Jay stopped the cart in mid-lobby to take a long look out the window. "It's probably a very nice lake. I grant you that the site looks hellish at the moment, but that's what lakes look like underneath. The question is, was this lake necessary, and I don't know the answer to that. I'm not a civil engineer."

The elevator opened, and they hurried to get the cart inside before the doors closed. Marion was silent until they arrived on the second floor. "Perhaps I'm being overly sensitive," she remarked. "But I think that if this valley had once been my home, I would be upset at seeing it so desolate."

"Well, Marion, he's had thirty years to get used to the idea."

She shuddered. "I don't think that would be long enough for me."

"Here's our room, 208." Jay fumbled for the key. "Are we meeting Erik back downstairs?"

"Yes. I told him ten minutes."

The key clicked in the lock, and he pushed open the door, signaling for Marion to enter first. She glanced at the quilted twin beds, the framed silk-screen prints of mountain scenes, and the little round table placed under a swag lamp. "It looks okay," she conceded. "Nouveau rustic motel."

At the far end of the room the floor-length curtains were drawn to keep out the evening sun. Marion pushed back the curtains and called out to Jay Omega, "Oh, goody! A view of the lake."

When they returned to the lobby ten minutes later, Erik Giles was sitting on one of the earth-tone sofas, leafing through a travel brochure on Ruby Falls. "In my day the big attraction was Rock City," he remarked. "Half the barns in the region had 'See Rock City' printed on the roof in white letters. I never did, though. Wonder if it's still in business."

Marion frowned. "I think that's down near Chattanooga. This part of east Tennessee seems fairly devoid of tourist traps."

Giles grinned. "Don't tell Bunzie. He might try to turn this into a permanent exhibit."

"Is he here yet?" asked Marion, trying not to sound starstruck.

"No. He must be on his way, though. There was an invitation to a cocktail party for the Lanthanides in the Franklin Suite at nine tonight, so apparently we're all getting together to socialize before the media gets here to cramp our style." He looked up at Jay Omega. "Speaking of the Lanthanides, I'm afraid that I must ask a favor of you. There was another message here, too. It was addressed to 'Whichever of the Lanthanides Arrives First.'"

"Interesting," said Jay Omega. "A door prize?"

"Alas, no. It's from George Woodard. He's stranded at the State Welcome Center with car trouble. He wants us to go and get him."

The invisible woman was enjoying her plane ride. At least she was registering ironic amusement at the fact that no one seemed to notice her or cared to speak with her. She was not enjoying the trip in the sense that she was actually *happy*; she did not particularly care for plane rides. But it was pleasant to be going on an unexpected vacation, and at the moment it was entertaining to contemplate the lengths to which this invisibility might extend. Could she get up and dance naked in the aisles? Could she sing at the top of her lungs? No, but she could certainly observe her fellow passengers without fear of return scrutiny. She was the closest thing there is to nonexistent: an overweight, middle-aged woman.

Perhaps, thought Angela Arbroath, such women were like General MacArthur's old soldiers: they didn't die, they just faded away. Angela, who had never been a beauty in the first place, had been fading away for twenty years now, and she thought she must have achieved the ultimate in nonentity. Now when she walked down the street, people pushed past her with their eyes staring straight ahead as if she were merely a pocket of dead air.

A different sort of woman might have been offended at this universal slighting of her humanity, but Angela Arbroath, who considered herself quite charming and not particularly human, thought it was a wonderful cover. It was like having a secret identity. Let people ignore me, she would tell herself; that way they will never know what they missed. It was odd that people assumed that quiet, unglamorous people were also meek and unintelligent. She was neither, but she didn't see any point in letting the whole world in on the secret. Her

friends knew what a special person she was, and
that was enough.

Thirty years ago she might have minded being
universally overlooked. But back then she still
cared what strangers thought of her; she still had
feelings to be hurt. Now she had adjusted very
nicely to a world of her own making, which centered
around her century-old cottage in Clemmons, Mississippi, and her garden of medieval medicinal
herbs. And of course, her mailbox. Angela had
assembled a carefully chosen family of cats, entertaining correspondents, fantasy and medieval history books, and a few eccentric old friends, and that
was her world. *The Soul selects her own Society—
Then—shuts the Door.* She had that line from Emily
Dickinson done in calligraphy and framed. It rested
on the mantel above the stone fireplace. On winter
evenings Angela would sit on her red velvet settee
beside the fireplace, with cats curled up all about
her, and she would answer letters to people without
really wishing they were there.

She leaned back in her seat and smiled with con-
tentment at her lot in life. Pat Malone would have
been proud of her—insofar as he would have given a
damn, she amended hastily. Poor old Pat. He was
the only one of the Lanthanides that she would
really like to see, and he was dead. A pity—she wondered what he would have thought of the mature
and mellow Angela, the one who would rather bake
zucchini bread than argue.

"About damn time," she pictured him saying.
"Arguing is a waste of time. You cannot convert a
fan; you can only enrage him."

But Pat might have minded that she had let herself go a bit. There was no getting past it: men were shallow. Even clever and unconventional ones like Pat Malone would probably prefer the sloe-eyed gamine of yesteryear to her present grandmotherly self, but even that didn't trouble her much. She still wore her hair long and straight, because it was the least troublesome thing to do with it, and her wardrobe ran to comfortable shifts, oversized jackets, and flat shoes, because fashion did not concern her either. For festive occasions she had homemade and hand-embroidered dresses in a medieval style, because it pleased her to wear them. Angela had come to terms with who she was, and had there been a psychiatrist in Clemmons, Mississippi, he would have pronounced her well adjusted.

Angela was still in high school when she began writing to the Lanthanides. One of them had written a comment in one of the fanzines she subscribed to, and he mentioned the Fan Farm. Their Tennessee address had reassured her somehow that these were *nice* boys. You never knew with the ones from New York or Minneapolis. Her mother had drummed it into her head that Yankees couldn't be trusted, that they weren't the right sort of people. After all, look what they did to Vicksburg. By the time she discovered the northern origins of most of the Lanthanides, they were solidly entrenched as her friends and confidantes, and she had become a fan publisher with her very own 'zine, reaching out to Yankees and other alien beings from coast to coast. She used the church's mimeograph machine, paying for her ink and paper supplies with money she earned on a paper route. The response was astonishing. For the first time in her life, Angela found herself *popular*.

She hadn't intended to be a self-published magazine editor. At first she merely wanted to correspond with the people she met through other people's 'zines, but a few samples of these grainy, amateurish efforts convinced her that she could produce a better one, and she quickly realized that it was much simpler to produce one magazine than it was to try to write twenty-five personal letters.

So *Archangel* had been born. Either by luck or uncommon good sense (she refused to remember which), Angela had written to Brendan Surn and Pat Malone and a couple of the fan-elite of the day, asking them to contribute articles to her first edition. And because most of them would have given an article to anyone who asked them nicely, they responded by sending her amusing and informative columns that she dutifully typed in on her father's old Underwood typewriter. When the issue was complete, she sent it to a few of the People Who Mattered in fandom, and suddenly she was a celebrity. People clamored for subscriptions to *Archangel*, and overnight she had a hundred new friends.

She would be the first to admit that *Archangel* was not the legendary fanzine that *Alluvial* was. It was generally acknowledged that *Alluvial*'s chief editor, Pat Malone, was brilliant, but because Angela had a less abrasive personality and was able to get along with almost everyone in fandom, she could get a wide variety of interesting articles

from almost everyone. By the time some of these
fans went on to become famous pros, Angela was
one of the most respected and influential amateur
publishers.

She smiled again, remembering the heady feeling
of acceptance in those early days. It was like being
cheerleader, prom queen, and secretary of the class
all rolled into one. And the letters were so *interesting*. They read the books that she read, and they
seemed absorbed in worthwhile subjects, like space
travel and future societies. Whereas her other correspondent, her dreary cousin Betty in Texas, only
talked about her boyfriends and what she wore on
dates. This was definitely an improvement.

Looking back, Angela knew that most of those
people were not her friends at all. They sent her lectures on their own pet obsessions with a word or
two of personalization, or they sent mimeographed
letters to who-knows-how-many correspondents.
Convoy duty was not her idea of a relationship, but
it took her a good many years to realize that. The
letters that were personal were mostly from unat-
tached young men, who viewed her as a rare prize,
because in the fifties women in the hobby were few
and far between. She had indulged in a few long-
distance romances with some of the more eloquent
souls, but the spark never survived an actual
meeting.

Over the years, though, Angela had become more
perceptive, and more selective about her friends,
and she had found some good ones and had managed to keep most of them for several decades now.
She no longer published *Archangel*, though. As the

years went by, she found that fans were getting younger and younger, and she no longer had much interest in communicating with the new bunch. She went to an occasional science fiction convention, upon prearrangement that friends she wanted to see would be there, but they paid little heed to the scheduled events, preferring to hold their own reunion. And every so often, someone would work up a privately published tribute to fandom, and she would be asked to include an article about *Archangel*, which she always did, reasoning that it was a debt she owed to the hobby in return for its earlier kindnesses to her.

Aside from that, she answered a few of the correspondents she chose to keep with *real* letters, and a score of less intimate acquaintances with a modest letterzine, really a round-robin letter in which she answered everyone in one letter and then sent copies to all of them. This lesser publishing effort she called *Seraph*, a pun both on *Archangel* and on the serif fonts she preferred in her IBM Selectric typewriter. Aside from these pastimes, Angela worked the night shift at the lab at the county hospital so that she could afford postage and cat food.

She had been surprised to hear from—she smiled at the conceit—MistralWorld, Inc. about the Lanthanides' reunion. The former residents of the Tennessee Fan Farm did not number among the friends she kept. She didn't suppose they had noticed, though. She still got eight-page letters from George Woodard about three times a year, but at least six of the pages were photocopied essays with no personalization whatsoever on them. They usually discussed the Woodard daughters, favorable comments received about *Alluvial*, and a bit of name-dropping: ". . . Had a nice note from my Maryland neighbor A. C. Crispin *(Yesterday's Son)* . . ." Occasionally George would dredge up a math puzzle, like Gauss's theorem of consecutive numbers, to amuse his readers, and once he had begun a mock-serious campaign to introduce another integer between two and three. He called it umpty, and encouraged his correspondents henceforth to count *one, two, umpty, three.* . . . Then between the numbers twelve and thirteen, one would insert the related digit *umpteen.* She wondered how many people got George's manufactured letter. Dozens, probably. Whenever she got one, she would skim the biographical monotony looking for the bits pertaining to herself (few, but close together, so that the page could be inserted into the pre-existing sermon). Then she would write back a cordial but inconsequential reply, similar to the tone of her letters to Cousin Betty, and George apparently never noticed that there was no real communication or sentiment between them at all. When Angela's mother died of a stroke, her letter to George went off as perfunctorily as ever, but with no mention of the family circumstances. She couldn't bear to receive a one-sentence-personalization condolence.

As for the others, she had lost touch with Bunzie and Surn, half afraid that if she did write to them, she would receive a reply from some secretary treating her as another piece of fan mail. Occasionally they would appear at a science fiction convention, but

she never looked them up. There was always too
much else to do in a short weekend. She and Barbara
Conyers exchanged Christmas cards, but she hadn't
heard from Stormy or the others in years, and the
fandom grapevine reported several of them dead.

She thought about the Substitute Con party, and
the long drive she had made to get there, using most
of her birthday money for gas! It would be strange
to see all those idealistic boys again as old men. In
retrospect, a lifetime was not very long. And what
strange bread upon the waters to have her 1954 gas
money expenditure repaid with a plane ticket from
Ruben Mistral (Inc.). She wanted to cry just thinking about the distance between then and now, and
about how short life is, and how easy it is to lose the
thread between people.

"Excuse me, ma'am, are you all right?"

Angela looked up into the concerned eyes of a
male flight attendant. He was about to hand a diet
Coke to her seatmate, and apparently he had
noticed her tear-stained cheeks. *Apparently he had
noticed.*

Angela Arbroath summoned a gentle smile. "Why,
I'm right as rain," she told him.

"It's no trouble at all," said Jay Omega for the
fifth time. "It isn't far to the State Welcome Center.
We passed it on 81 on our way in."

Erik Giles reddened and heaved a weary sigh.
"How like George Woodard to have car trouble! Do
you remember that character in 'L'il Abner' who
always had a black cloud over his head? That's
Woodard exactly. We used to call him Disaster Lad.

I think Pat Malone once wrote a Superman parody using Woodard as Disaster Lad."

"Cars are tricky things," said Jay Omega, to whom they weren't. "Marion once made me drive all the way to Roanoke to get her because her car wouldn't start. Turned out she hadn't put gas in it. Marion believes in mind over Mazda."

Erik Giles grunted in what may have been amusement. "Well, I hope this is the last of George's bad luck for the weekend."

As they rounded a bend, an open space between the oaks afforded them a glimpse of the dry lake bed. "It's a strange sight, isn't it?" Jay remarked.

Erik Giles shrugged. "Only because the hills around it are so green. Out west it wouldn't look strange at all."

"I haven't seen any sign of the town yet. I suppose everyone will visit that tomorrow when the reunion actually begins."

"I doubt if there will be much to see after all these years. In fact, I wonder how Bunzie can be so sure he'll be able to locate the time capsule."

"You must have had landmarks when you buried it."

"A fence and an old tree. Do you suppose they'll still be there?"

"I don't know. Traces of them may remain. Once you locate the town, you should be able to get your bearings and pinpoint specific landmarks."

"Perhaps so. I was just thinking how foolish we would all feel if we brought everyone here and then ended up finding nothing."

"Well, I hope you won't be disappointed." Jay

hesitated at broaching the touchy subject of money. "You weren't counting on the anthology sales to finance your retirement were you?"

Erik Giles stared. "Retire? You talk as if I were *old*. I shall be at the university for another dozen years. In fact, I have a hunch that Graham may be leaving to take a job at Carolina, which will put me in line for department head." He rubbed his hands together, smiling. "You see what I do to their deconstruction program then! I intend to enjoy myself hugely."

Jay, who still remembered the headache that resulted from his last discussion of deconstruction, hastened to change the subject. "I'm glad to hear that things are going so well," he said. "So you aren't considering returning to science fiction?"

"C. A. Stormcock is dead," said the professor solemnly.

They drove on in silence for the thirty miles that it took to reach the Welcome Center and Rest Area. Jay Omega enjoyed driving, and the rolling hills of east Tennessee provided the ideal setting for an evening's excursion. The winding road had been designed to accommodate the mountains. It clung to the hillside, a narrow path scarcely disturbing the rich vegetation that crept back on either side.

Jay didn't mind playing the Mechanical Samaritan, but he rather wished that it had been Surn or Mistral who had needed his help instead of Woodard, because he was sure that he'd be tongue-tied around writers of their stature, and an informal meeting over a disabled car would have done much to ease the tension for him. Still, he knew that he could count on Marion to be charming and chatty, and that was fine. He was glad to come along for a pleasant evening in the country if Erik wanted company, but apart from that, he had no agenda.

He was sorry when the two-lane blacktop ended at an overpass directing them onto the four-lane interstate. The rest of the drive was a less pleasant ramble, dodging trucks and staying out of the way of cars with Ohio license plates doing eighty. The shadows had deepened to a gray twilight when they finally reached the Welcome Center. Jay eased the Oldsmobile into the parking lot and began looking for the stranded George Woodard.

"Over there, I'll bet," said Erik Giles. "The old AMC Concord with Maryland tags."

Jay pulled into the space beside the white Concord and waved a friendly greeting to the distressed little man who was pacing the sidewalk in front of it. He was wearing tan walking shorts and a *Star Trek* T-shirt that held his physique up to ridicule. When he saw them, he hurried to the car and poked his head in the driver's window.

"Have you come for me?" he asked breathlessly. His glasses had slid down to the end of his nose, and his face was still sweaty from panic or the summer's heat. The air-conditioned Welcome Center stopped welcoming people to Tennessee promptly at five P.M.

Erik Giles summoned a brief smile as he climbed out of the car. "Hello, George!" he drawled. "Traveling by yourself?"

Woodard winced at the mention of a sore subject.

"Earlene had things to do at home," he said. "So I came by myself. Almost made it, too. Drove down from Maryland in eight and a half hours, and then the bloody contraption quits on me in the Welcome Center." He smiled. "I fancy there's an article to be written in *that* irony."

Erik nodded. "It isn't a leaky radiator this time, is it, George?"

Woodard intoned solemnly, " 'You may talk of Blog and Bheer when your fellow fen are near . . .' "

Jay Omega glanced at his watch. "Excuse me," he said. "Could you tell me what's wrong with the car?"

Woodard shook his head. "Henry Ford was a magician as far as I'm concerned."

"I mean, what did it do? What were its symptoms?" Jay persisted.

"It did nothing, and those were its symptoms." Woodard began to pace again. "I pulled into the rest area to—" He giggled. "—to jettison some recycled Pepsi, and when I came out of the men's room, the car wouldn't start again."

Jay looked thoughtful. "Could be a vapor lock. Did it make a noise?"

Woodard shrugged. "I think it laughed at me, but I can't swear to it." He turned away to speak to Erik Giles. "Are you still Stormy these days?"

"I prefer to be called Erik Giles," said the professor.

Jay Omega interrupted again. "I mean, did it crank when you turned the key, or did it click or what?"

George thought. "I think it clicked. I tried it umpteen times." He did not seem interested in the diagnosis, because he immediately resumed his previous conversation.

The volunteer mechanic waited patiently for a lull in the monologue. Finally George glanced at him again, and Jay said, "I hate to trouble you, but could you undo the hood latch for me?"

At this point, Erik Giles made a belated introduction, and George, upon learning that his mechanic was a science fiction author, became noticeably more cordial. He remarked that he had heard of *Bimbos of the Death Sun*, but had been unable to find a copy, and he offered to review Jay's next book in a forthcoming issue of *Alluvial*.

"The hood latch?" said Jay.

"We're in Tennessee now, Mr. Surn."

The plane ride had been uneventful, for which Lorien Williams was thankful. They had sat side by side in first-class seats, and throughout the flight Brendan Surn had stared out the window at the changing landscapes beneath them. Just east of the Mississippi, when cumulus clouds obscured his view, Surn went to sleep, awakening only when the green crests of the Smoky Mountains swelled beneath them, twenty thousand cloudless feet below.

This was one of Surn's good days. He had talked briefly, and he seemed to understand the purpose of the journey. Lorien hoped that things would go well over the weekend. She didn't want Mr. Surn to be hurt or embarrassed by the experience. She hoped that it would please him to see his old friends again.

"Sit here in this nice plastic chair, and I'll go and see about the bags." Lorien's face assumed an expression of sternness. "You won't wander off, will you?"

Smiling, he shook his head. "Not in Tennessee," he said carefully.

"All right, then. I'll be back as soon as I can." She hoped that she had brought enough money for the trip. They had Surn's Visa and American Express cards, and two hundred dollars in cash for cab fares and tips. That ought to do it. It had to, because Surn couldn't remember the automatic teller code to get cash with his credit card, and she didn't want to draw too much attention to them by asking for help.

"I have to be crazy to think I can pull this off," thought Lorien. "But what an opportunity—for both of us!" She had purchased a new wardrobe for the reunion, reasoning that people would be more likely to accept her as Surn's assistant if she were *not* wearing jeans and sandals. Since Lorien had never met an employee of anyone famous, she wasn't sure what sort of attire was required, but she decided that if she copied the style of the woman vice-president at Mr. Surn's bank, she ought to succeed in looking both respectable and businesslike. She had even had her hair done for the occasion. Catching sight of herself in a restaurant mirror, Lorien touched her newly styled tresses and frowned. "I look just like Marilyn Quayle," she muttered to herself.

Brendan Surn was a good deal more casually dressed, because as a famous Californian he was not even expected to own a tie. Lorien had studied the pictures on the book jackets of Surn's novels, and she had packed a "representative selection" of similar attire, adding his silver NASA jacket, a gift from the astronauts, in case it was chilly in Tennessee.

So far things seemed to be going well. Perhaps the Piracetam was working. Someone at the health food store had mentioned that the drug was used in Europe for Alzheimer's patients and people with memory problems, so Lorien ordered some. It wouldn't hurt to try, she reasoned. She wasn't sure if there had been any improvement. Sometimes he seemed fine and sometimes not, but she kept up the dosage in hopes that long-term effects would be more noticeable. If he didn't get any worse, that would be enough.

Brendan had done a couple of short telephone interviews concerning the reunion, and he had sounded fine. Lorien thought it odd that a man who couldn't remember how to turn on the stove could talk knowledgeably about literature, but she supposed that the things that would stay with him longest were the things that he cared about, not necessarily the simplest things he knew. She hoped that this meant he would remember the old days at the Fan Farm. If not, she could cover for him by staying close and changing the subject if things got awkward. There was only one problem Lorien Williams had not worked out: What happens if someone offers Brendan Surn big money to write another book? And what if he agrees to do it?

Managing Surn's business affairs and his laundry

were one thing, but Lorien was not at all sure that she was up to writing a best-seller.

While George Woodard talked about his teaching job and the next issue of *Alluvial*, speculated on the content of the next *Star Trek* movie (and whether there would be one), and lamented his health, Jay Omega probed under the Concord's hood for signs of trouble. The possibilities were legion. Woodard's engine looked like he had just followed an Exxon tanker through a mud hole. Disaster Lad indeed, thought Jay Omega, but immediately he felt ashamed of himself for this harsh judgment. Surely, he told himself, if George Woodard could have afforded the maintenance on this car, he could also have afforded to trade it in for a newer model. A few moments of study told him what the trouble was.

"It's your battery cables," he announced, fingering the wires barnacled with white corrosion at the terminals.

Behind him the conversation continued unabated. In Woodard's eagerness to discuss old times, he had apparently forgotten his car, his mechanical difficulties, and his new acquaintance. Not that it mattered. Fixing the car would take three minutes and required no assistance from the owner. Jay went back to his own car to get the wet rag and wire brush he would need to clean the battery terminals.

As he went past them, George Woodard called out, "Found the trouble, have you? I hope it's not expensive."

"I can fix it for nothing," said Jay Omega.

* * *

Bunzie hated people who accepted telephone calls on airplanes, which was unfortunate, because it was a practice that Ruben Mistral indulged in quite a bit. At the moment he was conferring with his office to reschedule meetings and to see who had left messages in reply to *his* messages. While he had his secretary on the line, he asked how the final arrangements for the reunion had gone. The response was reassuring. The chartered plane had taken off from LaGuardia at six, and the two hotels had declared themselves ready for the reunion and the editorial contingent.

Bunzie wondered what the reunion would be like, aside from all the hype. Did he really have anything in common with those guys anymore? It had been so long since he had talked about anything besides business that he wasn't sure he could carry on an ordinary conversation. And what if the guys were worse than boring—what if they didn't like him? Suppose they resented him for *going Hollywood*? Bunzie figured he had enough enemies throwing negative ions at him without inviting rejection from old friends. For one stifling moment he felt like faking an excuse not to attend and going home. But the plane full of book people had already left New York, and it was unthinkable that the auction should go on without him. The gang stood to make some nice money off this stunt, and it had been *his* doing. How could he think they'd dislike him?

Besides, he thought, these guys were his friends when he was broke and nobody. They had liked him then. There was even more reason to like him now. It was going to be all right.

Bunzie leaned back in his seat, watching the clouds roll by. Now maybe he could sit back and enjoy his friends and let the business take care of itself. He told Ruben Mistral to take the weekend off, and went back to reading the in-flight magazine.

> . . . One family returns
> every year on Memorial Day to row out
> and sink a wreath on what they think
> is the ancestral burial plot. But one
> of the older boys admits that he thinks
> an aging uncle confused the spot with his
> favorite fishing hole and they have
> for years been honoring a living channel cat.

—DON JOHNSON
"The Mayor of Butler"

CHAPTER 7

"I WONDER HOW it's going," said Marion for the third time.

"The reunion? Fine," said Jay Omega, spearing another forkful of barbecue. "Are you going to eat that last hush puppy, because if not—"

After the rescue of George Woodard from the Welcome Center parking lot, Jay had returned to the Mountaineer Lodge, leaving Erik Giles to go off to his private reunion party while he and Marion drove off in search of a decent restaurant. He wasn't entirely convinced that they had found one, but Marion insisted that it would be wonderful, and as far as the food was concerned, she was right. He wasn't too sure about the ambience.

The Lakecrest Café, as the place was called, sat on a mound of clay too small to be termed a hill, with its back to the narrow shore of Breedlove Lake. Marion had declared that the restaurant's name was either a reassurance for customers or a neon prayer that the lake's crest should go no higher than the bottom of the slope even during the spring runoffs. She conceded that it might also be a message to hydroelectric-happy Tennessee bureaucrats: the lake stops here.

The wooden building was at least thirty years old, and sported a rusting thermometer advertising Coca-Cola, fading posters from last year's fair, and a gravel parking lot full of pickup trucks, which, according to Marion, guaranteed the best food around. Jay muttered something about cholera, but she shushed him, and they went in.

Once inside, Jay's apprehensions began to subside. The green tile floor was well scrubbed, and the pine booths were free of graffiti. Fresh wildflowers sat on red gingham tablecloths, and the jukebox was playing quiet country songs at a reasonable volume.

As they slid into the corner booth, Marion laughed at his evident relief. "What did you expect?" she asked.

Jay pantomimed the strumming of a banjo and hummed a few bars of "Dueling Banjos," the theme from *Deliverance*.

"Honestly, Jay! What if someone sees you? Anyway, I thought you were a little more sophisticated than that. Wait until I tell Jean and Betty in Appalachian Studies that I found another *Deliverance* sucker."

Jay pretended to be studying the menu, but Marion saw him blush.

She went on. "Everybody has seen that movie, and from the way they've reacted to it, you'd think it was a documentary, but it wasn't. It was an allegory. The author, James Dickey, is a poet. Talking to someone from Appalachia about *Deliverance* is like talking about *Moby-Dick* to a member of Greenpeace. In both cases, you're confusing symbolism with reality." Marion waved her hand to indicate the rest of the café. "Do you see anybody in here who looks like one of those caricatures in *Deliverance*?"

Jay swallowed the last bit of hush puppy. "Well, there's a guy coming toward us. . . ." He nodded toward a large bearded man in jeans and a Charlie Daniels T-shirt. He looked like a cross between a linebacker and a bear.

Marion turned to look at him and her lips twitched but she said nothing.

"Don't worry, Marion!" whispered Jay. "I'll handle this."

"Howdy," said the man, easing into the booth beside Marion. "Did you all come for the show?"

"No," said Marion. "Is there one?"

"Well, most Thursday nights a few of us get together to do a little pickin'. Have a few beers." He eyed Jay Omega, who was noticeably paler. "Not too awful many knife fights, though," he added.

"We don't want any trouble," said Jay carefully.

Marion looked solemn. "What's a barbarian like you doing in a nice place like this?"

Jay's jaw dropped. "Marion!" he hissed.

She continued her scolding as if he had not spoken. "I mean, we come all the way from southwest Virginia, hoping for a little decent barbecue or some down-home cooking, and what do we find trashing up the place? A goddamned Joyce scholar!" She threw a hush puppy at him.

The bearded man grinned. "Shoot, Marion! What'd you wanna give the game away for? I really had your friend going there, and you know I just love *Deliverance* suckers!"

"Very funny, Tobe. What if somebody believed in that hillbilly act of yours? You could be perpetuating a stereotype, you know."

The big man sighed. "I reckon I could come in here in a Savile Row suit and a rep tie, and some people would still think the mountains were full of savages."

Jay Omega continued to look puzzled. "Is this the floor show?" he asked.

They laughed at his dismay. "Jay, may I present Tobias J. Crawford of the English department at East Tennessee State University."

"And one of the best clawhammer banjo players in these parts," Dr. Crawford added without a trace of modesty. "A bunch of us old boys from around here get together Thursday nights to play at the Lakecrest. Straight bluegrass. No ballad singing, dulcimer playing, academic storytelling, or Scottish country dancing allowed. Nobody in the group answers to 'Doc,' and the lawyer who plays bass has to tell people he's a truck driver."

Jay blinked. "You're another English professor?"

"That's right," nodded Crawford. "The woods are full of 'em in tourist season. Mostly they're backpacking on the Appalachian Trail, but a few of them are running around with tape recorders trying to pick up an authentic mountain folk song." He grinned. "I once gave a fellow from Carmel, California, a bluegrass rendition of 'Because I Could Not Stop for Death,' and told him it was a Child ballad that my great-great-great-grandpappy had brought over from England. He's probably tried to publish it in a journal somewhere by now."

Marion nodded. " 'Because I Could Not Stop for Death.' Very good. And I suppose you sang it to the tune of 'The Yellow Rose of Texas'?"

"Oh, sure. You can sing quite a few of Emily Dickinson's poems to the tune of 'The Yellow Rose of Texas.' "

To Jay Omega's further dismay, the two English scholars proceeded to demonstrate this literary discovery, amid giggles and spoons tapped on beer mugs for percussion. When the tribute to Emily Dickinson was finished, Marion wiped her eyes and attempted to speak. "You should see Tobe at an MLA conference!" she said between gasps. "But it was mean of him to scare you like that. Tobe, this is James Owens Mega, an electrical engineer who writes science fiction."

Crawford stuck out his hand. "Sorry to startle you," he said, "but when I saw you mime that banjo imitation, I knew you were discussing *Deliverance*, so I figured I'd come on over. We get pretty tired of that hillbilly crap."

Jay smiled. "I know what you mean. I have stereotypes of my own to contend with."

"Jay is the author of *Bimbos of the Death Sun*," Marion explained.

Tobe Crawford nodded. "That would take some effort to live down, I expect. Science fiction? Are you connected with that reunion going on in Wall Hollow?"

"Yes. Do you know Erik Giles from my department? It turns out that he was C. A. Stormcock, the author of *The Golden Gain*, who was one of the Lanthanides back in the fifties. He was invited back for the reunion, and because his health is not good we came with him."

Dr. Crawford looked interested. "Has the reunion started yet? There's been a ton of publicity about it. Newspapers, local television. I even saw an article that said *A Current Affair* was coming in to film it."

"I believe that's true," said Marion. "Did you see the interview with Mistral in *People* magazine?"

Tobe Crawford shook his head. "I get my news from the *National Enquirer*," he said solemnly.

Marion made a face at him. "That's right! Make English professors look bad, too, while you're at it! Anyway, I wouldn't expect a Joyce scholar to understand a complex field like science fiction, but these writers are very important in their genre, so all this publicity is to be expected."

"I hear that all sorts of movie types will be there. Have you seen any of those guys yet?"

"The Lanthanides are here, but all the business people arrive tomorrow." Marion gave Tobe Crawford a stern look. "I hope you're not thinking of taking your mountain man act on the road. Anyhow, I haven't seen any gullible city slickers. Tonight the writers are having a private party, so we haven't even met them yet."

"I've met them, but it was a long time ago," said Tobe.

"At a science fiction convention?"

"No. I remember when that bunch lived at Dugger's farm. I was just a kid then, so I didn't know any of them very well, but people used to think they were strange. I worked Saturdays in my uncle Bob McInturf's store, stocking shelves and sweeping up, and they used to come in every now and then to buy groceries. I figure that time capsule they buried was the pickle jar I gave them."

"Did they tell you what it was for?"

"Not that I recall. We didn't pay much attention to them, on account of them being so odd and keeping to themselves like they did. We knew Dugger's people, of course, and Jim Conyers is a good old boy—for a lawyer—but back then, people kept shy of them. I remember they set off some fireworks one time that damn near started a forest fire. Folks around here were about ready to run them off."

"I think they've mellowed since then," said Jay Omega.

"I didn't realize that you came from this part of east Tennessee, Tobe," said Marion. "So people here didn't know that the Lanthanides buried a time capsule?"

"Nobody would have cared. Those guys weren't famous back when I was a kid, so no one was particularly interested in what went on out there, as long as they didn't burn down the mountain." He grinned wolfishly. "A time capsule, huh? Too bad James Joyce didn't bury one of those."

Marion gave him an acid smile. "He'd probably

have dumped a box of Scrabble tiles into the canister and let it go at that."

Jay had begun to be afraid that the evening was going to degenerate into an English professors' version of sniper warfare. In his desperation to think of a new topic for discussion, he said, "You're the first local person we've met so far. What do you think of the drawdown?"

Tobias Crawford looked sad. "People hated that lake when they put it in. One old fellow compared the TVA's taking of our valley to the expulsion of the Cherokees on the Trail of Tears. When they announced the drawdown, I thought we'd all be thankful to see that lake gone, even for a couple of weeks, but now I don't know. It sure has dredged up a lot of memories."

"I wonder how it's going at the reunion," said Marion again. "Imagine—all the titans of science fiction in one little village!"

"Well, if they're as great as you say they are, I reckon they picked the right place to get together," said Tobe Crawford.

"What do you mean?"

"Wall Hollow. Haven't you heard how it got its name?"

Marion shook her head.

"Okay, I'll give you a hint. The present name of the town is a local corruption of the original. The town was settled in the early eighteenth century by German immigrants. Try saying it out loud. Wall Hollow."

"Wall Hollow," Marion repeated thoughtfully. "German . . ."

"Valhalla," said Jay Omega. "The home of the immortals."

Erik Giles had been reluctant to go to the reunion. For a long time he sat in his room, debating over whether or not to wear casual clothes instead of his white suit, whether or not to wear a tie, whether or not to improvise a name tag to spare himself embarrassment. And what if the others had changed so much that he failed to recognize them? Would that be a social blunder? In the end, hunger and boredom drove him out of his solitary bedroom, sporting a hand-lettered name tag drawn on a page of the nightstand note pad. He had folded it over his shirt pocket and secured it in place with the clip of his ballpoint pen. "Erik Giles, Ph.D.," the sign said, and in smaller letters beneath it he had written "Stormy." Fortified by that social insurance, the professor followed the arrows to the Laurel Room and steeled himself for the encounters to come.

It was a quiet party in a small banquet room. A photo mural of the lake in autumn adorned one wall, and the addition of chintz loveseats and potted plants instead of tables converted the space from banquet hall to salon. Soft canned music flowed from hidden speakers as an unobtrusive waitress glided about the room, retrieving empty glasses and offering hors d'oeuvres.

Thankful to go unnoticed, Erik Giles stood in the doorway studying the guests. The most familiar face was that of George Woodard, hunched over a little plate of appetizers, with a cup of punch balanced precariously on the arm of the sofa. He had changed

from his *Star Trek* T-shirt to a brown turtleneck
and polyester pants, and his black hair, grown long
on one side and combed across the top of his head,
shone like the surface of a bowling ball. Standing
near George was a plump, pleasant-looking woman
with braided hair and a medieval gown of green and
gold. She was talking to a florid fellow in a wrinkled
beige jacket and an open shirt. Giles caught a
glimpse of the gold medallion around the man's
neck and correctly deduced that this must be the
host of the party, "Bunzie" Mistral. The young man
hovering at Bunzie's elbow was either a relative of
someone in the group or, more probably, one of the
Mistral minions, on hand to see that things went
smoothly.

Turning his attention to the far end of the room,
Giles found Brendan Surn—by now a household
face—standing beside the lake mural with a secre-
tarial young woman in a navy blazer and skirt.
Surely not a wife, thought Erik Giles. She doesn't
look expensive enough to be the great man's consort.
Perhaps she was another one of the staff. The two of
them were talking quietly with a lean, distinguished-
looking man who was quite well preserved for sixty,
but more conservatively dressed than Surn or Mistral. Definitely not a movie person. Erik Giles tried to
remember who else was coming. It took him another
few minutes to remember Dugger's quiet boyhood
friend Jim . . . O'Connor? Conrad. Ah, he had it now.
Conyers. Jim Conyers. And the plump woman in
white linen at his side must be the fiancée of long
ago—Barbara. He had met her a couple of times,

years ago, but he could remember nothing about her. There probably wasn't much to remember.

Giles took a deep breath. This wasn't going to be so difficult, he told himself. He had a pretty good idea who everyone was already, and if any gaffes were made, there was no one important around to observe it. Things were going to go well, he thought, if only he could manage to be kind about his old acquaintances' follies, and if he weren't too over-bearing about his own scholarly importance. He straightened his name tag, squared his shoulders, and strode purposefully into the room.

Ever the genial host, Bunzie hurried to greet him, enfolding him in a bear hug, which Giles supposed to be the Hollywood equivalent of a cordial nod. He noticed that as Bunzie pulled out of the embrace, he sneaked a look at the name tag. "Stormy! Stormy! Stormy!" he intoned. "Great to see you again, kid!" Turning to the assembled guests, Bunzie announced, "Look, folks! It's Dr. Erik Giles—complete with name tag! And how about you, Stormy? Recognize the old gang?"

"I think so, yes," said Giles, edging away from his host. "How have you been, er—Reuben?" He pronounced it with the accent on the first syllable, the way Bunzie had said it in the old days, before he became the fashionable "Ruben," accent on second syllable, Mistral.

"It's still Bunzie," grinned Mistral. "Especially to family. And we're family, aren't we? Boy, when I think of those wonderful times we had back on the farm."

"It would have been nice to have central heating," said Giles.

"Well, Dugger could afford it now, couldn't he? After we sell this anthology for a bundle . . ."

"Poor Dugger. I wish he were alive to see this. He could have bought another farm somewhere. And wouldn't Curtis Phillips love to see his name coupled with Lovecraft's in scholarly articles?" Erik Giles looked around the room. "This is a reminder of what we've lost, isn't it? Curtis, Deddingfield, Dale Dugger? Intimations of our own mortality."

"You forgot Pat Malone," said Bunzie.

Giles shrugged. "I don't miss Pat. He was a cynical pain in the ass."

Bunzie's smile was all-forgiving. "Poor old Pat. Such an idealist! He was trying to be sophisticated, that's all. But he was a great mind, and in his own way, he thought the world of us."

"Well, perhaps." Erik Giles didn't want to beatify a departed nuisance, but it would have been rude to disagree. He shook Bunzie's hand. "Good to see you again."

He made his way toward Brendan Surn, the farthest point in the room from the effusive Bunzie and the limpet Woodard.

As he approached them, Brendan Surn turned his attention from the Conyers couple, his face lighting up in a warm smile. "Hello, Peter!" he called out. "They told me you weren't coming."

The little mudhen secretary looked stricken. "Mr. Surn!" she gasped. "This is Erik Giles. You remember. Mr. Mistral was telling us that he's a college professor now."

Brendan Surn looked blank for a moment, but then he put out his hand and smiled again. "Erik Giles. Of course. In that white suit of yours, my next guess might have been Mark Twain."

They all laughed merrily to cover the awkward moment. Then the secretary offered her hand to Giles. "I'm Lorien Williams, Dr. Giles. I'm Mr. Surn's assistant."

"Lorien?" echoed Giles.

She blushed. "I was born in the sixties, when my parents were heavily into Tolkien. And before you ask, no, I don't have a brother named Gandalf. Anyway, it's an honor to meet you. And you know Mr. and Mrs. Conyers, of course. We were just talking about the movie version of *Starwind Rising*."

"Er—yes," said Giles, trying to remember a movie he had seen once ten years ago. "Too bad they had to leave out so many of the subplots, but I suppose a nine-hundred-page book presents many problems for screenwriters."

"So you live over in Virginia now?" said Barbara Conyers, who was the family conversationalist.

"Yes. I teach at the university. I don't get over this way very often."

"Jim and I still live in Elizabethton. Jim is semi-retired now from his law practice, and we have a little nursery of trees and bedding plants. I've always loved working with flowers. And our daughter Carol lives over in Johnson City. Her husband is at the university, and they have two little ones, Andrew, who is four, and Amy Allison, two-and-a-half."

Giles turned to Lorien Williams. "Is this your first trip to east Tennessee?"

She nodded. "First trip east of Idaho. There are a lot of trees here. In California I get homesick for trees sometimes."

"You should see the country when the lake is full," said Barbara. "Especially in June when the mountain laurel is in bloom. It's about the prettiest place on earth then."

"I find it interesting to see the valley exposed again after all these years." Giles nodded toward the mural of Breedlove Lake.

"I know," said Barbara earnestly. "It's strange, isn't it? Like digging up an old grave. I swear Jim's been having nightmares about the whole thing. He wakes up sometimes of a night in a cold sweat. He talks about water running down the walls."

Conyers frowned. "Probably indigestion," he grunted.

Barbara chattered on. "Still, I guess it's a good thing they did decide to drain the lake, because otherwise, you all would never have been able to recover your stories, would you?"

Lorien Williams nodded excitedly. "Isn't it wonderful about the time capsule? After all these years, new stories from Peter Deddingfield and Curtis Phillips! I've read everything they ever wrote."

Jim Conyers looked solemn. "I don't care much for myself. Barb and I are happy as we are, but maybe after all these years Dugger will finally get something published. Wish he could have been around to enjoy it."

Barbara sighed. "He would have been so proud of

all his friends. They've all become so famous." Giles's frown reminded her that this was too sweeping an accolade. "And even the ones who aren't celebrities are doing *real* well," she amended. A glance in George Woodard's direction suggested that she knew better, but was going to leave it at that anyhow.

A new voice chimed in. "I wonder what Pat Malone would have thought of all this hoopla."

Giles turned to see the woman in medieval dress smiling up at him. There were lines around her eyes and at the corners of her mouth, but she had an appealing air of youthfulness about her.

"Angela Arbroath, Stormy," she said, offering him a much beringed hand. "I published *Archangel*. Remember?"

"Yes, of course," said Giles hastily, giving her an awkward peck on the cheek. "*Archangel*. Quite a nice little magazine, as I recall."

Angela blushed. "Well, it wasn't a patch on *Alluvial*, of course, but Pat Malone was a much better editor than I was. And of course, he could offer articles by Surn and Deddingfield. You wouldn't believe how much *Alluvial* sells for today."

Giles gave her a mirthless smile. "One dollar per issue, I believe."

"Oh. Of course. George still publishes something called that, doesn't he?" She paused for a moment, trying to think of something kind to say about that. Finally she blurted out, "Well, you certainly are looking well, Erik!"

"And you haven't changed a bit," he assured her. "And of course you were here the weekend we decided to put that time capsule together. You even sent us back a story, didn't you?"

"That I did," grinned Angela. "And if Bunzie is the magician he thinks he is, it'll keep me in my old age."

"Do you remember what you wrote?" asked Barbara Conyers.

"Not really. Something with a woman protagonist, I think, to annoy the guys. In most of *their* early works the women were like cheeseburgers—they were either trophies or dessert."

Erik Giles laughed. "Remind me to introduce you to Marion Farley," he said. "I believe you two are soul mates."

It was nearly ten o'clock. The supply of hors d'oeuvres had dwindled to a few selections that nobody wanted, and the champagne had been abandoned in favor of decaffeinated coffee, but the talking was louder and more animated than before, and frequently punctuated with laughter. As the reunion rekindled their memories of each other, the Lanthanides had pulled the couches close together, and they all sat around in a circle, arguing about subjects they hadn't cared about in decades.

None of these subjects concerned science fiction, science, or literature in general. In the years since the dissolution of the Fan Farm, they had resolved all their uncertainties about those subjects to their own satisfaction, and they were past the need to discuss such matters. What still rankled was the personal issues.

"I didn't know that was moonshine you kept in

that mason jar in the bathroom. And anyway, it took the paint off my brush, didn't it?" After all these years, Woodard was still stung by Bunzie's old grievance. "Besides," he added petulantly, "I probably saved your life by using it up. Drinking that stuff can make you go blind. It gives you lead poisoning, I believe."

Giles laughed. "Speaking of that sort of lead poisoning, remember that issue of *Alluvial* that Curtis and Pat Malone put out when they were stinking drunk? 'An Interview with Cthulu.' And they filched a couple of love poems that Deddingfield wrote to Earlene Riley and put those in. I thought the post office was going to send the feds in after us when that issue went through the mails. Remember the verse about 'Your succulent nipples spark fusion in my teeming loins . . .' Ugh! And Deddingfield wasn't even embarrassed. He swore he wrote it from memory!" Hearing a silence instead of indulgent laughter, Giles looked up to see shamefaced smiles on the faces of the others. George Woodard had turned scarlet, and seemed intent upon a petit-four.

Finally Conyers said quietly, "Well, Peter always was an old lying hound, wasn't he?"

Erik remembered that George Woodard referred to his wife as Earlene. A glance at Woodard's red face told him that it was the same girl. Girl! She must be sixty now. They had met her at an East Coast S-F convention. He wondered if she still attended them.

To break the silence, Angela said, "Do you remember how much Dale hated Erik's jazz records! Pat told me that Dale wrote a story once contending that jazz was the sound of alien invaders fine-tuning their spaceships' engines."

Erik Giles looked puzzled. "I can't remember having any special fondness for jazz. Well, perhaps I did. I fancied myself a bohemian in those days."

"I remember you used to argue incessantly about whose turn it was to do the dishes," said Brendan Surn.

"We were always arguing incessantly about something," said Bunzie. "That's what adolescent intellectuals do. Bicker. Protest. Whine. Censure. But we laughed a lot, too."

"Dissent is the sign of an active and inquisitive mind," said George Woodard, for whom bickering had remained a way of life. "In *Alluvial* I welcome disagreement from freethinking individuals, exercising their First Amendment rights. Speaking of *Alluvial*, I'm planning to write this up in a forthcoming issue, and I'd welcome some guest columns. How about you, Angela?"

Angela looked away. "I'm not sure I have the time, George. I'll see. Okay?"

"I guess we ought to talk about the reason we're all here," said Bunzie, drawing a well-scribbled index card out of his hip pocket. "The business part of this reunion starts tomorrow. I thought we'd begin with an introductory meeting here at our hotel. Jim, I think you agreed to give the media people some background on Wall Hollow and the construction of the lake?"

"Yes. I did some research, and I can answer anything that isn't an engineering question. History, facts and figures, local legends, and so on."

"Good! Colorful anecdotes will make good copy for feature stories. I leave it to you." Bunzie consulted his notes. "After the introduction here, we will make our way down the hill, where several small motorboats will be waiting to take us to Dugger's farm. Expect to pose for pictures during this process. We have boots for all of you."

Tentatively, Lorien Williams raised her hand. "Excuse me, but how can boats get around out there if there is nothing left but mud?"

Bunzie's smile was intended to make her feel at ease. "Good question, Lori!" he beamed. "You know, the best thing we could have used would have been those hovercraft things they use in the swamps of the Everglades. What do they call them? Whatever. Anyway—" He shrugged. "Try to find those swamp boats in east Tennessee. Try to find a *bagel*. But rowboats they got. So we rented a couple, complete with outboard motors and navigators. The boats will stay in the original channel."

Jim Conyers felt the need to translate. "When they drain the lake, Miss Williams, the water doesn't go away entirely. The Watauga River simply returns to its original banks and flows through the valley just as it did before the lake was formed. We will travel on the river."

"But once we get to the farm, we slog it out on foot," said Bunzie, wagging a playful finger. "So don't forget your boots!"

Taking the silence that followed for assent, Bunzie resumed his lecture. "Now, as to the time capsule itself. That's the real reason for our being here, and we don't want to disappoint all those editors who have come in search of treasure, do we? Does anybody remember any landmarks that might still be standing, to help us in locating it?"

Jim Conyers was tired. Ten o'clock was usually his bedtime, since he got up at five. But Barbara seemed to be enjoying herself, so he stayed. All the talk was making him sleepy, though. It seemed to him that all the Lanthanides ever did was talk aimlessly and wait around for something to happen. He had forgotten that feeling of waiting; he'd always had it at Dugger's farm. Everybody seemed to be killing time, *waiting* for something, and while they waited they talked, but nobody ever seemed to know what they were waiting for, and nobody ever tried to make anything happen. And, as far as he could tell, nothing much ever did happen at the Fan Farm. Except a lot of feuds between one another over trivialities. They could sulk for three days over a magazine cover that one liked and the other didn't. Finally, everybody just got tired of sniping at everybody else, and one by one, they left.

Now, thirty-five years later, here they were again, the dearest of old friends, remembering Wall Hollow as if it had been a paradise of sweet accord. The feuds were forgotten. He wondered if dredging up the past would bring the old enmities to the surface again. Perhaps not. If their lives did not touch at any point, what could there be left to quarrel over?

He studied the aging Lanthanides. Bunzie still seemed amiable and enthusiastic, but the lines about his mouth and an occasional sharp look at his assistant suggested that he could also be a demanding tyrant. And Giles had come to the reunion, but he seemed embarrassed to be reminded of his youthful foray into fandom. Jim didn't know what to make of Surn. He seemed like the patriarch of the reunion, but his detachment could mean anything. Angela Arbroath seemed happy, and Jim figured that was good enough. He expected less from women, and he knew it, but he told himself that his generation couldn't change the way it saw the world, and it saw women as lesser beings. He hadn't expected much of Angela, and he had not been disappointed.

Only Woodard had not changed. He had grown older without growing up, still living for his fanzine and his pen pals as if there were no other goals in life to aspire to. At least the others who had stayed in science fiction had gone on to bigger accomplishments: novels, films, and in Surn's case a Medal of Freedom from the President. But for George it was still 1954. Jim sighed at the waste. By rights, Woodard ought to be allowed to live an extra fifty years, so he'd have time to *do* something if he ever emerged from his cocoon.

"Have you seen the lake?" Lorien Williams was asking Bunzie.

"Not *lately*!" said Bunzie, laughing loudest at his own joke.

"It looks like a giant hog wallow right now," said Angela. "That mud must be knee deep out there. How are you all going to get around in it?"

"Small boats in the wettest parts," Bunzie told her. "And after that, wading boots. I brought a case of them, all sizes."

"A lot of people are upset about this drawdown," said Barbara, leaning forward confidentially to impart the local point of view. "You know, they didn't move all the graves when the TVA made the lake back in the fifties, and some people are afraid that there'll be bodies floating in the mud when the water recedes."

Angela Arbroath gasped. "Where is Dugger buried?"

"Somewhere else. The lake was already here by that time," Jim told her.

"I've heard that some pilots in private planes have flown over the valley and reported seeing bodies floating in the channel," Barbara insisted.

"Catfish," said her husband. "Those channel cats can get up to six feet long."

Barbara Conyers tossed her head. "Well, I just hope y'all don't stumble across any unearthed corpses when you go out hunting your time capsule."

"I hope not, too," said Bunzie. "The film crews couldn't use that sort of footage for promotion."

"Speaking of skeletons in the valley," said a new voice, "I should think we had quite enough of our own."

The Lanthanides looked up to see three new-comers standing in the doorway: a dark-haired woman and a young man who looked startled by their companion's outburst, and the speaker him-self. He was a gaunt man in late middle age, and his somber outfit—a black jacket over black shirt and trousers—emphasized the pallor of his skin. He leaned on the door frame and studied the group with a smile that might have been derisive or challenging. It was anything but friendly.

Bunzie decided to ignore the impertinence. Frowning at the intruders, he waved them away. "I'm sorry!" he called out. "This is a private party. The Lanthanides will not be giving interviews until tomorrow."

The younger couple turned to leave, but the man in black still stood in the doorway, enjoying the disturbance he had created.

Erik Giles stood up. "They aren't reporters, Reuben. At least, two of them aren't. These are my friends Jay Omega, the writer, and Marion Farley, from my department. They came with me. I'm afraid I don't know the other gentleman."

Jay Omega looked apologetic. "We met him in the lobby as we were coming in," he explained. "He was looking for the reunion. He said that you would know him."

The Lanthanides looked questioningly at each other. No one spoke. Bunzie nodded to his assistant, signaling him to be ready to handle an awkward situation. "I don't think any of us knows the gentleman," he said dismissively. "So if you will excuse us—" The man in the doorway smiled. "It'll come to you, Fugghead."

"My God!" whispered George Woodard, peering at the stranger. "It's Pat Malone!"

Pseuicide—The fannish term for faking someone's death. Since most of fandom is conducted by mail, hoaxes are relatively easy to perpetrate.

CHAPTER 8

"WHAT WAS THAT all about?" whispered Marion when the door to the reception closed behind them.

Jay Omega shrugged. "I guess they knew him. What shall we do now? Call it a night?"

Marion glanced at her watch. "Not until I find out what's going on. Why don't we go out to the lobby and get some coffee? That way, we can waylay Erik when the party breaks up, and try to find out what's going on."

Her companion stifled a yawn. "All right. If you insist, but I don't see—"

"Shh!" Marion gestured toward the closed door of the banquet room. "Someone may come out unexpectedly. It would be a considerable blow to my self-esteem, not to mention my professional standing, if someone came out and caught us loitering in the hall like a couple of groupies. Let's talk about it over coffee."

Several minutes later, Marion had commandeered the coffee shop booth with the best view of the lobby, and she was hunched over a steaming mug of black coffee with the furtive air of an unindicted co-conspirator. Jay Omega, whose attention had been captured by a piece of Dutch apple pie, was doing his best to humor her.

"I'm sure they didn't mean to be rude," he said. "They seemed quite upset."

"It's all very strange," she murmured, stirring furiously. She kept casting sidelong glances at the hallway to the banquet room as if she were expecting a stampede, but all was quiet.

"He's another one of the Lanthanides, isn't he?" said Jay. "When we met him in the lobby, and he said that he was Pat Malone, I assumed that he was an editor or a film person, and that he was joking, but Woodard seemed to recognize him."

Marion scowled. "Woodard called him Pat Malone, which is ridiculous. Pat Malone has been dead since 1958. Everybody in fandom knows that. I know that and I wasn't even in fandom in 1958. I was in diapers!"

This was something of an exaggeration, but Jay wisely did not correct her arithmetic.

"I admit that it *sounded* like Woodard said 'Pat Malone,' but it's impossible. Pat Malone is dead. All the books say so."

Jay smiled. "That would explain the shocked looks on the faces of the rest of them."

"It certainly would," snickered Marion. "Pat Malone! I wonder how he found out about the reunion?"

"Ouija board?" suggested Jay Omega, trying to keep a straight face.

Marion, who had gone back to trying to figure things out, acknowledged his wit with the briefest of smiles. "Very clever. Actually, his knowing about the reunion is probably the least part of the mystery. Thanks to the dramatic effect of the drained lake, and to Ruben Mistral's excellent publicists, this reunion has been covered in everything from computer bulletin boards to the *National Enquirer.* You'd *have* to be dead not to know about it."

"I wonder if Elvis will show up," Jay mused. "He's from Tennessee, too, isn't he?"

"Don't be silly," said Marion. "Elvis Presley is dead."

"That doesn't seem to have stopped Pat Malone," he pointed out. "Can you explain that?"

Marion nodded. "I think so. Mark Twain said it best: *All reports of my death have been greatly exaggerated.* Actually, in fandom such misinformation isn't even uncommon. Fans chiefly correspond by letter and by hearsay, so it's very easy for someone to start an unsubstantiated rumor, which soon gets repeated as fact farther along the grapevine."

"Somebody said he was dead, and nobody checked?"

"Hardly anybody ever checks *anything* in fandom. Remember all the garbage that came out in fanzines after *Bimbos of the Death Sun* first came out? People thought 'Jay Omega' was a pseudonym for half of SFWA."

"I told you not to read the amateur commentary on my book," said Jay, downing the last of his milk. "It only upsets you. Even *good* reviews upset you."

"I couldn't believe how shallow most of those reviewers were," said Marion, momentarily distracted. Then, noticing her companion's amused smile, she decided to jettison the tirade. "Well, never mind about literary criticism! The subject at the moment ought to be history. Apparently we have just witnessed the debunking of a death hoax of thirty years' standing."

"Hoax?" Jay looked bewildered. "So you're saying that somebody deliberately made an announcement that Pat Malone was dead, and everybody just believed it and let it go at that?"

"Something like that. Given the mentality of fandom, death hoaxes are inevitable occurrences. Some people do it as a practical joke; some declare themselves dead in order to get rid of people who otherwise will not go away; and some people do it in order to annoy the person they report as dead. Back in the fifties, fans were taking up a collection to bring the brilliant Irish fan Walt Willis to Chicon II in Chicago, and a neofan named Peter Graham sent out postcards announcing Willis's demise."

"Why?"

"Apparently because Peter Graham felt like it, and because his parents had given him a postcard mimeo and he wanted to use it. He knew that it would cause a sensation because Willis was so popular. Most people realized that the postcard was a hoax at the time, because he had misspelled 'diphtheria,' and because it seemed strange that an Irishman's death announcement should be postmarked San Francisco."

"I suppose Walt Willis was pretty upset about it."

"I hear he wasn't. People said that when he got to the U.S., he charmed everyone by answering his telephone, 'Peter Graham speaking.'" Marion smiled at the memory of one of fandom's finest hours.

"But, of course, you don't approve," said Jay solemnly.

Marion looked stern. "Death hoaxes are cruel and pointless. I wonder who started this one?"

"I wonder why Pat Malone didn't bother to set anyone straight?"

"That may be what he is doing right now." Marion sighed. "I wish Erik Giles would come out. That is one conversation I'd give anything to hear."

"You may get your chance tomorrow," Jay told her. "Someone is going to have to explain his presence to the media people. Still, thirty years is a long time to wait to correct a mistake like that, don't you think?"

"I don't know. From what I hear about the personality of Pat Malone, he may have staged the hoax himself. And I know why everyone was so quick to believe in it."

"Why?"

Marion sighed. "Wishful thinking. Before Pat Malone died, he created a stink in fandom that lasted for decades. A lot of people will be dismayed to hear that he's back."

Alluvial—Volume 7, Number 4
June 16, 1958

***Special Issue of ALLUVIAL
dedicated to Pat Malone***

IN MEMORIAM PAT MALONE
By George Woodard, Editor

One of the most powerful, if strident, voices in fandom has been stilled by no less a censor than the Grim Reaper himself, who swept down with his black wings in the night, and carried off Patrick B. Malone, on June 8 in Biloxi, Mississippi.

Word has reached me here in Maryland that Pat Malone has died, and, since this information has not been generally released and since it concerns a fellow Lanthanide, I consider it my somber duty to relay that which I know concerning his passing to the late, great Pat's many associates in the realm of science fiction fandom. According to Jack L. Bexler (editor of JACKAL'S MEAT), he (Jack) received a letter from his (Pat's) widow, Ethel Lucille Malone, who resides in Cupertino, CA. (She did not write to me, one of Pat's oldest friends in fandom, but that is another matter.) Why he died in Mississippi is not clear to this writer. Bexler relates that Pat Malone had been sick for a number of years with a tuberculosis-related illness of some kind, and that he finally died of it this month, in great pain. His body was donated to the Washington Medical School, by his own instructions.

Pat will be remembered by his myriad correspondents as one of the founders of ALLUVIAL, one of the leading fanzines of this decade, but he is even better known as an incisive critic of the social order, the Jonathan Swift of fandom, the stinging gadfly of all he surveyed. He is the author of one SF novel, *River of Neptune*, which is unfortunately out of print, but somewhere in the Library of Congress, his name will be listed for all time.

Who among us has not felt the barbed tongue of Patrick B. Malone? Of course, he will also be remembered for his perceptive analyses of the works of Jules Verne, and for his detailing the fulfillment of Verne's scientific prophecies (e.g. the submarine), but it is his fan-related writings which will make his name ring down through the ages. His opus *THE LAST FANDANGO* (privately mimeographed) is a classic of social commentary, and it revolutionized the heretofore timid accounts of fan politics and convention activities.

He left the editorship of ALLUVIAL in 1955, when he left the Fan Farm, and I have carried on. I like to think that Somewhere, he will keep reading, and will say, "Well done, Woodard!"

He is gone, and those of us who were his friends will miss his crisp forthrightness. His enemies have lost a chance to change his opinion of them. And we shall not see his like again.

GEORGE WOODARD, ED.

GOODBYE AND GOOD RIDDANCE, PM!
A Guest Column By Jack L. Bexler

Providence, Rhode Island
June 1958

I write to bury Pat Malone, not to praise him. Speaking no ill of the dead smacks of hypocrisy and I'll have none of it, so I will at least do Pat the courtesy of being as forthright as he was, and not pretend that death has improved him. (Though I thought it might.)

I never met Pat Malone face to face, but I have certainly felt his typewritten wrath in various altercations that ran between *ALLUVIAL* and *JACKAL'S MEAT*. One such return salvo was sent back to me unopened in mid-June by Ethel Malone from Cupertino, California, enclosed in a letter saying that her husband Pat was dead, and so, ironically enough, it was his chief enemy who was given the task of announcing his death to his friends. (If he had any.) I only regret that, unlike Mac-Duff, I cannot also bring them his head.

Others will have to eulogize Pat Malone, the man. I knew him as a typeface with one half the "S" missing. It summed him up very well. The half-essed Pat Malone. He came from a dull, but respectable background, and perhaps being something of the alienated intellectual, the perpetual rebel, made him decide to leave the little college town of his birth, and begin his odyssey—to make a fandom of hell, and a hell of fandom.

He found others of his kind through the S-F magazines of the 'Forties, and later drifted onto the Fan Farm in Wall Hollow, Tennessee, where a mimeograph machine salvaged from a redneck's junkyard launched his career as a fan publisher. *ALLUVIAL* was born, and its regularity and reasonably good quality (he had a lot of other people's talent to draw from, and he used it well) quickly made him a celebrity in the genre. Not that Pat cared much about that. He contended that it didn't pay anything, and that the people singing his praises were "nobodies," so Pat tried to make the leap to pro-dom.

He managed to write one novel, *River of Neptune*, which sounded to me like a rewrite of some of Jules Verne's ideas (most notably "The First Men in the Moon"), but I am not a literary critic. I just know what I like, and in my opinion Harlan Ellison has a better chance to be famous than Pat Malone does.

That one "real" book did not make a happy man of Pat Malone. He didn't become famous with his little paperback yarn. He didn't become the darling of the literati. And he still didn't have any friends. The fact that there is only ONE book by Pat Malone further suggests that it was a fluke, rather than an indication of any real literary talent.

He gained much more notoriety from *THE LAST FANDANGO*, because people are invariably drawn to sleaze, however mendacious it is.

Pat Malone was a failure. He failed at life. He failed at fandom, his retreat from life. And he failed at being a writer, his retreat from fandom. His well-publicized and unprovoked attacks on well-meaning associates in the hobby testifies to his basic instability and to his own misery, which he attempted to alleviate by inflicting it on others.

I do not mourn his passing, and upon contemplating his life and his death, I do not think they let him in to heaven. If they did, I don't suppose he likes it much.

JACKAL BEXLER

GOOD NIGHT, SWEET PRINCE
In Remembrance of Pat Malone
by Angela Arbroath

(*REPRINTED FROM ARCHANGEL, JULY 1958,
ALL RIGHTS RESERVED.)

(Jack L. Bexler writes that Pat Malone has died in Mississippi. And I write this partly in sorrow for the loss of an old friend, and partly to let you know that I have no further details to give you on his actual passing. I did not know that Pat Malone was in Mississippi, and I believe that he was down near the Gulf, whereas I live up near Memphis, TN. Please don't send me any more letters asking for details. I don't know anything about Pat's death! What follows is a tribute to his life.—A.A.)

It has been several years since I saw Pat Malone, so perhaps the person who has died is not, in the emotional sense, the man that I knew, but, for the annals of fandom, wherein lies his best hope to be remembered, it falls to my lot to eulogize Pat Malone.

On a personal level, I can only say that I liked him as a friend and respected his talent, and then I must try to explain him to his many adversaries, because Pat Malone was truly a stormy petrel, whom few people appreciated and virtually no one understood.

Pat Malone was an idealist who valued intellectual

qualities above material possessions, and he very much wanted to be a part of a special group of dedicated and intelligent people. If he could have come to terms with God, he would have become a Jesuit, I think. As it was, he opted for a group of people who wrote with spirit and enthusiasm, made strong friendships (bickering aside), and who built an environment in which intelligence and verbal skill rather than race, social aptitude, sex, or family background determined one's position. Aldous Huxley aside, let us hope that this is the Brave New World. It is certainly the world in which Pat Malone wanted to live.

When his newfound paragons fell short of these utopian expectations, he took them to task for it. He hated the pettiness of some fans, and he was contemptuous of "Big Name Fans," who sought to become celebrities in what Pat considered a solemn intellectual order. He was forthright in his criticisms, and he made people angry. So long as what he said was true, Pat didn't care how people felt about its being said.

But he wanted to love us. I think that the civilization described in his novel *River of Neptune* is an idealization of fandom: the Marilaks are us as he would have liked us to be.

There is not much to say about my personal relationship with the young Pat Malone of the Wall Hollow fan farm. We wrote for a long while and drew mind-close, and later we came together as physical beings, and it was a very special time. I would have liked for us to have grown old together. I'd like to think of us 42 years from now, parking our air-car on a hilltop in Kenya and watching the Millennium come up like thunder, while we reminisced about sixth fandom, and all the wondrous things our old friends had done and been, but such a future was not to be.

Three years ago Pat Malone went out of our lives, and now he has even left our planet. I wish that I could have said good-bye to him before he went, so that I could have tried to tell him that even a stormy petrel is a wondrous creature to his friends.

ANGELA ARBROATH

In the Lanthanides' private party, no one was singing "Auld Lang Syne," and their expressions of shock and dismay left no doubt as to which way they would vote on the question of *should auld acquaintance be forgot?*

Only Angela Arbroath had summoned a tentative smile for the man in black. His expression suggested that he was receiving just the reception that he had expected, and was quietly enjoying it. While the others conferred in a buzzing undertone, he helped himself to straight Scotch and examined the hors d'oeuvres tray without favor.

"Is it really you, Pat?" ventured Angela, coming close to peer at him.

The stranger looked up from his perusal of the label on the bottle of Scotch. After a moment's study of the blushing middle-aged woman, he countered, "Am I to assume that somewhere in there is the former Angela Arbroath?"

She refused to be offended. "I do believe it *is* you, Pat Malone!" she cried. "I don't know of another soul who could be so offensive and ill tempered on such short notice and little provocation. You just want to see what I'll say! Well, here goes. You don't look so hot yourself, Patrick. I don't think I'd have known you." She gave him a hug. "Now where the hell have you been since 1958?"

He smiled, nodding to the others who had clustered around to hear his answer. He addressed them all. "Fandom may be a microcosm, children, but the rest of the world out there is reasonably large. I got lost in it. I found better things to do."

Ruben Mistral was scowling. Before anyone else could speak, he stepped between the stranger and the rest of the guests, as if he were protecting them from an assassin. "Just a minute, folks!" he announced in his crowd-control voice. "Before anybody says anything else to this individual, I think we should consider the possibility that this is a publicity-seeking impostor. This is a media event, you know."

The dark man smiled down at him. "Ah, Bunzie, don't tell me you've finally learned to look before you leap! If you had been able to do that in 1954, maybe Jim here would have checked the car radiator before we left for Worldcon, and we wouldn't have been left high and dry in Seymour, Indiana."

Bunzie reddened. "Well, who made us late in the first place, Malone? *You* said you were going to set the damned alarm clock for six-thirty. And when did we wake up?"

Jim Conyers eased his way to Bunzie's side. "If in fact this is Pat Malone," he reminded his host.

With raised eyebrows and a cold smile, Pat Malone was scanning the group. "Conyers," he nodded. "Always the sensible one. Let me guess. You're an attorney now?"

"More or less retired. But still cautious." Conyers seemed pleased to have been pegged so well.

Pat Malone studied the others. "Brendan, of course. My old sparring partner. And—"

"Erik Giles," said the professor quickly. "Good to see you again, Pat."

The gaze moved on. "And—unless someone brought his father to this little get-together—this must be Georgie Woodard."

Woodard managed a feeble grin. "I still publish *Alluvial*, Pat."

"No, George. You put out a silly bit of drivel purporting to be *Alluvial*. That 'zine, I assure you, is deader than I am." Malone reached for the bottle of Scotch and took it with him to the loveseat. "Are you all going to stay in shock much longer? This one-sided chat is getting a bit tiresome."

"We thought you were dead, Pat," said Angela. "We wrote tributes to you. How could you put us through all that grief when all the time you were alive, probably off somewhere laughing at us!"

"You were grieved?" He sounded surprised. "Well, *some* of you weren't. I wonder if it's too late to sue Jackal Bexler for libel?"

"Yes," said Jim Conyers.

"I thought so." He gave a little mock bow. "But thank you for your professional opinion, counselor. Anyhow, I rather thought that after *The Last Fandango* came out, I was more feared than esteemed. In fact, I'll bet some people have been looking over their shoulders ever since they heard the news of my untimely death, hoping that it wasn't a hoax."

"But why did you do it?" asked Lorien Williams.

Brendan Surn, who had been listening with uncharacteristic attentiveness, patted her hand. "I expect that Malone considered an obituary the most dramatic form of resignation from fandom. Didn't you, Pat? And with a death announcement, you not only got to rid yourself of old associates, you also got to hear exactly what they thought of you. I've often thought that Peter—"

"Peter Deddingfield is really dead, Brendan," said Erik Giles sharply. "He was killed by a drunk driver nine years ago. Besides, he was never the adolescent hoaxer that Malone has proven to be."

Pat Malone's dark eyes blazed. "Was I such an artful dodger, gentlemen? Or were you simply a bunch of rumormongers who couldn't be bothered to check your facts?"

Ruben Mistral felt that things were getting out of hand. Signaling for silence, he resumed his role as spokesman for the group. "Okay, Pat. We'll skip the whys and the wherefores. You're not dead. How did you find out about this reunion?"

"You do yourself an injustice, Bunzie. The publicity that your people have put out has ensured that everyone on the planet had a chance to hear about this event. As one of the Lanthanides, I considered myself invited."

Bunzie nodded impatiently. "No question about that. You had a story in the jar, too. But listen, the rest of us have agreed to certain business details. Percentages, representation by one agent, rights offered for sale. I hope you're not planning to come in as a maverick and queer the deal!"

Pat Malone's eyes widened in feigned innocence. "Now I ask you, Erik, would I queer the deal?"

Erik Giles blushed and turned away.

"I did wonder, though, about the wisdom of digging up old sins."

"What do you mean by that?" Ruben Mistral demanded.

"Oh, you know, Bunzie, little things that were no big deal in the early fifties, but might be now. Now that some of us are Eminent Pros." His tone was mocking.

"Such as?"

"Remember that phrase that a certain member of the Lanthanides paid me a six-pack for? On one occasion, I happened to remark that when I was a child, I had always been puzzled by the phrase 'for the time being.' I took it literally. I thought there really was someone called the Time Being, and that people did things for him."

"That's the basis of Peter Deddingfield's *Time Traveler Trilogy*!" cried Lorien Williams. "You mean it was *your* idea?"

"Worth a lot more than a six-pack now, don't you think?" asked Pat Malone. "What's it in now, its twenty-seventh printing? And then there's that story that Dale Dugger and Brendan Surn collaborated on. It read a lot better when you won the Hugo for it in '65, Brendan, but the original idea was Dale's, wasn't it? And remember how grossed out we all used to be because George Woodard—"

"That's enough, Pat!" Erik Giles shouted above the others' murmuring. His face was red now, and his eyes bulged from their sockets. "You could be asking for a hell of a libel suit."

Pat Malone smiled. "Public figures? Truth is a defense? Right, Jim boy?"

Conyers, the attorney, shrugged and glanced uneasily at the others. "I wouldn't venture to give you an opinion. But I don't see what you'd gain by embarrassing a bunch of your oldest friends."

"Gain?" Malone surveyed the scowling group and seemed pleased with the effect of his announcement. "Didn't *The Last Fandango* teach you anything? I'm an idealist, folks. And you fat cats have sold out. You all think you're the Founding Fathers of the Genre. Look at old Thomas Jefferson Surn over there in his NASA jacket. I think it's time somebody reminded you of what a bunch of half-assed adolescents you used to be, and how little difference there really is between who made it and who didn't. A lot of luck, maybe, and—" he looked directly at Bunzie"—more than a little ruthlessness."

"So you came back to screw us, did you, Pat?" asked Erik Giles.

His tormentor surveyed the room again. "Speaking of matters procreational, I see that Earlene Riley and Jazzy Holt aren't here. I'll bet no one has even *mentioned* their names."

George Woodard attempted to muster his dignity. "My wife was unable to attend."

Malone whistled. "Oh, Georgie, Georgie, you didn't." He turned to Bunzie. "Which one of 'em?"

Bunzie reddened. "Earlene."

"Ah. *Succulent nipples.*" His grin broadened as he

watched the others' discomfort. "Well, George, I hope you're man enough for the job. Where is Jazzy Holt? Lounging under a lamppost in Biloxi? *Hello, sailor.* No, I suppose not. After all, she's sixty, too, isn't she? Funny how people in our memories don't age."

Lorien Williams had recognized the name. She leaned over toward Conyers and whispered, "Does he mean Jasmine Holt, the famous S-F critic?"

Pat Malone overheard the question. "She was a critic, all right. She once told me that my dick looked like a tadpole sleeping on two apricots. Another *expert* opinion," he said, grinning at Jim Conyers. "Where is the randy bitch? Not still collecting virgins at S-F cons, surely?"

"She lives in London now," said Bunzie. "Although she wasn't one of the Lanthanides, I did invite her to attend the reunion, because of her—er—connections with the group, but she declined, telling me to use my own discretion about the disposal of the shares of Curtis Phillips and Peter Deddingfield. She doesn't need the money. Of course, there would have been some legal question about her entitlement anyway."

"She was married to both of them," Lorien Williams explained. She was pleased to finally be in the know on a bit of Lanthanides gossip.

"Separately?" smirked Pat Malone. "Or did you all take *Stranger in a Strange Land* as a directive from God?"

"I think that's enough, Pat," said Brendan Surn quietly. "There is nothing to be gained by rumormongering, as you put it a few minutes ago."

Bunzie looked relieved that order had been restored. "That's right, Malone. I asked you before, are you going to abide by the business arrangement already established?"

"Certainly, count me in. I'm sure you drove a shrewd bargain, Bundschaft." He ambled toward the door. "I may have another little project to pitch to the editors, though. Strictly on my own. Good night, all." Without waiting for anyone's reply, he was gone.

Bunzie stared dejectedly at the closed door through which Pat Malone had just left. "What the hell do we do now?"

Why have you come here
to this place you say
you never liked, where
mockingbirds read your mind . . .

—DON JOHNSON
"The House in the Woods"
from *Watauga Drawdown*

CHAPTER 9

THE REUNION WAS only seven hours away, but no one
was sleepy. The full moon shone on the newly resurrected Watauga River, which coursed again in its
original channel, a ribbon of light in the muddy
wasteland of the valley. In the long grass on the
hillsides above the shoreline, crickets chirped in a
ceaseless drone. It was a peaceful night in the
mountains, but no one forgot that when the sun rose
to reveal the barren lake bed, the dead would be
back among them. Indeed, one of them had returned
already.

After Pat Malone's invasion of the Lanthanides'
reunion, no one wanted to talk anymore about old
times. Within a space of ten minutes, everyone at
the reception in the Laurel Room had pleaded
fatigue or the lateness of the hour, and had retired
to their own rooms to ponder the evening's events.

Jim Conyers had been unmoved by the encounter,
and he felt a thickening in his senses that he knew
was a craving for sleep, but Barbara, who was out-
raged, wanted to discuss it.

She sat on the foot of the bed, staring at herself in

the mirror as she did her customary one hundred strokes a night with her hairbrush. Her shoulder-length curls—still a rich shade of chestnut (now obtained from a bottle)—shone in the lamplight, and her face seemed as unlined as a young girl's.

"That certainly was a performance tonight!" she remarked, brushing vigorously.

"Bravado," said Jim, stifling a yawn. "The Lanthanides loved to make scenes. They used to remind me of a bunch of Shetland pony stallions: terribly fierce and sincere, but so insignificant as to be comical."

"Well, it was a revelation to me," said Barbara, checking out his expression in the mirror. "I never knew that all those sexual high jinks were going on up at Dale's place."

Conyers shrugged. "They weren't, really. Jazzy Holt was somebody the others met at a science fiction convention. She never even visited the farm. They—er—got together at conventions, and spent the rest of the time writing soulful letters to her. She married Curtis after he left Wall Hollow, in '56, I think, and they divorced pretty soon after, about the time of his nervous breakdown."

Barbara sniffed. "Curtis Phillips was always crazy, if you ask me. Not that the rest of them were much of a contrast. Anyhow, it's a good thing for you I didn't know about such goings-on in 1954, Jim Conyers, or I'd have thought twice about marrying you." Another thought occurred to her. "What about Earlene Riley and Angela Arbroath? You can't say they didn't visit!"

"Angie was a high school kid, and built like a pipe

cleaner back then. Not exactly a femme fatale. Most of us treated her like a kid sister. And Earlene was a pudding-faced girl who used sex to build her self-esteem."

Barbara stared. "Jim! Do you mean she thought she was worth something because that pack of drips wanted to sleep with her? Lo-ord God! They would have slept with an Angus heifer if they could have caught one!"

Jim's smile was rueful. "Well, *I* wouldn't have!" he told her. "I had the prettiest girl in east Tennessee as my one and only."

She put down the brush and came to hug him. As he enfolded her in his arms and lay back on the bed, he thought how good his life had been, and for the thousandth time he was glad he had never told Barbara about that one little incident with Earlene Riley. He wondered if Pat Malone remembered it.

Several rooms farther down the hall, Ruben Mistral was pacing, while his preppy minion, still wearing a coat and tie, sat at the writing table by the window, notebook at the ready, in case there were instructions to be carried out. "He's not dead!" said Bunzie for the umpteenth time. "The son of a bitch isn't dead!"

The minion, a recent USC film school graduate named Geoff, ventured an opinion. "Excuse me, sir? Are you *sure* he's really Pat Malone? We never asked to see his driver's license."

Bunzie snarled. "Of course it's him! He may not look the same, but there's nothing wrong with that steel trap he calls a mind. His memory is perfect!

Why couldn't he have gone ga-ga instead of poor old Brendan? Did you notice how out of it Surn was?"

"Not especially, sir. I had never met him before. He did seem less forthright than Mr. Malone."

"So did Attila the Hun. I should have known Pat's death was too good to be true! At that party tonight he remembered enough damaging tidbits to keep the *Enquirer* presses rolling for a month! If he tries to get chatty in front of the reporters, so help me I'll kill him!"

"Would you like me to see that he is barred from the activities tomorrow?" said Geoff, whose job was to anticipate such assignments.

It was tempting, and Bunzie hesitated, thinking of the serenity of a reunion without the Lanthanides' stormy petrel, but as appealing as the suggestion was, it was too risky. "He'd call a press conference the minute our backs were turned," he sighed. "He'd use the hotel fax machine to blitz the media. By the time we schlepped back to the hotel with the time capsule, he'd probably be booked on Oprah, Geraldo, *and* Donahue! I think we're going to have to take him with us—so that we can keep an eye on him."

Geoff, whose threshold of modesty was considerably lower than his boss's, doodled a question mark on his note pad. "Has he really got all that much to tell? It was a long time ago, after all. Sounds like boyish pranks to me."

"That's a point," murmured Bunzie. "Maybe you're right. After all, we live in a world where Supreme Court nominees smoke pot, and elected officials get caught screwing around. Compared to that, we're small potatoes."

Geoff thought of adding, "And since you're not as famous as all that, who'd care," but he thought better of it. Instead he said, "It's not as if there were any terrible secrets within the group."

Bunzie was silent for almost a full minute before he replied. "No, I suppose not. But you can never tell what will strike the public fancy in the silly season! Remember when a moose fell in love with a cow and made *Newsweek*? All the same, I want you to stay with him tomorrow. Keep him away from the reporters! And the editors, too! Don't let him get off by himself with anyone."

"Sure. No problem." Geoff was careful not to react to this pronouncement. Privately, though, he was thinking, Holy shit! I wonder what those guys were up to back then!

"It went fine tonight. Just fine," said Lorien Williams for the third time. "You were great! Have you taken your medication yet?"

Brendan Surn, who was wearing his homespun monk's robe, was sitting on the edge of his bed, apparently unmoved by the evening's events. He had smiled his vague smile as Lorien helped him change clothes, and he watched the end of a television movie while she got into her pajamas. In response to Lorien's question about his pills, he looked about him for clues that he had taken it, a glass of water, the bottle of pills, but there was no physical evidence to jog his memory. He shook his head, giving her that helpless little smile that meant he didn't know.

Lorien rummaged about in her suitcase. "No, of course you haven't!" she announced. "I hadn't even unpacked them yet. Here, open the bottle while I get you some water."

Surn worked diligently on the childproof cap. From the bathroom, Lorien called out to him over the sound of running water, "Did you enjoy the evening?"

He thought about her question until she returned. "Yes, it was quite nice," he said, accepting the glass from her.

"It was interesting to meet them all," said Lorien, sitting down on the edge of the bed to continue the chat. "I wish I could have met Curtis Phillips and Peter Deddingfield, though."

Brendan Surn frowned. "Weren't they there?"

"No, Brendan," said Lorien gently. "They are dead. It was Pat Malone who came back. And I don't own anything of his that I could get autographed."

He gave her a vague smile. "Pat Malone forgot that he was dead."

Lorien, who was never sure whether or not Surn was joking, thought it best to overlook that remark. "Well, you are going to have a long day tomorrow, Brendan!" she said briskly. "There will be a lot of reporters and a lot of unfamiliar situations. Let's go through it all again, shall we? And then I think you should get some sleep."

"I'm not tired," said Surn. "Is there some work that I should be doing?"

His assistant stifled a yawn. "Do you want to

finish your monthly letter to that fanzine you contribute to?" She went over to a small suitcase and extracted a sheaf of papers and a mimeographed journal bound in yellow construction paper. "I've made the notes here about the topics you wanted to comment on to each participant."

Although *Phosgene* was a science fiction fanzine, or more specifically a letterzine, its subjects ranged far afield of the genre. Any given issue might contain essays from various contributors on the subject of Central European politics, solar energy, abortion, or tropical fish diseases. Subscribers would write letters about whatever they cared to discuss, and in the next issue everyone else would comment, usually briefly, on each of the opinions expressed. The fact that almost no one had the slightest pretension to expertise on any of these topics did not deter them from pontificating. Indeed, one might suppose that anyone who had any proficiency in the subject would not be there in the first place, because he could find a better forum for his ideas, i.e., a place where they might actually have some influence. As it was, the *soi-disant* philosophers of fandom preached at each other while the world went by. Offering sermons from the mount of his celebrity to the subscribers of *Phosgene* was one of Brendan Surn's few vanities.

Lorien Williams consulted her notes. "Let's see . . . We have Lois Hutton talking about women in combat, and you wanted to say . . ."

Surn waved his hand. "Tell her that NASA experiments proved that middle-aged women would make the best astronauts. Surely they could be equally effective as soldiers." He giggled. "Besides, who'd miss them?"

Lorien wrote everything down except for that last comment. She felt that Surn was a prisoner of his generation, but that he should be protected from the scorn of his more enlightened younger acquaintances. "The next writer is Gareth Whitney from Culpeper, Virginia."

"Yes. I like him. Tell him that I agree with him that even if A. P. Hill had not been shot, he would not have survived the Civil War, for reasons of health, and that while I cannot agree that he was the equal of Stonewall Jackson, I do think that as a brigade commander, he was exceptional."

Lorien scribbled down this reply. "Ready for the next one? They're arguing about Harlan again."

Surn smiled. "Oh, Harlan. Leave them to it. They're having such a good time, and he can take care of himself. I won't comment. What else?"

"Worldcon."

"San Francisco," sighed Surn. "Snog in the fog!"

Lorien looked away. "It's in Orlando this year, actually," she said in a tone of studied casualness.

"It doesn't seem very long ago," mused Brendan Surn, staring out into the dark void of the Watauga valley. "The San Francisco Worldcon. And living here. But they all look so old. Did I write a story about that once? About a man who comes out of a daydream to find that he has aged fifty years in two minutes?"

Lorien patted his hand. "That was Fredric Brown, Brendan. In *Nightmares and Geezenstacks*." Sometimes she felt that remembering titles and authors was all the help she could give him, but he seemed pleased at this shared memory.

"So it was," he said with a sudden smile. "I *remember* it!"

Erik Giles looked down at his third cup of coffee. "I really shouldn't be doing this," he remarked. "Either I'll pace all night or I'll have to sleep in the bathtub."

Angela Arbroath patted his hand. "Go on, Stormy! Have a caffeine orgy. After the shock we've had tonight, we ought to be drinking something a lot stronger than coffee."

On the other side of the table, Jay and Marion glanced at each other, wondering if this could be considered an opening for the introduction of a touchy subject. Shortly after the reunion party disbanded, Erik had come wandering out into the lobby, still chatting with Angela Arbroath, and Marion had hurried out of the coffee shop to snare them with the promise of coffee. So far, introductions and pleasantries had dominated the conversation, but now the hour grew late, and the other tables in the coffee shop had emptied one by one until they were alone. Now seemed like a good time to discuss the dramatic events of the evening's reception.

"I imagine it gave you quite a shock," said Jay Omega, "and it's partly our fault, for which I apologize. We ran into the fellow just as we were coming back from dinner. He was coming through the front doors with his suitcase at the same time we were entering, so naturally I helped him with the doors."

Marion smirked. "Virtue is its own punishment."

"Then when he asked me where the Lanthanides reunion was being held, we couldn't very well plead ignorant. I told him that outsiders were not permitted to attend, but he just smiled and said that he was invited."

"And, of course, I asked who he was," said Marion, taking up the tale. "Jay wouldn't have challenged him, but I'm much more assertive. Imagine my surprise when he said he was Pat Malone. It was on the tip of my tongue to say, 'But you're dead'; however, even I can't manage to be that abrupt."

Jay smiled. "You underestimate yourself." To Giles and Angela Arbroath he explained, "In order to convey the impression that he was expected at the party, the fellow said, 'I expect the Lanthanides have been looking high and low for me,' and Marion muttered, 'I thought those were the places to look.' "

"We figured it out, of course," said Marion. "We came in here for coffee and talked it over. It was a death hoax, wasn't it?"

"Apparently so," said Erik Giles dryly. "Even if I believed in resurrection of the body, I don't think the deity would waste it on Pat Malone."

"It was inconsiderate of him," said Angela Arbroath. "Just the sort of silly prank that fifties fans went in for, not caring about the feelings of those who were taken in by it."

"I suppose he came back to get in on the money and the notoriety?" asked Jay.

"I hope so," said Erik. "It would be much more like him to come back in order to upset things, don't you think, Angela?"

She considered it. "Not out of sheer mischief," she said at last. "But I will grant you that Pat was an idealist, and if he thought any of you were selling out, or capitalizing on your old days at Dugger's farm, then he might very well feel self-righteous about putting a stop to things."

"But he's over sixty now, too!" Erik protested. "Surely he could use a bit of cash as badly as the rest of us!"

Angela stared at him. "How odd!" she cried. "I've only just realized that we don't know a single thing about the resurrected Pat Malone! We were all so much in shock that no one thought to ask him what he has been doing all these years. We treated him as if he really were a ghost."

"Even if he did come to spoil things, how much trouble could he cause?" asked Marion. "You all are a bunch of *writers*. How many guilty secrets could you have?" She laughed at her own joke.

Everyone else looked thoughtful.

George Woodard had brushed his teeth, put on his striped pajamas, and cried a few tears of sheer frustration. Now he was ticking off a list of his most sympathetic friends, trying to decide if there was someone he could safely call to discuss the current crisis, but he could think of no one who wouldn't be delighted at the irony and embarrassment of it. George realized that he could crank up the science fiction rumor mill with one phone call, but in doing so, he would not receive one word of consolation or consideration for his plight. It wasn't worth it. Let everybody find out from someone else. He couldn't be bothered.

Earlene was not the first person he thought of to call, but her name did come up in his ruminations. He decided against it. She would probably force a full account of the evening's confrontation from him, and somehow she would contrive to blame George for the fact that it happened at all. Serves you right for going, she would say. No, Earlene would not be pleased that Pat Malone remembered her so clearly. George wasn't pleased, either, of course, but he consoled himself by thinking that it certainly wasn't true.

It had been true thirty-five years ago, but the "hot little number" that Malone recalled had cooled off to glacial proportions several decades back. Now she gave every appearance of being able to fall into a deep sleep as soon as her head hit the pillow. George puzzled over this apparent contradiction in the essence of reality. How could something which was technically true be so utterly false? The polite fiction maintained by everyone else—that Earlene was a dull little housewife—was certainly more accurate, but it ignored a good portion of her life. It was as if Earlene were two people: he had married one, but was forced to live with the other.

For a brief moment, George caught himself wondering if the old Earlene would have continued to exist had she married Pat Malone, but that thought was too damaging to his ego for him to dwell on it for long. He rummaged in his suitcase for the emergency Baby Ruth he had hidden in a sock, and began to quell his anxieties in his customary manner.

In the Holiday Inn in Johnson City, the editors and reporters had taken over the cocktail lounge. They were glad for a chance to get together, although such meetings were far from rare. They just didn't happen in New York. All of the occupants of the lounge worked in Manhattan within a half mile of each other, but in order to socialize, they had to attend conferences in various cities, or turn up as fellow lecturers at a writers' workshop somewhere. If this were a Thursday night in New York, a third of them would be doing their laundry; the other two-thirds would still be at the office.

The fact that Johnson City was a relatively small town did not unduly depress them, because (1) while many of them had fled to New York from small towns, they were well able to tolerate small doses of rural Americana; and (2) the publishing business *is* a small town.

Although the editors were ostensibly camped in Tennessee to engage in a bidding war, their camaraderie was unaffected by the potential rivalry. They were veterans of many such campaigns, and it was, after all, someone else's money that they were playing with. Except for the possibility of added prestige for a literary coup, which might result in money or perks, the Lanthanides Anthology Auction might as well be a Monopoly tournament. Their attitude toward the other group of professionals present—the various media representatives who had turned up for the occasion—was cordial, but more reserved. They didn't want to seem overly interested in the glitz business, and until one of them owned the current project, they had nothing quotable to say anyhow. Besides, editors secretly fear that journalists have the Great American Novel stashed in typing-paper boxes in their closets, and that given proximity to a book editor, they will try to market it. The editors' dread of becoming a literary hostage—trapped in a corner, listening to an endless plot summary—kept them packed into a tight little herd for protection. They imagined the reporters circling them like lions, seeking to pounce upon the weakest member of the herd.

The journalists in turn kept to their own corner of the lounge, swapping war stories about covering the vice-president, discussing software, and exchanging interesting fax numbers (Billy Joel's, for example). They were equally wary of the editors, who, after all, might want to get their names in the paper or might be seized with a guilt-ridden urge to wave to the folks on TV. Among themselves they also swapped horror stories about the most obnoxious "civilians" who had tried to impose on them lately.

At the beginning of the evening the two factions had staked out opposite sides of the room, holding court around their own tables, with occasional furtive glances toward the other enclave, but as the evening wore on, and sobriety wore out, some of the braver souls began to exchange pleasantries across professional lines, and by midnight, the room had become one large mob of *pros*, driving less determined tourists to their rooms to contemplate *The Best of Carson*.

Sarah Ashley, agent for Ruben Mistral and architect of the Lanthanides package, had hosted a prime-rib dinner for the group earlier in the evening, but she had wisely refrained from discussing business except to say that she for one felt privileged to be present at the making of a science fiction legend. After dinner, she had thanked everyone again for coming to the party and had gone up to her room, leaving the pack to speculate on the next day's events.

They had managed to avoid the subject for a good two hours, but finally weariness with the usual topics prevailed, and an Australian with one of the tabloids called out, "What do you make of this bit of grave robbing that's going on tomorrow?"

"The Dante Gabriel Rossetti syndrome," said Lily Warren, an editor who got her start in publishing with a university press.

"What has baseball got to do with it?" asked the *USA Today* reporter.

Lily winced. "Rossetti was a nineteenth-century English poet. When his wife died, he buried some of his unpublished work with her, and then about a year later he . . . went back and dug them up again."

"Geez," said *USA Today*. "Is anybody buried with the time capsule?"

The tabloid reporter had pulled out his pocket notebook and was already composing his lead.

"I wonder if Sarah Ashley would consider splitting up the package," mused Enzio O'Malley, one of the New York editors.

Lily Warren shook her head. "She'd be crazy to agree to that. Think of the publicity value in the time-capsule anthology story! Every book club in the country will grab it, for starters. Then there's the other sub rights. Films, foreign—"

O'Malley sighed. "I know, but I was thinking in terms of actual literary merit." He ignored the snickering of his colleagues. "You see, we own Brendan Surn's back list, and he really is one of the great writers of the genre." More snickering. "I was thinking that it might be nice to acquire just his story—for a lot less money, of course—and put it in a new anthology of his short fiction."

"No way," said Lily. "The package is too valuable as a whole. Besides—" She hesitated.

"Exactly," said O'Malley. "Selling that piece would gut the whole collection, because Surn's story might be the only thing in there that isn't crap."

"Oh, come on!" another editor protested. "Surely, Curtis Phillips—"

"Curtis Phillips was a fruitcake, and you can never tell whether he was being brilliant or deranged on this particular writing binge. Suppose he just raves for twenty pages? And most of the other contributing authors were one-book wonders, whose early work may turn out to be worthless." Enzio O'Malley downed the last of his beer. "Sarah's asking us to take a hell of a gamble here. I'd buy anything of Surn's in a minute, but the whole package? I don't know."

"Suppose it *isn't* any good?" asked another editor.

Lily Warren chuckled. "Goodness has nothing to do with it. The very act of paying serious money for this collection in an auction will make it famous, and the publicity generated by this reunion is priceless. Half the country will know about this collection months before the pub date. By the time the publisher runs major ads, books the old geezers on the morning talk shows, and intimidates the sales force with a six-figure print run, every rube in America will have heard of it, and thousands of them will buy it for the novelty value alone. Didn't *The Satanic Verses* sell big, despite the fact that no one actually read it? Oh, this time-capsule gimmick will sell, all right. Sarah Ashley is no fool when it comes to marketing."

O'Malley stared mournfully into his empty beer mug. "The critics will savage it, and the S-F crowd, which is notoriously poor, will wait for the paperback, and you'll have to eat fifty thousand hardcover copies of a shit-awful book," he said mournfully.

The other editors fell silent. Enzio O'Malley's pessimistic, and probably accurate, assessment of the package had brought an unpleasant note of reality to the revels. For a moment they were forced to contemplate whether they actually ought to be trying to publish *good* books, instead of shilling for hyped books. But the feelings of gloom were brief, and almost instantly succeeded by a universally held conviction that Enzio O'Malley's negative comments were designed to throw them off the scent. Obviously, he had been issued firm orders by his publishing masters to acquire the time-capsule anthology at any cost. Silently they began to wonder what kind of money or treachery it would take to beat him out of it.

Jay Omega couldn't sleep. The party in the coffee shop had broken up an hour ago, and now the hotel was dark and quiet. He lay on the side of his bed, unable to relax, listening for night sounds and replaying the day's events in his head. Marion, unused to Lakecrest beer and long hours, was sleeping peacefully, but Jay was still wide awake. He thought he might have been able to fall asleep if he could have lain in bed and read a hard-science fiction novel, full of technical monotony, but the light would have disturbed Marion. He told himself that he needed to sleep because of the eventful day that would begin in just a few hours, but that only made him more alert. The more he pursued oblivion, the more restless he became. Finally, giving in to his own anxieties, he slipped on his jeans and sweatshirt and crept from the room. Perhaps a walk in the cool night air would calm his thoughts and allow him to sleep.

He crossed the deserted lobby and left the building, with the glass door swinging noiselessly behind him. The moon shone above the ridge of oak trees, and the air was crisp and cool, but the parking lot smelled of oil and burnt rubber. It was not a place he wanted to linger. Jay hurried away from it and found the path through the rhododendrons that led down to the edge of the lake. Now the steep moss-strewn trail ended in a gully of dry red clay, ringed like redwoods from the lapping waters of the receding Watauga.

Jay stood alone in the darkness, thinking that it was quiet, because like most country people he didn't register the ceaseless whine of crickets as noise. He looked up at the full moon, a small silver disk hanging above the distant hills, and saw it only as a dry lake bed suspended in the black sky. It illuminated the few clouds hovering near it, but there was no reflecting shine from the dark emptiness of Breedlove Lake, no response from the dead land.

Jay felt a disquieting urge to walk forward into the dark basin of the lake without caring where it would take him or whether he came back at all. Such moodiness was rare for James Owens Mega. Usually, he dealt logically with problems that he could solve, and he wasted little time fretting over the rest, but the Lanthanides troubled him. They seemed to him to be various projections of his own future: Erik, the sedentary academic who had given up writing; Mistral, the Hollywood mogul who had turned his hobby into an empire, and was universally accused of selling out; or George Woodard, who had allowed his alternate universe to consume his life, and lived in poverty and failure as a result. He supposed that Brendan Surn was the most enviable of the company, but he, too, presented a grim specter of a writer's future: obviously suffering from some mental impairment, he lived alone and friendless, except for his various business caretakers and the young nurse/companion who looked after him. Jay could see himself in any of those existences, and he did not like what he saw. Do writers live happily ever after, he wondered.

He was still pondering that waking nightmare when he heard footsteps on the path above him, coupled with the sound of rhododendron branches being brushed aside. The crickets fell silent. At last the figure stepped out from the shadows of the trees, and Jay could see the dark, emaciated figure of Pat Malone wending his way carefully over the rocks and coming toward him.

"You couldn't sleep, either," he called out softly to Malone.

The older man shrugged. "No. You're the young engineer, aren't you? I thought there would be a lot of sleepless people tonight, but I wasn't expecting one of them to be *you*."

Jay Omega sat down on the concrete ramp that had been a boat dock. Now it lay two hundred yards up from the shallows of the receding lake. "My sleeplessness wasn't on your account," he told Malone. "I was contemplating my own mortality, I guess."

"You could always come back from the dead," came the reply from the shadows. "I did."

"It's odd that you should turn up. I was just wondering what you had been doing for the last thirty years," said Jay. He explained his feelings about the other Lanthanides, and his own unwillingness to become like any of them in succeeding decades. "I had hoped that your life turned out happier than theirs," he concluded, straining in the darkness for a glimpse at Pat Malone's expression.

The responding voice was grim. "Was I any better off than they were? Not in the sense you mean, perhaps. I had to be somebody else, that's all. Tonight feels like a kind of resurrection for me. I'm not sure that I care for it, but I had to come."

"The others didn't seem pleased to see you," Jay remarked. "I wondered about that."

Malone laughed. "You *wondered*? Didn't you ever read my little mimeographed masterpiece called

The Last Fandango? I drummed myself out of the hobby once and for all in that, and along the way I made some very unpleasant but true observations about certain prominent jerks in fandom. The more perceptive of the Lanthanides might assume that I was here to do more of the same."

"Are you?"

"I wouldn't be Pat Malone if I didn't. I am legend."

Jay was puzzled. "We were talking about you tonight," he said. "We all wondered what you have been doing for the last thirty years. You never said."

"Yes, I did. I told you that I had become somebody else. Come to think of it, they all did that, didn't they? But I'm not sure I like the people they turned into. Mistral who is somebody with a capital S. And your professor friend, who is trying to live down his years in fandom. But even the silliest of them—Woodard—came to terms with the real world when it came down to raising kids and making a living, but he trades on his youthful associations to impress neofans. George Woodard: a big-name fan! Some idealists, huh?"

"All except Curtis Phillips," said Jay Omega.

"Yes, I guess that's what happens to people who don't conform. They get locked up. But Curtis was more free than any of them, I think. He got to keep on being himself."

"And you didn't?"

"I could have. But I didn't want to end up like Curtis, so I traded my freedom for—" He seemed to think about it. "For respectability. A different kind of freedom."

Jay thought he understood. "I know. I faced that

as a teenager. You have to conform to make money, and in our society, having money is the only way to keep yourself really free. So I became an electrical engineer instead of a journalism major, and now I can afford to do some writing, because—"

Pat Malone began to walk away. "I must go," he called back as he disappeared up the path into the darkness. "You weren't at all who I expected. Go to bed."

"Who ever you—" Jay's words echoed in the hollow stillness. Malone was gone. Go to bed, mused Jay. I suppose my elders have spoken. As he headed back toward the lodge, he was surprised to find himself yawning. "Tomorrow," he said aloud, "I will wonder if I dreamed this."

CHAPTER 10

AT TEN O'CLOCK in the morning—the late hour being a concession to the long commute from Johnson City—the Lanthanides reunion officially began, with a coffee-and-doughnuts briefing in the Mountaineer Lodge conference room. A gaggle of sleepy editors and journalists was herded in to the meeting, where a smiling and surprisingly un-jet-lagged Ruben Mistral greeted them personally and steered them toward a sympathetic waitress, who was dispensing the coffee.

Two dozen metal folding chairs had been set up facing a varnished pine lectern, and in the front row sat George Woodard, looking like a mud slide in his khaki safari outfit. He had a lap full of doughnuts, and a cup of milky coffee wedged precariously between his knees. Iridescent flakes of doughnut glaze clung to the corners of his mouth, and his black hair, lank and oily, lay in a collapsed wave across his forehead. He looked more subdued than usual, daunted perhaps by lack of sleep, the presence of reporters, and the aura of show biz emanating from the ringmasters of the show. He had been hoping for a better breakfast, at the reunion's expense, but failing that and with the prospect of lunch uncertain, he had stocked up on greasy, sugar-encrusted doughnuts as his only sustenance. They did not sit well on his already upset stomach.

Geoff, minion of Ruben Mistral, seemed to be hosting the briefing, and he had chosen to reflect this authority by masquerading as Indiana Jones. He sported a battered fedora, khaki vest and pants, and even a stubble of beard over his weak chin, as a tacit reminder of the rigors of the day's expedition. He had omitted the Indiana Jones trademark bullwhip and pistol as a concession to the solemnity of the occasion.

Beside him, cordial to the milling crowd of editors, journalists, and well-wishers, but not courting them, was Ruben Mistral, resplendent in a buttondown linen Basile shirt, yellow pleated trousers, and alligator loafers, the latter being evocative of the valley's current swampy condition but hardly appropriate for traversing it. He was drinking his coffee out of a Royal Doulton porcelain cup in the teal and gold Carlyle pattern. He searched the crowd for the missing Lanthanides, and spotted Erik Giles and Angela Arbroath talking to their two professor friends. Conyers and his wife were chatting with a young woman in jeans and a Villager shirt, probably a local reporter. Where were the others? A glance at his Rolex told him that it was time to start the briefing.

For an instant, Mistral considered sending George Woodard in search of the stragglers—he was certainly expendable—but this was a task that required efficiency and speed, both of which were well out of Woodard's range of abilities. Geoff was doing the technical part of the spiel, so he couldn't be spared. He looked around for another minion and finally decided to draft one.

A moment later, a jovial Bunzie-like Ruben Mistral appeared at Giles's elbow. "Good morning, kids!" he beamed. "We'll be ready to get underway in just a moment, but not everybody is here yet." He hesitated for effect, and then brightened as if inspiration had just visited. "I wonder if I could ask a favor. It would certainly speed things up if someone would go after our missing comrades. That is, Brendan Surn and—" a faint expression of distaste punctuated his request "—and, of course, Pat Malone. What a guy! We resurrect the time capsule, and Pat comes back from the dead. Would you mind locating them and bringing them to our little briefing?" He turned his cold smile briefly on Jay Omega, and then, reconsidering, he directed his gaze at the person he considered to be of lowest rank in the foursome. "How about it, dolling?" he said, placing a fatherly hand on Marion's shoulder.

Dr. Marion Farley, who had flunked people for less, managed an expressionless "I'd be happy to" and left the room.

"That's good," said Mistral, glancing at his watch again. "Look at the time! I think I'd better start anyway. The first part is just background. They won't miss much." He hurried back to the lectern to call the meeting to order.

"Ladies and gentlemen. And editors . . ." He waited for the polite laughter before continuing. "I want to welcome all of you to Wall Hollow, Tennessee. The year is 1954. Geez, I wish it was. Gas was eighteen cents a gallon back then. Anyhow, before I introduce my fellow Lanthanides, I'm going to turn Sarah Ashley loose on you to talk about money and percentages, and all that stuff we writers just don't understand." The groan in the audience was presumably from Mistral's editor, who knew better. "Then I'm going to turn the program over to my associate, Geoffrey L. Duke, who will fill you reporters in on the engineering details of this endeavor. After that, we hit the boats!"

Even when she was seething, Marion was efficient. First she checked the restaurant to see if the absentees were finishing up a leisurely breakfast. They weren't. Then, after obtaining the missing Lanthanides' room numbers from an intimidated young receptionist, Marion attempted to commandeer the desk phone, but before she could pick it up, it rang. In the interests of time Marion decided to take the more direct approach of going after them personally. Since both Surn's and Malone's rooms were on the second floor, she decided that taking the elevator up one flight would be faster than waiting for the desk clerk's phone.

She was a bit annoyed at missing the introductory remarks from Mistral, but she was pleased at having kept her temper. Marion was fond of saying that women Ph.D.s do not have to strive for humility: it hunts them down on a regular basis.

Since Brendan Surn's room number put him closest to the elevator, Marion tried him first. She tapped lightly on the great man's door, wondering if she would now be mistaken for a chambermaid. "Mr. Surn! The Lanthanides reunion is about to start!"

After several moments the door opened and Lorien Williams peered out with a worried frown. "Is it nine o'clock already?"

Marion was relieved to see that she was dressed, as was Brendan Surn, who had also come over to the door. They both wore blue sweatsuits and new white running shoes. Marion refused to allow herself even to think any snide remarks about Brendan Surn. He looked tired. "It's a little past nine now," Marion told them. "Would you like me to show you the way? They're serving coffee and doughnuts there if you haven't had breakfast yet."

"That will be all right," said Surn, reaching for the door.

"I'll get the room key," murmured Lorien.

"There's one other missing person," said Marion. "Pat Malone. You haven't seen him, have you?"

"Pat Malone is dead," said Brendan Surn in his gentle way, as if reminding her of an obscure current event.

Lorien Williams hurried over and took him by the arm. "No, Brendan," she said. "It's Peter Deddingfield you're thinking of that's dead. And Curtis Phillips. We saw Mr. Malone last night, remember?"

Marion took a deep breath. "I'll just go and find Pat Malone, then. Someone at the desk will show you to the conference room." She turned and fled down the hall, and her cheeks were wet.

Geoffrey Duke had taken his place at the lectern in the conference room and was giving background information to the press. Behind him were two enlarged black-and-white photos, labeled "Wall Hollow 1954" and "Wall Hollow Today." They were taken from the same spot on a mountainside over-looking the valley. The first picture looked like a calendar illustration of a New England town. It showed a small village of white houses and a steepled country church nestled among the oak trees in a green valley. It conjured up images of Norman Rockwell paintings and old Frank Capra movies.

The second photograph was hardly recognizable as the same spot. The two main roads of the village were still visible, outlining the dimensions of the town, but only a few of the stone buildings remained standing, surrounded by craters marking the sites of the houses, and the blackened skeletons of oak trees. The scene, a study in mud and desolation, evoked comparisons with disaster photos: bomb sites, and towns laid waste by hurricanes. People would study the first picture of Wall Hollow, glance at the second, and then look away at nothing for a few moments before they went back to what they were doing.

Geoffrey Duke consulted his notes on the technical aspects of the drawdown, and called the conference to order. After a few words of welcome, he plunged into his well of statistics. "Breedlove Lake has a water surface area of sixty-six thousand acres, extending sixteen miles upstream," he said to the furiously scribbling reporters. "The dam, which is three hundred and eighteen feet high, is thirteen hundred feet thick at the base and produces fifty thousand kilowatts of power with its two generators."

"How did they construct the dam?" asked the *Times* reporter.

"They selected a deep, narrow mountain gorge and filled it with three million cubic yards of dirt and rock. The dam's core is one million four hundred eighty-four thousand and seven hundred cubic yards of compacted clay, surrounded on either side by two million cubic yards of rock."

"Where'd they get all that rock?"

Geoff was ready for that question. "Three quarries near the construction site. They loosen the rock with coyote tunnel blasts using Nitramon."

"Using *what*?"

"It's a brand name for ammonium nitrate. Dupont. Digging and loading the blast tunnels took weeks."

"What about the people in the valley?" asked Sarah Ashley. "Did they just get kicked off their land?"

"No. The TVA bought the town for thirty-five thousand dollars."

Murmurs of disbelief came from the crowd. "What if people didn't want to sell?"

Geoff shrugged. "That was too bad, I guess."

"How many people were relocated?" asked another

journalist, who was trying to calculate how much each family received.

Geoff consulted his notes. "More than a hundred early on in the project. Seven hundred and sixty-three at the closing of the dam. Eighty-five percent relocated in the east Tennessee counties of Carter and Johnson. Five percent left the state. Including, of course, most of the Lanthanides."

Bunzie whistled a few bars of "California, Here I Come" and waved for Geoff to continue.

"The drawdown, which began six weeks ago for the purpose of repairing the dam, was effected by opening the sluice gates—"

Jay Omega was sitting in a front row seat beside Erik Giles. "I wonder what's keeping Marion," he murmured.

"I don't know. She may be dawdling on purpose to miss this technical spiel," Giles suggested. "I'm surprised that Malone isn't here, though."

"I doubt if he'll miss the boat," said Jay Omega. "He seemed very keen on the reunion."

Erik Giles grunted. "Are you familiar with the fairy tale *Sleeping Beauty*?" he asked.

"Sort of," said Jay. "Why?"

"Pat Malone reminds me of the bad fairy at the christening."

In the second-floor hallway of the Mountaineer Lodge, Marion knocked again. "Mr. Malone!" she said, more loudly this time. "Are you awake? The reunion sent me to get you!" She put her ear to the door, straining to catch the sound of the shower or the television. All was silent. Marion began to become concerned. After all, she told herself, they are rather elderly. As she straightened up, trying to decide what to do next, she caught sight of the maid, pushing her cleaning cart around the corner by the elevator.

"I hope I'm not about to make an idiot of myself," Marion muttered, hurrying to intercept her.

A few moments and several explanations later, the chambermaid, muttering, "I'm not real sure we ought to do this," used her passkey to unlock the door of Pat Malone's room. As the door swung open, Marion called out, "Mr. Malone! Are you all right?"

An instant later they could see that he wasn't. The smell of vomit and voided bowels reached them and made them draw back, even before Marion saw the stiffening form of the room's occupant, sprawled across the sill of the bathroom. "You call," she said, nudging the maid out of shock, "I'll see if there's anything to be done for him."

While the maid was spluttering into the telephone, attempting to make the front desk understand the situation, Marion knelt beside the body of the recently resurrected Pat Malone. His eyes stared up at her, sightless, with the same glare that had so daunted the Lanthanides at last night's reception. Steeling herself for the sensation of touching dead flesh, Marion reached for his wrist, confirming the absence of a pulse. This time, she thought to herself, there could be no doubt of the death of Pat Malone. This time he wasn't coming back.

Bunzie was in the midst of telling his highly romanticized version of the burying of the time capsule to a captive audience. Each time he mentioned one of his fellow Lanthanides, he prefaced the name with superlatives: the late, great Dale Dugger, the macabre genius Curtis Phillips, and the literary legend Brendan Surn. The more perceptive of the journalists might have noticed that Ruben Mistral did not really discuss any of the stories actually put into the time capsule by himself and his comrades, but perhaps they did not notice this omission, since Mistral was a charming and well-polished speaker. He seemed to be winding down the litany of reminiscences when a balding man in a dark suit appeared at the door and motioned for Mistral's attention.

The ever alert Geoff Duke hurried to the back of the room to confer with the hotel employee. "What is it?" he hissed, grasping the man's elbow and propelling him out of earshot. "We're in the middle of our presentation here."

The hotel clerk was a study in unruffled dignity. "We thought you ought to be notified, sir. One of your party has passed away."

"Oh, shit!" murmured Geoff, caught off guard by the news. "I was afraid one of those old geezers might croak from the excitement. . . ." His voice trailed off when he caught the disapproving glint in the listener's eye. "I mean, what a shock. I can't believe it. What a complete tragedy. Which one of them?" His mind was furiously manipulating publicity options concerning the untimely demise of the literary legend Brendan Surn. Perhaps a cremation and hasty burial in the mire of the ruined farm in place of the time capsule? Visions of *Newsweek* photos danced in his head. He wondered if he could safely paraphrase the Gettysburg Address in the eulogy: *But in a larger sense, we cannot dedicate, we cannot consecrate, we cannot hallow this ground.* His hustler's reverie was cut short by the hotel manager's reply.

"The guest was registered as a Mr. Pat Malone," he said carefully. "I believe there was some trouble over his unexpected arrival last night?"

Geoff cringed. Obviously, the waiters had been gossiping. "His attendance had not been anticipated," he agreed. "Of course, his old friends were delighted to see him."

This bit of social whitewashing cut no ice with the Mountaineer Lodge. "It was our duty to notify the sheriff as well as the medical authorities," he said solemnly. "I came to notify you so that you could break the news to the folks in your conference."

Geoff's pallor and expression suggested that he might welcome the medical authorities himself. "We won't have to call off the boat trip, will we?"

The hotel manager relented. "Probably not," he said. "I expect that it will take them all day to figure out what he died of, and to get all the medical details attended to. If everyone will agree to be available for questioning tomorrow, then I see no reason why you shouldn't go ahead with your plans today. After all, the old gentleman may have simply succumbed to a heart attack."

Pat Malone didn't get heart attacks, thought Geoff Duke grimly, he gave them.

Marion didn't know why she had agreed to stay with the body until the authorities arrived. Perhaps it was a tacit acknowledgment that fandom was a family—or at least a tribe—and she felt a sense of loyalty to another of her kind, both of them self-imposed exiles from the clan. Or perhaps it was a lingering respect for one of the legends of science fiction. She wished that she had been given another chance to talk with fandom's stormy petrel, but stranger though he was to her, she could not leave him lying on the cold floor of a rented room with no one to pay him last respects.

Marion sat on the edge of the double bed, trying to look anywhere but at the shrunken form in the doorway of the bathroom. Irrationally, she felt that it would be an invasion of Pat Malone's privacy to stare at him in his final humiliation, sprawled in vomit on the cold tile floor. But she knew that the body should not be moved, and that no cleaning up could be done because there might have to be an investigation into the death. She also knew that it would be a mistake to touch any of the deceased's possessions in the hotel room, but when boredom and anxiety made her restless she decided that there would be no harm in looking. And if she felt it necessary to pick something up, she could use a tissue to avoid leaving fingerprints. Thus fortified with the tools and rationalization for her actions, Marion began to examine the deceased man's possessions. Above all, she wanted to know where Pat Malone had been between deaths.

His suitcase sat on top of the low chest of drawers, with its lid propped open against the wall. It was a cheap vinyl bag of medium size, without an identification tag on its handle. Inside it were a couple of shirts and changes of underwear and a worn collection of paperbacks: *The Golden Gain*, Brendan Surn's latest paperback reprints, and an issue of *Fantasy and Science Fiction* containing Peter Deddingfield's first (and worst) published short story. These books were bound with a thick rubber band, enclosing a note that read "Get Autographed." Lying loose in the suitcase were a book club edition of Deddingfield's *Time Traveler Trilogy* and a copy of Pat Malone's only published novel, *River of Neptune.* On impulse, Marion picked it up with her tissue-shielded hand, wondering if the author had made any notations in his personal copy, but when she flipped through the pages of the yellowed paperback, she found that the pages were unmarked. On impulse she turned to the title page and found an inscription in faded red ink: "To Curtis Phillips, A Slan for All Seasons, from Patrick B. Malone." She looked through the other books, but found no writing of any kind, except a rubber-stamped notation in the front of the Brendan Surn novel: USED—$1.

"Why would he have Curtis' copy of his own book?" Marion wondered aloud.

She patted the clothing in the suitcase to see if there was anything else concealed inside it. Nothing was hidden in the clothes, but a bulge in a side pouch of the luggage revealed a bottle of prescription medicine. "Elavil," the label said, and the pharmacist listed was located in Willow Spring, North Carolina. Most interesting of all was the name of the patient, neatly typed on the prescription label: Richard W. Spivey.

"Now who the hell is that?" asked Marion, peering at the corpse as if she expected an answer.

While Sarah Ashley was explaining literary auctions to the reporters, Ruben Mistral went out into the hall to confer with his minion. The arrival of the hotel manager had not gone unnoticed by Mistral, even though he gave no sign of it as he rambled on in his reminiscences. The expressions and body language of Geoff and the hotel man had told him that something was amiss, and he had seized the first opportunity to leave center stage and find out what was going on.

"Pat Malone is dead," said Geoff, in tones suggesting that his chief concern was the possibility of being shouted at for the inconvenience of it.

Ruben Mistral opened his mouth and then closed it again, wondering just exactly what it was he felt, and, more importantly, what he *ought* to be feeling. He couldn't even say that he was shocked, because he hadn't really got used to the idea of Pat Malone being alive in the first place. As far as any of them were concerned, Pat Malone had been dead for thirty years. It was no good resurrecting him for an hour, then killing him off again and expecting anyone to be shocked about it. It was a relief that he wouldn't be around to make trouble, of course. Pat had always had a genius for making trouble.

An instant later he realized that by dying, Pat Malone had caused the maximum amount of trouble imaginable. The tabloid reporters would start grinding out ghost and murder stories, forgetting the time capsule, and even the other papers would dutifully report it, and overshadow the reunion story, because death is more interesting than anything else.

"Don't worry," said Geoff, misinterpreting his stricken look. "It was a heart attack. I don't believe he suffered."

"Too bad," growled Mistral.

"And the hotel manager said that we could go ahead with the day's activities as planned. He has called the sheriff and the medical people, but he thought you might want to make the announcement to the reunion group."

Ruben Mistral reached an instant decision. "Why?" he said. "It had nothing to do with us."

"I'm sorry?" said Geoff, expressing not regret but total confusion.

"We all thought Pat Malone was dead, right? So we didn't mention him in the press releases or the brochures. The press never knew about him at all. So why bring him up now? It will only distract them from the real story. I'll tell the others privately in a few minutes, and instruct them not to discuss it with anyone." Somewhere deep in his consciousness, Bunzie was deploring the unfortunate necessity of having to behave this way, but after all, he told himself, the Lanthanides who are still alive could use the money.

"Are the boats here yet?" he asked.

Geoff glanced at his watch. "They should be. Shall I go and check?"

Mistral nodded. "I'll start herding the group down toward the lake, before any of them can spot an

ambulance or a cop. Once we get them out in the
boats, everything will be—" He broke off suddenly
as a sandy-haired young man in jeans emerged from
the conference room. "Not leaving, are you?" he
asked heartily.

"No," said Jay Omega. "I just wondered where
Marion was. Excuse me."

While Sarah Ashley explained terms like "bidding
floor" to the more conscientious journalists, the
Lanthanides were chatting together, waiting to be
summoned for the boat trip. Brendan Surn and
Lorien, who had arrived late, helped themselves to
coffee and doughnuts and then joined the group in
the front row. Jim and Barbara Conyers came up to
join them, exchanging pleasantries with Angela
Arbroath and passing around pictures of the grand-
children.

"I think he was hoping they'd have pointed ears,"
joked Barbara. "The three-year-old can already say
the whole thing: *Space, the final frontier . . .*"

Erik Giles consulted his watch. "It's nearly ten. I
wonder what happened to Marion. She's going to
miss the boat if she isn't careful."

"She came and got us about twenty minutes ago,"
said Lorien Williams. "Isn't she back yet?"

"She'll turn up," said George Woodard, who was
bored by the troubles of others. "Do you think they'll
provide us with Dramamine for the boat ride?"

Angela Arbroath smiled. "I don't think there will
be much turbulence in shallow water, George. But
you might want to stop drinking coffee. There's no
place to pee in an open boat."

"Where is Pat Malone?" asked Barbara Conyers.

"Maybe he overslept," said Woodard. "He was always completely irresponsible. I, for one, won't miss him."

"I will," said Angela. "I forgot to ask if he's still married."

Brendan Surn smiled and patted her arm. "Wouldn't you rather have Pete Deddingfield?" he asked playfully.

"I'm sure she would," said Lorien hastily. "What a guy!" She didn't want to have to explain again who was dead and who wasn't to Brendan Surn.

Ruben Mistral emerged from the crowd of reporters just then, looking grave. "Before we head down to the boats, I need a word with you," he said, pitching his voice to a discreet undertone.

"What's wrong?" gasped Angela, taking a mental tally of who was present.

Mistral looked faintly disapproving, as if he were anticipating hysterics. "Just a little bad news," he murmured. "But the important thing is that we must not discuss this with any of the media people present."

"Who died?" asked Jim Conyers.

Mistral winced at the plain speaking. "It's Pat Malone, I'm afraid. He wasn't looking too well last night. Heart attack, I imagine. It's something we have to face when we get to be our age. But you know how reporters are. We wouldn't want to distract them from the real story, would we?" He looked sharply at George Woodard, traditionally the weak link in the chain. "After all, if we make a fuss, it could diminish the importance and the monetary value of our time capsule. Not to mention the possibility of our being detained by the police for questioning."

The Lanthanides looked at each other nervously. Finally Jim Conyers said, "I don't see any harm in keeping quiet about this for the time being. It isn't obstructing justice to refrain from mentioning a death to a bunch of reporters and book editors."

"Exactly!" nodded Mistral, visibly relieved.

"None of their business," said George Woodard.

Angela Arbroath was pale, and her eyes were red-rimmed. "I suppose you know best," she murmured. "But it *was* natural causes?"

"Sure," said Mistral. "What else could it be?"

"Marion, what are you doing in here?"

When Marion hadn't reappeared at the briefing, Jay Omega had gone in search of her. He had checked the coffee shop and the lobby without success, and finally he decided to look in the room to see if she had been taken ill. As he made his way along the second-floor hallway toward their room he had noticed an open door, and when he glanced inside he saw Marion Farley, gazing out the window at the barren expanse of red clay between the pine-topped slopes. She did not turn to face him until he had repeated the question.

When Marion stood up, he could see that she looked ill.

"Are you all right?"

She pointed toward the bathroom. "Pat Malone," she said grimly. "He's dead again."

He looked in the direction she pointed, and for the

first time he noticed the blue-robed body sprawled partly inside the bathroom. Jay looked from Marion to the corpse and back again, half expecting everyone to burst out laughing and say "Gotcha!," but the look on Marion's face was solemn and strained, and he was forced to believe that it was true. As he came toward her, he became aware of the smell, and this convinced him beyond any doubt that there had indeed been a death.

"What happened?"

Marion shrugged. "He was like this when I found him. I checked to make sure that he was dead—no pulse—and other than that, I left him alone. The maid was with me when I found him, and she saw to it that the authorities were called. I'm sorry I didn't come back, but I couldn't leave him. I kept thinking to myself, This guy wrote *River of Neptune*. I know that doesn't make him anything extraordinary, but—well, to me it does. I'm an English professor. I'm a *fan*." There was a catch in her voice. "I even wanted to get his autograph."

Jay put his arms around her. "Far be it from me to talk you out of revering writers," said the author of *Bimbos of the Death Sun*. "But there really isn't anything that you can do here."

"I know, Jay. I said I would stay until someone came for the body, though. You understand, don't you?"

Jay sat down in the armchair by the window and motioned for her to sit on the bed. "I'll keep you company," he said. "We'll make it a two-person wake. It's too bad about the old fellow. I think he was looking forward to this. Wonder where he's been all these years."

"I wonder *who* he's been all these years," said Marion. She told Jay about the medicine bottle issued to someone other than Pat Malone.

Jay looked puzzled. "An alias? That seems strange. I wonder how the police are going to notify his next of kin."

Marion looked sadly at the crumpled figure in the doorway. "I wonder if he has any," she said.

"Didn't that old fanzine of yours say that he had been married?"

"Thirty years ago," said Marion. She gasped. "I wonder if *she* knows he isn't dead. I mean, he is, but I wonder if she knew that he didn't die in 1958."

Jay Omega shrugged. "Won't the police handle all that?"

"I don't know," said Marion. "If it was natural causes, they might not try too hard. And it might take them weeks or months. Damn it, I want to know who Pat Malone was for the last thirty years! I wonder if he had any ties in fandom!"

"I brought my portable computer," said Jay diffidently.

"Of course you did. You never go anywhere without it!" snapped Marion. "So what? Are you going to compose the eulogy?"

"No, but I may be able to find out some things about Pat Malone in a hurry. You remember Joel Schumann?"

"An engineering student of yours? Sort of."

"He gave me a phone number that might be

helpful. Joel is known around the department as the Napoleon of hackers."

Marion looked interested. "An FBI of nerds! It might work. When can you start?"

"This evening after the boat trip," said Jay. "The rates go down at five."

> *—Francis Towner Laney's epitaph in*
> *fandom. (The term is used*
> *figuratively for one whose coming*
> *always portends trouble.)*

CHAPTER 11

AT TEN FORTY-THREE in the morning, a gaggle of rubber-booted literary tourists waddled down the red clay slopes of Breedlove Lake and clumped onto the concrete boat ramp, which now stopped two hundred yards from the water's edge. Above them towered hillsides of clay and rubble, once submerged beneath the lake and now forming a desolate canyon beneath the pine-topped hills surrounding it.

Beside the boat ramp, a rocky mountain stream bubbled down the hillside, headed for the distant lake water. Before the drawdown the stream had been swallowed by the expanse of Breedlove Lake, existing only as a current within the reservoir, but now it had been freed to course through its own eroded canyon, through seasons of silt, as it cut its way to the muddy waters of the great Watauga, pulsing again through the heart of the valley.

The concrete of the boat ramp ended twenty feet down the slope, succeeded by a flat graveled plain that might once have been a road. Another hundred yards on—and thirty feet down, had there been a

lake—the road fell away into a series of curving
rock ridges, spiraling down to a shelf of brown clay
that was the new shoreline. Except for deep gullies
that had trapped the ebbing lake water, the valley
was visible again, and once more the Watauga
River, artery of the region, was a discernable conflu-
ence, kept within its banks by the release of its
overflow through the sluice gates of the TVA dam.

Three boats waited in the shallows of the river.
Two of them were outboard motorboats, capable of
ferrying five passengers and operated by leathery
good old boys in windbreakers and fishing caps.
Obviously, they had hired out their private vessels
for the day's expedition for a little excitement and
some easy money. The third craft was the large,
flat-bottomed sightseeing boat on loan from the
Breedlove Marina, which, with its red awning, and
its Tennessee flag flying, would hold twenty passengers. It was used by the marina for its regu-
larly scheduled tours of the lake area, a particularly
popular outing during the warm months of early
autumn, when the changing leaves on the oaks and
maples turned the surrounding mountains into
bands of flame and gold.

Geoff Duke led the party of editors and journalists aboard the sightseeing boat, and Ruben Mistral
motioned for the Lanthanides and their guests to
climb into the motorboats to begin their quest for
the time capsule on Dugger's farm. Mistral, now
sporting a gold-braided captain's hat, mounted
the newer-looking motorboat that was obviously
intended to be the flagship of the expedition. He was
joined by Brendan Surn and Lorien, and Jim

and Barbara Conyers, all of whom looked as if they were attending a funeral. Mistral patted Conyers's shoulder, and smiled encouragingly at the others, but he received only tentative smiles for his efforts. Jay Omega and Marion Farley, who had made a belated appearance at the point of embarkation, joined Erik Giles, Angela Arbroath, and George Woodard in the second outboard.

When everyone was comfortably seated and, at the helmsmen's insistence, corseted with orange life preservers, Ruben Mistral gave the signal for the boats to cast off, and the journey began. One by one the vessels glided out into the channel of the amber-colored river, heading upstream toward the sunken village of Wall Hollow and the farms beyond it. In the second craft, the boatman, who had introduced himself as Dub, admitted to Marion that this was his first stint as a lake guide, but he allowed as how he was a lifelong resident of the area and was willing to make conversation if anybody had a mind to ask him anything.

"Where is the town?" asked George Woodard, surveying the sea of mud surrounding the channel.

Dub smiled. "This lake is seventeen miles long, buddy. It'll take us a good hour to get there, I reckon."

They rode for a while in silence, past black trees spangled with snagged fishing lines and lures that clung to the dead branches like spiderwebs. There was an eerie stillness about the valley, and the slowness of the churning outboard made their passage seem like a nightmare journey through a surreal landscape. It might have been a deserted battlefield or the scene of some sudden disaster: the overriding feeling in the barren and silent valley was one of death and irreparable loss.

Marion shivered. "It's so eerie in this wasteland. Lines from T. S. Eliot keep running through my head."

"I know," murmured Angela Arbroath. "I've never seen a place so desolate in bright sunshine. It even feels cold. Do you suppose that it's Pat Malone that is making me feel gloomy?"

George Woodard's piggy face became animated with alarm. "Angela!" he hissed. "We aren't supposed to talk about you-know-what."

Marion looked at him with ill-concealed contempt. "I found the body," she said.

"Did Mistral ask you not to tell anyone about Malone's death?" asked Jay.

Angela nodded. "He didn't want the reporters to find out. He thought it would distract them from the reason we're here. I can't believe that Pat Malone is dead."

George Woodard stared at her. "I can't believe he's alive!"

"Yes, it takes some getting used to. I'd said good-bye to him all those years ago, and then suddenly he's back, and—"

"In all my life I have loved but one man, and I have lost him twice," said Marion dreamily. Noting her companions' puzzled looks, Marion hastened to add: "That's from *Cyrano*. It seemed appropriate."

They floated on in silence for a while. When they passed under the concrete arch of the Gene C.

Breedlove Bridge, looming half a mile above their heads, envious spectators leaned over and waved at the makeshift flotilla. Its passengers craned their heads to peer at the pink blobs high above them, and a few of them returned the greeting.

George Woodard, lost in thought, barely noticed the bridge at all. He was pondering the death of Pat Malone and envisioning a memorial issue of *Alluvial*. After giving the matter careful consideration, George had decided not to demean himself and his phone bill by activating the S-F grapevine, but he concluded that the prestige of his 'zine depended upon his being the final authority on the Lanthanides reunion and on the Malone affair. He was, after all, both an old comrade of Malone's and an eyewitness. Why should the other 'zine publishers have the story. If he established himself as the authority on it (surely none of the other Lanthanides would bother), he could be invited as Fan Guest of Honor to any number of conventions in the coming year, which would mean that he would have his way paid to these conventions and the really good ones would give him plaques for his wall commemorating his status as Fan Guest. Pat Malone owed him that.

He considered his material for a memorial issue. New eulogies would have to be solicited, of course, and perhaps some samples of Pat's writings could be included. Would Pat's recent undeath affect the copyright laws, he wondered. Would anybody even *believe* that Pat Malone had come back? No one had thought to take any pictures of him. Perhaps it would be best not to mention him at all, but, of course, he had unimpeachable witnesses. And besides, hardly anyone ever questions the veracity of anything in fandom. The memorial issue was sure to be a big seller in fannish circles. He wondered if he could afford to double the number of copies for this issue.

George, for one, was not sorry to see Pat Malone dead. The late Pat's sneering reappearance at the Lanthanides reunion had been a forceful reminder of how little he had missed the scornful, bullying Malone. George was always twice as inept when Malone was present. With painful clarity now, he remembered Pat Malone's old practical jokes at his expense. There was the shaving cream in his bed, and the phony acceptance letter from *Weird Tales*, and the campaign Pat and Curtis had started at a Knoxville con to "cure" George's virginity. Well, perhaps he ought to forgive them that one. Earlene had volunteered to effect the cure, and George had fallen hopelessly in love with her. Sometimes, though, he wondered if she had done it in hopes of getting the attention of Pat Malone.

Had Earlene ever loved him? Were those sadistic jokers from the Fan Farm ever his friends? And did he like who he was; had he ever liked himself?

George looked out at the barren lake bed, wondering if his life had been a mortal version of Breedlove Lake: a pleasant, opaque facade, covering up a whole lot of nothing.

In the bow of the white motorboat Ruben Mistral struck a pose—like stout Cortes silent upon a peak in Darien, the *Times* reporter had quipped. Several of his colleagues scribbled down the phrase, unaware that Keats was being quoted. (*USA Today* reported the phrase as "a mountain in Connecticut.") Mistral's expression of solemn dignity suggested that he was leading an expedition up the Amazon rather than taking a boat ride in conjunction with a business deal. Occasionally, though, he forgot to provide a photo opportunity for the journalists' boat, and he would sit back down beside Brendan Surn and attempt to converse over the noise of the outboard motor.

"Great to see you again, Brendan!" he said, patting the older man's shoulder. "It's been too long! About the only time I get to see you these days is at those damned science fiction cons!"

Lorien Williams raised an eyebrow. "Don't you like cons?"

Mistral's smile wavered, and he glanced at Surn for his cue. "Have you ever been to one?" he asked.

"Of course," said Lorien. "I've been to—"

"I mean, with Brendan. I've never seen you at a con with Brendan."

Lorien shook her head. "No. I haven't had that honor yet."

Mistral snorted. "Honor! Did he tell you about the time he took a manuscript-in-progress to a con so that he could read from it, and one of the fannish bastards stole it? That was in the days before copy machines, too. Or the time one hot little number sneaked into his room with a passkey, and he had to call hotel security? She was underage, of course."

Brendan Surn smiled vaguely in Lorien's direction. "Not all fans are bad, Bunzie. *We* used to be fans."

"We didn't behave the way these punks do today," growled Bunzie. "They've gone a long way past water balloons. The only reason I go to cons these days is to see old friends. This reunion is perfect. Old friends, and no fans."

Lorien Williams studied him thoughtfully while she waited for Brendan to rise to the defense of fandom, but the old man turned away, staring at a rusting oil barrel that lay half buried in the Watauga mud flat.

After an hour's journey upstream, they began to see more skeletal trees in the mire, and the remnants of stone walls loomed ahead of them on the port side. "Yep," said Dub the helmsman in response to the unspoken questions. "That's Wall Hollow coming up on the left there. Not much of it left, is there? That stone building over there was the jail, and next to it was the Azalea Café. It was built out of river rocks cemented together. It has held up real well. Of course, most of the town was made of wood, and it's all gone. You can still see the roads, though." He pointed at the patches of asphalt visible in the plain of red mud. "That would have been Main Street."

"It doesn't look like a town anymore," said Marion, staring at the desolation.

"No, but it puts me in mind of a funny story," said Dub, who seemed to be the least affected by the ruins. "At the time the town was condemned by the TVA to make way for Breedlove Lake, there was a mayoral race going on in Wall Hollow, and strange as it may seem, the election was hotly contested. And one old boy said, 'I don't know what those politicians are getting so het up about. The next mayor of Wall Hollow will be a catfish.'"

The passengers laughed politely, and Angela asked him whether he had gone to the new Wall Hollow, the one that the TVA constructed on the other side of the lake for the refugees.

Dub rubbed his chin and steered for the deepest part of the river. "No, ma'am," he said after a bit. "I moved on over to Labrot Cove, about five miles from here, where I had some kin. I didn't want to lose anything else to that lake there." He shrugged. "Of course, that was a good while ago. Over the years I have got used to it, and now I go fishing over in here without giving it another thought. Why, many's the time I've hauled in a big old channel cat, and said to myself, 'I believe I've done caught the mayor.'"

Erik Giles had been studying the asphalt lines in the mud, trying to get his bearings from the remnants of buildings left as clues. He pointed to a barren hillside in the distance. "Keep going," he said. "Dugger's farm was just up that hollow. The river will take us most of the way."

The trio of boats glided past the ruins of the old train depot and passed within the shadow of the old stone gristmill, a shell of a building still standing against the deluge of pent-up lake water. The only sound for several minutes was the click of camera shutters from the flat-bottomed tourist boat as the photojournalists recorded the occasion.

Once past the wreckage of the old river bridge, the Watauga snaked between smooth red hills that for years had been merely shallow places in the lake. Now they were mounds of rubble, ringed like redwoods with the concentric circles of ebbing waves. The river sank into a narrowing valley, past smooth stretches that must have been pasture land, and at times it flowed only a few feet below the level of the asphalt remnants of a country road. The asphalt gave way to a stretch of pebbles, and then the road vanished altogether into mud the color of rust.

"This used to be a beautiful place," said Erik Giles in a voice that was little more than a whisper. "It was so green and peaceful. And we were such kids then. We thought 'happily ever after' was just a question of waiting long enough. We just didn't understand the randomness of our existence." He laughed bitterly. "Now, of course, we know better. Now, I'd say this is a pretty good metaphor for the way life is: it seems beautiful and endlessly deep while you're young, but little by little the water—the life—slips away, and you are left with nothing."

"Do you know where you are yet?" the pilot of the lead craft asked Ruben Mistral.

Mistral shrugged. "The moon?"

The boatman forced a smile. "Best I can recall, Dugger's farm ought to be in the next quarter mile or so, and you'll be wanting to leave the boat there, I reckon, and do some walking around."

"Yes," said Mistral. "It's just hard to get your bearings in this wasteland. Conyers, can you tell where we are?"

"I think so," said the lawyer. "See that outcrop of

rocks up the hill there, just below the pine trees? I've stood on Dale's front porch many a time staring up at that thing. In the twilight—from a certain angle—it looks like an Indian. If the foundations of the farmhouse haven't sunk into the mud, we ought to see them right about now."

A few moments later they rounded a bend, removing a looming sandhill from their line of sight. "Look!" said Lorien Williams, pointing to a swampy plateau partway up the slope. "Is that a chimney?"

It was. There was a gently sloping hollow between two bare hills, and within its basin a pool of lake water had settled, covering the foundations of Dale Dugger's farmhouse with its own riparian shroud. A two-pronged remnant of a locust tree rose out of the shallows, and twenty feet past it, a crumbling rock chimney protruded from the orange water.

"We found it," said Mistral. "Start looking for a place to dock."

The three boatmen maneuvered their vessels toward an outcrop of boulders on the bank of the river. One at a time they were able to drift in close enough so that the passengers could climb out of the boats onto the rocks and make their way up the slope toward the site of Dugger's farm. Ruben Mistral, the first to disembark, repeated his landfall several times for the benefit of the cameramen, and then he created another photo opportunity by assisting Brendan Surn from the boat and pointing solemnly toward the ruined chimney. Together they scrambled up the rocky bank, picking their way along the driest parts of the lake bed, trailing a gaggle of camcorders and journalists in their wake.

The other members of the party were left to clamber up the river bank as best they could, without the encouragement of the media or the editors.

"This is certainly a grim occasion," Marion whispered to Jay. "I feel like a gatecrasher at a funeral."

"Remember that we're here to see that Erik doesn't overdo it," said Jay. "Maybe you can cheer him up. He doesn't seem very happy."

Marion looked about her. "None of them do. Isn't it odd how things broke down so quickly into matters of status? Mistral stays mostly with Surn—the two pros, associating mainly with each other. And Conyers and his wife are talking to Erik—the sober ex-fans in coalition. That leaves Woodard and Angela, who were never anything but fans. But maybe I shouldn't mention this to you, Jay. After all, you're a dirty old pro."

He sighed wearily. "I just accidentally wrote an S-F novel, okay? I didn't mean to apply for citizenship in the Twilight Zone."

"I don't think you can apply, Jay. I think fandom takes hostages."

"Be careful where you step, George," said Angela Arbroath, grabbing his elbow. "That puddle may be deeper than you think."

George Woodard, who hadn't even seen the mud hole he nearly plunged into, blinked out of his reverie and thanked her. "I was just thinking about the time we stayed up all night listening to the plotting of *Starwind Rising*," he said. "The moon was shining low beneath that branch of the locust tree, and it filled the whole horizon. As we listened to that story, I could actually *see* the story happening. I remember picturing one of the heroes looking just like Conyers. You know, he always did have that clean-chiseled all-American look. It was just like a movie going on in our heads. Once I found myself searching the surface of the moon, looking for traces of the domed cities, and I remember checking to see if my helmet was on. My helmet! I'd forgotten I wasn't in a spaceship orbiting the moon."

Angela smiled. "I didn't know Brendan had talked about his books in such detail to you all."

George flushed. "Actually, it was Dale who told that story. But I'm sure he'd discussed it beforehand with Brendan!"

Angela nodded. "I suppose so." She looked around the valley and then at the chimney rising out of muddy water a few yards away. "I guess I remember Pat better than anyone else from the Fan Farm. Sometimes he'd tell me what all of you were up to when he wrote to me."

"Do you still have the letters?" asked George eagerly. "I'm planning a memorial issue of *Alluvial*."

"No, George. I wouldn't let anyone see those letters without first obtaining Pat's permission, and I guess that isn't going to happen, is it?" Seeing his disappointment, she went on. "There isn't much in them that would interest fandom, anyhow, George. Like most men, Pat talked mostly about himself. And he tried to carry on a long-distance romance with me, which worked better on paper than it did in real life." She smiled ruefully. "Like a lot of things in fandom."

Their conversation stopped when a reporter approached them, tape recorder in hand. "Can you tell me what your thoughts are at this moment?" she asked breathlessly.

George Woodard squinted at her. "Are you from *Locus*?"

After twenty minutes of site inspection, interspersed with photos and interviews, Ruben Mistral signaled for everyone's attention. When the crowd stopped milling around and stood in a respectful huddle around him, he stalked over to the black husk of a tree a few hundred yards from the chimney pool. The tree stood at the foot of a gently sloped mound of red clay, scored by a series of upright posts, each about four feet high.

"This is what remains of the fence," Mistral announced. "The first landmark. And that is the tree that we used as the second marker. This, ladies and gentlemen, is the very spot on which, thirty-six years ago, the Lanthanides buried their time capsule. It is time to resurrect the past. It is time to begin the digging. I will go first."

Mistral's contribution to the retrieval effort was to remove exactly two spadefuls of mud—the second was for good measure, in case someone's first photo did not turn out well. After that, each of the Lanthanides was invited to be filmed wielding the shovel, before the actual work of unearthing the jar was turned over to the three boatmen, under the direction of Geoffrey Duke. All four had donned khaki coveralls for the messy job of excavating a mud hole.

Marion clutched Jay's hand. "What if it isn't there?" she whispered.

He groaned. "Don't even think such a thing!"

"Well, what if it isn't? Everybody in fandom knew it was there, didn't they? Suppose crazed science fiction fans from Knoxville—"

"Hush, Marion!"

"I wonder if anybody will ever make such a big deal over your unpublished stuff."

"I doubt it," said Jay. "They certainly haven't been overly enthusiastic about the *published* stuff."

Several yards away from them, Brendan Surn was leaning on Lorien Williams's arm and smiling benignly at the diggers. "Aren't you excited about this?" asked Lorien, smiling up at him.

"Why, yes," said Brendan Surn mildly. "Yes, thank you. It's very nice."

Lorien's smile froze in place. That was the answer Brendan always gave when he was fading out of the here and now and hadn't the least idea of what was going on. No more interview questions today, she thought. She wondered how she would field the questions for him.

While the digging was going on, Ruben Mistral took up a position a safe distance away from the mudslinging, which he watched with an expression of dignified expectation. A few of the reporters tried to bait him with fanciful questions, such as "What if you find a skeleton?" or "What if the time capsule isn't there?" but he only smiled at them and refused to be drawn into any negative speculation. Privately he was wondering how the authorities were dealing with the problem of the late Pat Malone back at the Mountaineer Lodge, and he was wondering whether he ought to take any steps to suppress the news of his death. So far so good, he told himself. There would be time to worry about damage control later. First, let them find that damned jar.

Digging in mud wasn't easy. The sides of the hole kept collapsing in on it, and water seeped up from the bottom as they dug. The three diggers were soon transformed into identical mud-caked gingerbread men. When fifteen minutes of digging had elapsed, taking the hole to a depth of three feet, several people who obviously knew the Lanthanides' proclivities remarked that none of them were energetic enough to have buried anything so deep. Geoffrey Duke reminded these doubters that mountain streams had carried silt into the lake bed for more than three decades, depositing layer after layer of extra soil on top of the original cache.

The editors, who had grouped together at the back of the crowd, for fear of being invited to dig, eyed the excavation efforts nervously. "Suppose it isn't there?" asked Lily Warren.

Enzio O'Malley shrugged. "You ask them to write their stories from memory and you get better stuff, because now they've been pros for thirty years."

"What about the dead ones?"

"Even better. You get Mistral or Surn to give you a general description of the plot, and then you farm out the story to somebody famous who can really write. I'd like to see Robert McCammon write the

Curtis Phillips story. Maybe Michael Moorcock for
Deddingfield's stuff. Now that anthology would be
worth publishing!"

Lily Warren gave him a sour smile. "So, Enzio, you
will actually be disappointed if they find anything?"

"I wouldn't say that. But if I acquire the rights to
it, I'll make sure the contract says I get to request
some rewriting."

The Del Rey editor heaved a sigh of exasperation.
"If Enzio had been given the Ten Commandments
on Mount Sinai, he would have had them down to
six before he left the summit."

A clink of shovel on metal drew gasps from those
nearest the hole, and the crowd surged forward.
"We got it!" shouted Geoffrey Duke, wiping his forehead with a mud-stained forearm. "I see a lid down
there!"

"Easy, fellas!" said Mistral, elbowing his way to
the side of the pit. "Don't break the glass now. That
water would completely ruin the contents."

Marion went up and hugged Erik Giles. "They
found it!" she cried. "I'm so happy for you!"

"I hope it's worth it," said Giles sadly.

One of the diggers jumped into the rapidly collapsing hole and, knee-deep in muddy water, fas-
tened a rope around the neck of the jar. While he
pushed and rocked the jar to free it, the others
pulled on the rope, and moments later it gave,
sending the digger sprawling into the side of the
mud hole as the brown encrusted jar slid to the
surface amid cheers from the onlookers. With a tri-
umphant flourish Geoff Duke wrapped the un-

opened jar in a clean plastic sheet, while the other mud-caked diggers helped their comrade out of the hole and headed for the river to rinse off as best they could.

At Mistral's insistence, the Lanthanides grouped around him, smiling sheepishly into various camera lenses, as their leader held the jar aloft like a recently bagged trophy.

"Here it is!" yelled Mistral. "The Dead Sea Scrolls of Science Fiction!"

"Are you going to open it, Mistral?" asked one of the reporters.

"Not in the middle of this pigsty," he retorted. "It's too valuable for that. Let's go on back to the lodge, and we'll clean this thing up and let you get a look at it."

"When can *we* look at it?" yelled one of the editors.

"Photocopies will be made of the material, and you will have until tomorrow morning to read the contents, and to deliver your sealed bid to Sarah Ashley."

Another reporter waved her hand above the crowd. "Mr. Mistral!" she called out. "One more question! Isn't that the highway up there beyond those trees?"

Mistral looked up, just as a car whizzed past a few hundred yards above their heads. Just past the grove of oak trees up beyond the boundary of the lake, the road curved around the mountain, running parallel to the lake for a stretch before it snaked away again. Mistral grinned ruefully and held up his hands.

"Could you tell us then why we had to take boats to get here?"

Ruben Mistral grinned at her. "I wasn't sure how to recognize Dugger's farm from the road. It isn't always that close to the lake, you know. Besides, honey, the boat trip makes better copy," he told her. "But anybody who wants to hitchhike back has my permission." With that he handed the jar back to Geoffrey Duke for safekeeping, then turned and ambled back down the hill toward the river. After a moment's pause, the entire troop of muddy followers plowed along after him.

He wanted to pound on their doors, call them out
in their housecoats and frowsy pajamas,
and tell them in clear words
that time buries itself like a river under a lake
that river feeds, that though the past is irretrievable,
nothing left down there is gone.

—DON JOHNSON
Watauga Drawdown

CHAPTER 12

JAY OMEGA AND Marion Farley were not invited to
the remainder of the afternoon's events. When the
three boats had safely moored again at the Mountaineer Lodge boat ramp, Ruben Mistral gave
everyone an hour's break to get cleaned up from
their muddy trip upriver. At that time, he informed
the Lanthanides, they were to assemble in the
downstairs conference room to witness the official
opening of the time capsule, to be followed by interview sessions with the journalists. The editors who
did not want to observe the publicity marathon in
action were urged to attend a private screening of
Ruben Mistral's latest movie, *Laser Nova*, after
which photocopies of the time-capsule contents
would be issued to them, and they would be
returned to their hotel in Johnson City to prepare
for Sunday's auction.

"You ought to try to talk to Ruben Mistral sometime this weekend," Marion told Jay. "Did you bring
along a copy of *Bimbos of the Death Sun*? Maybe he
could help you sell the movie rights."

Jay shook his head. "Just what I need—to be famous for writing *Bimbos of the Death Sun*. It was bad enough when it was a paperback original that no one could ever find."

"But think of the money, Jay!"

"Think of the dean of engineering, Marion. Try to get tenure with something called *Bimbos of the Death Sun* on your vita!" He smiled at her expression of disappointment.

She sighed. "Tell me about trying to get tenure! My department hires two tenure-track people for every *one* position. I wish I could have become a professor in the good old days, like Erik Giles did. Back then you got tenure more or less automatically, just for hanging around for a few years without screwing up. I don't know if he's *ever* published anything. Whereas I have to spend every waking moment grubbing up some obscure footnote—"

"I see," said Jay. "So you think that if I could make a career out of science fiction I could escape all that hassle."

"You could. Ask Isaac Asimov about academia some time."

Jay smiled. "Ask practically everybody else about low advances and an uncertain income. Anyway, thanks for trying so hard to make me famous, Marion. But it takes more than talent to be Ruben Mistral, and I don't think I've got it. Anyhow, we have more important things to do. Can you find the hotel manager and see what he knows about Malone's death?"

"I suppose so. But is this really any business of

ours? Shouldn't we at least consult Erik before we do anything?"

"I talked to Pat Malone late last night after the party. I kind of liked him." He grinned. "Maybe I'm becoming a Pat Malone fan. Anyway, this is between me and him. Will you help?"

"I said I would." Her eyes narrowed suspiciously. "What are you going to do?"

"I'll be up in the room mobilizing the troops."

Marion hesitated. "Look . . . you're not going to get arrested for breaking into the files of the U.S. government, or AT&T or anything. Are you?"

"Me? A hacker? Not a chance. Besides, I doubt if government records would be much help. What we need is a lot of people from a lot of different places to make phone calls for us and ask the pertinent questions."

"And what makes you think that a bunch of fans from all over the country would be willing to help you out in this investigation?"

Jay grinned. "Are you kidding, Marion? These are people who will argue for days over the meaning of a phrase in a *Star Trek* episode, and I'm going to give them a chance to solve a mystery concerning fandom's greatest nemesis—Pat Malone! If what you've told me about fandom is correct, I think they'll jump at it."

"They probably will," sighed Marion. "It is, after all, gossip that can be rationalized as a public service inquiry. Go to it! You'll put the KGB to shame."

The ceremony for the opening of the time capsule was set for four o'clock. The small conference room seemed to be lit by lightning, so frequent were the flashes from the photojournalists' cameras. The Lanthanides posed separately, together, and in a series of group shots clustered around the now-unmuddied time capsule. The huge glass jar had been cleaned with a succession of wet Mountaineer Lodge towels before the meeting began, and it now occupied the place of honor on a table in the front, covered in a shining white dropcloth.

"I suppose he couldn't find any red samite," muttered Lily Warren, who was unfavorably reminded of the Grail legends.

Ruben Mistral waited until the flashes dwindled to an erratic few before he took his place as master of ceremonies of the Grand Opening.

"Ladies and gentlemen," he intoned solemnly. "We are about to engage in time travel. Remember that a Greek philosopher—I forget which one—said that time is a river, and that you cannot stop time, because you can never set your foot in the same place twice. But today we found that river of time, just as it was thirty years ago, before the lake was created, and we embarked on that river in search of—" he smiled at his own conceit "—in search of our lost youth. Those were the days when we were fans, idolizing the tale tellers and the dream merchants, and we put all our hopes for the future—our writing, our precious brain children—into this one fragile vessel and sent it forward to the future to wait for us." He patted the lid of the time capsule.

"For thirty-five years it has waited. Through war, and flood, and the untimely deaths of some of our beloved comrades, this little vessel of silicon has held our brightest hopes. And today we went back to get it. The time has come to open it. Ladies and gentlemen, it is a solemn moment when one comes to terms with one's youth. May I have a moment of silence, and the assistance of Brendan Surn, in opening this reposit of our youthful ambition?" He was gratified to see that a number of reporters appeared to be taking down his speech in shorthand. In the back of the room, camcorders were rolling.

After a moment's hesitation, Brendan Surn, assisted by Lorien, made his way to the table where the time capsule sat, gleaming under the camera lights. Mistral removed the cloth, revealing a jumble of papers and other objects crammed into the translucent pickle jar. He motioned for Surn to take hold of the side of the jar, while he gripped the other side. "It may have rusted shut," he explained to the assembled witnesses.

On cue Geoffrey Duke advanced from the sidelines holding a flat rubber mat, which was in fact a large jar opener. He tapped expertly on the top of the lid and then applied the opener, wrenching it with considerable force. After two more tries, the lid opened, amid cheers from the audience. With a little bow to Mistral, Geoffrey made a hasty exit, leaving his boss to tilt the jar forward to give people another view of the contents.

"I suppose I'd better take this stuff out," he murmured. "I hope I can remember what all of it is." He reached into the jar and pulled out a propeller beanie. "I believe that was yours, George." In carefully neutral tones he read the attached tag. "By

1984, all the world's intellectuals will be wearing these."

George Woodard hunkered down under waves of laughter. "We were *kidding!*" he protested.

Mistral reached back into the jar. "Oops, better be careful with this. A movie poster of *War of the Worlds*, liberated from the Bonnie Kate Theatre in Elizabethton. I'll bet that's worth something these days." He looked at the other Lanthanides. "What are we doing with this stuff?"

Jim Conyers smiled. "In 1954 we said we'd donate it to the science fiction hall of fame."

More chuckles from the audience.

Sarah Ashley stood up. "Since the happy day of such a repository has not yet come, perhaps we could use these things as a traveling exhibit, when it's time to publicize the anthology." She smiled as polite applause approved her suggestion.

"Okay," said Mistral. "Thanks, Sarah. Good idea. Now, what else . . . picture of a dog."

"That was to fool the aliens," said Erik Giles.

"Good plan. Here are the manuscripts. I'm afraid they're not in accordance with your submission guidelines, guys." Groans from the editors in the audience. "Geoffrey, if you'll take these away to be photocopied." He peeked at one page of the stack of papers and grinned. "Angela, do you still circle your i's?"

"Sometimes, Bunzie. Do you still misspell weird?"

He sighed. "She knew me when, folks.—What else? There's an envelope in here, addressed to the Lanthanides from John W. Campbell Jr."

"That's right!" cried Woodard. "Remember, we

wrote to him and asked for a letter to the future that we could include in our time capsule. And we never read it. Open it! Let's see what he said!"

Mistral began to tear the flap on the yellowed envelope. "John W. Campbell Jr., as many of you may know, was the legendary S-F editor from the Golden Age of Science Fiction. He discovered most of the great ones—"

"Except us."

Mistral forced a laugh. "Well, I think everybody got their share of rejection slips from Mr. Campbell. Let's see what he has to say to the future." He pulled out the letter and scanned a few lines.

As the silence grew longer, Jim Conyers called out, "Well, Bunzie? What does he say?"

Mistral reddened. "It's on Street & Smith letterhead, and it's from Campbell's secretary, Kay Tarrant. It says: 'Mr. Campbell regrets that he does not have the time to reply to your request. . . .' " He stopped reading amid the shouts of laughter. "Let's see what else is in here."

"A jar of grape jelly in case Claude—that's an old inside joke from fandom, folks. We might as well skip it. And here's some old magazines—"

"—Which are very valuable," said George Woodard, unable to contain himself. "If they go on display, I must insist that every care be taken—"

"Make it so," said Mistral with a smirk. "Now, let's see. We have an August 1928 issue of *Amazing*, signed by both E. E. 'Doc' Smith and Philip Francis Nowlan."

"Worth four thousand dollars. Minimum," said Woodard.

"Some Ray Bradbury fanzines; old comic books, no doubt valuable; copies of *Alluvial*; letters from various people . . . Carl Brandon, Sgt. Joan Carr."

"Those people didn't exist," Jim Conyers reminded him.

Mistral raised his eyebrows. "That ought to *really* make them worth something."

For the benefit of the press Jim Conyers explained about hoaxes in fandom, and how a fan might assume several personas in letter writing, since early fans seldom met.

"Thanks for clearing that up, Jim," said Mistral, calling the meeting back to order. "Here we have Curtis Phillips' beloved copy of H. P. Lovecraft's *Outsiders*, annotated by himself and Lovecraft expert Francis Towner Laney."

Erik Giles spoke up. "Unfortunately, as I recall, Curtis's comments were based on his interviews with the demons themselves, and contain their comments about Lovecraft and Laney."

"They *liked* Laney," chuckled Brendan Surn.

"The volume is priceless," declared Woodard.

"Well," said Mistral. "That's about all the interesting stuff. Thank you all for coming to this momentous occasion. The Lanthanides will hang around up here to chat with the press, and the rest of you can go and hang out in the bar until the bus comes. Or come look at the exhibits here."

"Make sure your hands are clean," Woodard warned.

Sarah Ashley heaved a sigh of relief. Her blond hair was still immaculately coiffed and her gray suit was perfect, but there were lines of strain around her eyes, and her face was drawn. The interviews were over now, the exhibits had been removed, and only she and Ruben Mistral were left in the conference room with the empty pickle jar, which now looked very ordinary and unimpressive.

She set down the assortment of papers on the desk in front of Ruben Mistral and began to wipe her soiled fingers with a moist tissue. "Well, you old rogue," she said, smiling at her most audacious client. "You've done it!"

Mistral's eyes widened in mock innocence. "I don't know why you doubt me, Sarah. Isn't it everything I said it was?" He patted the humble pickle jar as if it had just won the Derby.

"Miraculously, yes," she said dryly. "I suppose the handwriting will have to be analyzed, and perhaps the paper tested to certify age. Depending on how picky the purchaser is about authentication. But I shouldn't think there will be any problems whatsoever in going ahead with the auction tomorrow. You really did produce the lost works of the genre. Thank God. I had visions of looking foolish in front of thirty million people."

"The time capsule is absolutely genuine, Sarah. The sleight of hand was in the hype," said Mistral with a feral smile. "I took what is perhaps a mediocre collection of juvenilia and parlayed it into the Dead Sea Scrolls of Science Fiction."

"Yes, I heard that. Nice catch phrase."

"It should be. I paid an ad agency five grand to come up with it." His manner grew conspiratorial. "Incidentally, while we're being candid, there is one little matter I need to discuss with you, Sarah. We had an unexpected visitor turn up last night, and now he's dead."

She listened expressionlessly while Mistral explained the reappearance of Pat Malone and his sudden death some twelve hours later. When he had finished his recital, Sarah Ashley's eyes narrowed. "I do dislike coincidences. It was natural causes, of course?"

Mistral shrugged. "What else? I didn't talk to the police, of course, but nobody has said anything, so I thought it best not to mention the incident to the press."

"Very prudent. Perhaps tomorrow you might tell the story to the winning bidder, in case he wants to use it in publicizing the anthology. By then the news stories we need will have been filed with their respective publications, don't you think?"

Mistral nodded happily. "That's all right, then. I guess it's all over but the photocopying."

"And the bidding. But you must let me worry about that."

Locked in the attic of Ruben Mistral's consciousness, Bunzie pounded and pleaded to be let out, but his chances of having any say-so in the proceedings was nil. He might mourn his old friend in private, and even wonder about the circumstances of his death, but this was business, in which he was never permitted to interfere.

Marion knew that her appearance in the manager's office wasn't going to brighten his day any. The long-suffering hotel official had already endured a peculiar, media-infested science fiction get-together, the murder of one of the guests, and the arrival of police on the scene to disrupt the normal routine and intimidate the other patrons of the lodge. All he needed now was a self-appointed amateur sleuth wasting his time with ingenuous questions. Marion hoped she didn't look too much like a scatterbrained crank.

She phrased her request to the desk clerk with what she hoped was polite authority, and after a few stammered objections and a five-minute wait, the clerk led her back to the office of Coy A. Trivett, manager of the Mountaineer Lodge. It was a small, sparsely furnished room, decorated with framed photographs of mountain scenes and a hardware-store calendar from Elizabethton. The carpeting matched that in the lobby, and the worn chintz loveseat had been salvaged from the lobby seating area during last spring's renovations. Trivett himself, a blond man in his thirties, looked like a high school athlete who was thinking of running to fat. At the moment he wore the tentative smile of one who has resolved to be civil despite all temptations to the contrary.

"Is everything all right?" he asked in the anxious tones of one who knows better.

Marion introduced herself, placing a slight stress on the honorific "doctor" with which she prefaced her name. She found that use of her title helped to prevent people from mistaking her for an idiot. "It was I who found the body," she explained. "And I just wanted to see how the investigation was going.

In case the police want to talk to me," she added in an inspired afterthought.

"I believe they will," Trivett told her. She noticed a lingering trace of a local accent in his carefully precise speech. "I had a call from them a little while ago, and they asked whether your group would be staying on through tomorrow. They said they'd be over in the morning to talk to you people."

Marion's eyes widened. "Do they suspect foul play?"

"They didn't say exactly. But they took the fellow's medicine along with them for testing. Were you a friend of his?"

"I had just met him," said Marion. "But he was rather famous. I guess most people in science fiction have heard of Pat Malone."

The hotel manager blinked in surprise. "Who?"

"I suppose he wasn't exactly a celebrity outside the genre, but, believe me, in science fiction, Pat Malone was a name to conjure with."

"Ma'am, who are you talking about?"

"Pat Malone. The gentleman who died here last night."

Trivett frowned in confusion. "Was that his stage name or something?"

"No. Why?"

"Because the dead man was a Mr. Richard Spivey. At least according to his driver's license. I don't know anything about a Pat Malone."

On the editors' bus, en route to the Johnson City Holiday Inn, Enzio O'Malley was complaining loudly to all and sundry. "Some of this stuff is *hand-*

written!" he wailed. "I haven't had to read handwriting since I edited the college poetry magazine!"

"Be thankful it's legible," said Lily Warren. "I was afraid they'd find a time capsule filled with muddy water—that is, if they found anything at all."

"This is going to take me hours to read."

"Fortune cookies take him hours to read," muttered the Del Rey editor sotto voce.

"Has anybody looked at any of this stuff?" asked Lily. "I wondered if some of these stories are early drafts of pieces they rewrote and published later. I'd hate to pay six figures for a draft of *Starwind Rising.*"

"This story by Dale Dugger is pretty good," said a short dark girl who couldn't have been more than twenty-three. She had recently been transferred from the romance division to science fiction, and she was still unfamiliar with her new territory. "Has he got a back list?"

After a few moments of stifled laughter from her rival editors, Lily Warren said gently, "No, Debbie. Dale Dugger died of alcohol-related disorders in Nashville. He isn't significant."

Enzio O'Malley scowled. "Well, at least we can assume that he wasn't a temperamental old bastard like the famous ones."

"I thought Mr. Conyers was very nice," said Debbie.

Lily Warren sighed. "He's just a lawyer. The famous ones are Surn, Mistral, Phillips, Deddingfield, and possibly Erik Giles, who wrote the C. A. Stormcock book."

"He thinks he's famous," said O'Malley. "I asked

him to autograph my photocopy of his time-capsule short story, and he refused point blank."

Lily Warren laughed. "I always suspected you of being a closet fan, O'Malley."

"Are all the authors represented in the manuscript?" someone else asked.

Lily flipped through the pages of faint typescript and badly photocopied holograph manuscripts. "I don't see Deddingfield," she said. "Everyone else is there."

Someone from the back of the bus called out, "Has anyone read the story by George Woodard?"

"I'm saving that for late tonight," said O'Malley. "For a sedative."

"All right," said Jay Omega. "I think I can fly this thing."

As soon as Marion had gone, Jay went out to the car and retrieved his Tandy 1400HD laptop from the trunk. At nearly twelve pounds, it was a bit heavy to be a portable machine, at least compared to the latest technology, but Jay was used to it. He liked the keyboard and the backlit screen, and he couldn't see any point in dropping a thousand bucks on a newer model just to save himself a few pounds of luggage. He could write books on it, send faxes with it, and, when he hooked it up to a telephone, he could access the world.

Several minutes later he was back in his room establishing a command center. He had dragged the round worktable over beside the bed, within reach of the telephone wall jack. He unplugged the touch-tone phone on the nightstand, and in its place he plugged in the computer modem. He set up the computer in the center of the worktable and attached it to the modem.

Now all he had to do was make some phone calls.

Jay Omega took out his wallet. Tucked away with his Radio Shack credit card, his SFWA membership, and his frequent flier ID was a cardboard Guinness beer coaster with Joel Schumann's telephone number scribbled on the back. Beneath that was a second number, inscribed: Bulletin Board—J.S., Sysop. It was this second number that he needed. The notation beside that number indicated that Joel Schumann was the systems operator (i.e. sysop) for an electronic bulletin board to which a number of computer enthusiasts in his area subscribed. Through Schumann's bulletin board, users could contact other people on other bulletin boards anywhere in the world, but because everyone wasn't always logged on, it could take days for the right person to receive a message. Jay decided that he needed some advice before proceeding. Although he dutifully paid his twenty-dollar yearly dues to keep the system operating, bulletin board chatting wasn't something he had much time or inclination for. Once a week he checked the messages to see if someone were trying to reach him, and occasionally he scanned the screens of typewritten conversations to see if anything more substantial than *Robocop* was being discussed. Most of the time it wasn't, so he let it go at that. Now, though, he needed some advice, and he was pretty sure that Joel Schumann was the place to start.

Jay dialed the number, hoping that one of the

four lines was free. A click told him that it was, and almost instantly his screen lit up with the logo of Joel Schumann's bulletin board. Jay logged on and typed in his password: *Frodo*, which was the name of Marion Farley's cat. He had no idea how she had come up with that name, and it never occurred to him to ask. After a moment's pause the system pronounced him cleared for entry and informed him that he had seventy-two minutes to spend before being disconnected.

"I hope that will be enough," muttered Jay. After a moment's thought, he typed in a message to "ALL": PLEASE ADVISE. I NEED TO CONTACT S-F FANS FROM ALL OVER THE COUNTRY TO TRACK DOWN A MISSING PERSON. URGENT AND IMPORTANT MATTER. TIME IS LIMITED. I'M IN A MOTEL NEAR JOHNSON CITY, TN, USING LAPTOP. PLEASE ADVISE FASTEST AND MOST EFFECTIVE WAY TO CONTACT FANDOM.—J. OMEGA.

After reading through the lines to make sure he hadn't misspelled anything, Jay transmitted the message and logged off. Now he had to wait for somebody to read his message and leave a reply. Because it was a Saturday he knew that it wouldn't take long for an answer. He decided to call back in half an hour. While he waited, he ambled over to the television and began to flip through the channels, testing his theory that at any given hour of the day, *Star Trek* is always playing somewhere. It wasn't, but he did find an old episode of the British series *Blackadder*, a program which Marion ranked somewhere between chocolate and sex. He had settled back on the bed, happily immersed in a parody of court life in the sixteenth century, when Marion burst in.

"You won't believe what the hotel manager said!" she cried.

Jay turned down the volume on the set. "Try me."

"He said the dead man was someone called Richard Spivey."

"He could have changed his name, I suppose. It would have made it harder for fandom to track him down. Did you look in his wallet?"

Marion shivered. "No. I didn't want to search the corpse. That's why I'm an English major. But he did have books autographed by some of the Lanthanides."

"To Spivey or to Pat Malone?"

Marion considered it. "Neither, that I recall. One of them was to Curtis Phillips *from* Pat Malone. Maybe he got it back when Curtis died. It seems strange, though, doesn't it?"

"Everything about Pat Malone is strange. I don't suppose you were able to find out how he died?"

"Mr. Trivett doesn't think they know yet. But he did say that they took his medicine bottle along to be tested."

"What was in it?"

"Elavil. Prescribed to Spivey. And before you ask, I have no idea what that is. *You're* the science person, not me."

"Is there anybody here with any medical background? Maybe we could ask them."

Marion ticked each of the Lanthanides' names off on her fingers. "Angela!" she said. "She works in a hospital, doesn't she? I suppose you want me to see if she knows what Elavil is."

Jay Omega glanced at his watch. "I think I can call the bulletin board back now to see if they have any advice for me. You might also ask Angela for any information on Pat Malone's supposed death in 1958. What authority did they have for believing him dead? While you're at it, ask her if she's positive that he was Pat Malone."

"They certainly acted as if he was," said Marion with a grim smile. "He created more stir than Ted Bundy at a beauty pageant."

"I wonder if Ruben Mistral contacted Pat Malone's next of kin about the time capsule. See if you can find the answer to that one, too."

Marion sighed. "This has a familiar ring to it. I talk to people while *you* talk to machines."

"No, Marion," said Jay with wounded innocence. "I'll be talking to people, too. I'm just using machines to do it."

"All right," she sighed. "I'll go and grill the suspects." At the door, Marion hesitated and looked back. "Jay, you don't really think he was murdered, do you?"

He shrugged. "I haven't given it much thought. I'm sure the police will tell us. Right now I just want to know who he was."

When Marion had gone, Jay went to his computer and typed in *Alt-D* and then *M* to allow him to manually enter the electronic bulletin board phone number from the Guinness beer mat. He typed in the number, hit return, and waited while the computer dialed the number. After two rings the line was answered, and after he typed in his identification, a welcome screen from the bulletin board asked him if he wanted to check his electronic mail. He hit *return* and found that there was one message waiting. He pressed *R Y, return.*

After a moment's pause the message appeared:

TO Dr. Mega—FROM Sysop. SUBJECT: Please Advise. All right, all right, I'm here. You didn't have to shout. (Don't use all caps next time.) Remember when I made you subscribe to Delphi? I know that all you use it for is to snag cheap air fares, but it does have other uses. I hope you can remember your password. If so, call the Tennessee local TYMNET number, 615-928-1191, and log into Delphi the way you do at home. Go to CONFERENCE, then type WHO. This will list current conference conversations. Hopefully you will see a conference name that looks promising for your line of inquiry. You don't need to join it. You can issue the command WHO IS <User Name>, and that will give you a profile of the people currently in the conference: where they live, what they like, etc. If you want to talk in their conference, type JOIN <Conference name or number> and then you can barge in and start asking them questions. If your topic is really offbeat, you can create your own conference, and let the strange ones find you. (What have you gotten yourself into now, Dr. Mega?) I'll be around for most of the evening in case you get in further trouble, need bail money, whatever. May St. Solenoid be with you. JS.

Jay made notes of the instructions in Joel's message, sent a quick reply of thanks to him, and logged off the bulletin board. Then he turned off the television, yawned and stretched, and sat down at the keyboard of his computer. "It's going to be a damn long night in fandom," he muttered.

Marion found Angela Arbroath in her room recuperating from a marathon session of nostalgia and journalism. "I hope I'm not disturbing you," said Marion, strolling past Angela into the room as if she were sure of her welcome. "This must have been quite an exciting day for you!"

Angela, who was wearing a flowered kimono and leather thongs, looked tired. She had scrubbed off her makeup, so that her lips had a bloodless look to them and her wrinkles stood out in high relief against her pale skin. "I guess the news about Pat sort of overshadowed all the rest of it," she said apologetically.

Marion sat down on the unused one of the twin beds, and settled in for a long chat. "I am sorry about what happened to Pat Malone," she said. "I didn't know him, but I found the body, you know, so you can imagine how it has made *me* feel. I wondered, though—are you certain that it *was* Pat Malone?"

The older woman smiled. "He knew things that only one of the Lanthanides could have known. You weren't there, were you, when he turned up at the party last night? Within minutes they were all bickering as if it were more than thirty years ago. He knew just what to say to infuriate them." She sighed. "He always did."

"Can you think of anyone who might have wanted to kill him?"

"Hon, I can't think of anyone who didn't. At one time or another, Pat Malone antagonized every correspondent he ever had, every close friend, every sweetheart. Did you ever read *The Last Fandango*?"

"No. I've certainly heard about it, though. Was it ever actually published?"

"In a manner of speaking. It was mimeographed and distributed by the Fantasy Amateur Press Association. And in the book he severely criticized the Fantasy Amateur Press Association."

Marion nodded. "Yes, I knew about that. I've never seen one, though."

"It was nothing fancy. Just pages and pages of typing. No illustrations, no sophisticated typesetting, nothing to make it visually pleasing. Nothing to make it pleasing, period." She looked away. "I cried when I read it. He said so many awful things about all the people that I knew. And the worst of it was, I couldn't really deny any of it. It's just that he saw them so uncharitably." She smiled bitterly. "And about me? Oh, he said that I lacked only beauty to be a femme fatale. He was most unsparing of people's feelings. But, of course, he was hardest on himself."

"In what way?"

"He wanted people to know what an idiot he thought he had been for succumbing to fandom, so he outlined his whole experience in getting involved

in science fiction, and he outlined the disillusionment that made him leave."

Marion tried to temper her excitement. "Did he
mention the Lanthanides?"

"Yes, of course. He said that Surn was pompous,
and George was a fool, and he was critical of everyone, but the most damning thing he did was simply
to chronicle their bickering, and their naïveté, and
their youthful arrogance. He made them—and himself, you understand—look like arrogant clowns.
And then he proceeded to do the same thing to the
rest of fandom as well."

"Could anyone who read *The Last Fandango* have
known the things he talked about last night?"

Angela looked puzzled, but she considered the
question. "I don't think so," she said. "He mentioned
a few pranks that weren't included in his memoir. If
he had written down every stupid thing they did,
his book would have been longer than *War and
Peace*."

"So he knew a lot of embarrassing secrets?"

"I suppose so. Not that anyone ought to care
about who was sleeping with who after so long a
time." She smiled reflectively. "But I guess Barbara
Conyers just might at that. Anyhow, why did you
ask me if he knew anything dangerous? He wasn't
murdered."

"Not that we know of," Marion admitted. "But it
seemed possible. The hotel manager told me that
the police took Pat Malone's prescription medicine
along with them. It was Elavil. We wondered if you
knew what that was."

Angela Arbroath sat up straight. Her expression became thoughtful. "*Pat Malone* was using Elavil?"

"Apparently so. Or at least he had it in his possession. The name on the bottle said 'Richard Spivey.' What is it?"

"Amitriptyline. It's used to treat depression." She seemed to have forgotten Marion's presence. "That would explain a lot. He used to get so caught up in wild schemes—like fandom—and then later he would berate himself for having wasted his time on them. Yes, I suppose he might even have been manic depressive. Although, I have to say that he didn't seem to behave much differently last night from the way he was in the old days, so I don't see that the medicine was doing him much good."

"I wonder if they've notified his next of kin. Did he have any? I thought you mentioned once that he was married."

"That was in the fifties," Angela reminded her. "And his wife was about ten years older than he was. Don't ask me to explain *that*. I do remember that there was a lot of chauvinistic letter writing in fandom in those days, with those runty little shits asking each other what he saw in *her*. Nobody ever thought to marvel that she'd seen anything in *him*. Well, as I say, it's a long time ago. She may have died."

"Maybe so. By the way, have you ever heard of Richard Spivey?" asked Marion, trying to appear casual.

Angela shook her head. "If he's a new writer, don't expect me to know him. I haven't kept up."

"I don't know who he is," Marion admitted. "But I

sure do wish I knew what killed Pat Malone so conveniently. Not that the police would confide in me."

"Get Jim Conyers to ask them. He's a lawyer around here, and he's probably old friends with the sheriff."

Marion looked at her with renewed respect. "What a perfectly simple, brilliant idea."

Angela nodded. "Well, I hope you find out something," she said. "As cantankerous as Pat was, I never wanted him to be dead."

There was a soft tapping at the door. "I'll get it," said Marion, eying her hostess' kimono. She went to the door and eased it open. "Yes?"

Lorien Williams stood there, twisting her hands and looking anxious. "Excuse me, is Miss—um—you know, Angela. Could I speak to her, please?"

Marion glanced back at Angela, who waved for her to let the visitor in.

"Is anything the matter?" she asked as Lorien edged past her, head down and slouching. Behind her, Marion looked over at Angela and mouthed: Who knows?

"I wondered if you could take a look at Mr. Surn," she said to Angela. "I think somebody said you were a nurse."

Angela paled. "What's the matter with Brendan?"

Marion said, "Shall I call an ambulance?" She was remembering the huddled form of Pat Malone, slumped on the bathroom floor.

"No. It isn't that bad. I mean, it isn't a heart attack or anything. It's just that sometimes he has . . . well, bad spells. There are times when he doesn't know me, and he gets very angry. I don't blame him, of course. I'd get angry, too, if—" Lorien's voice trailed off uncertainly.

Angela looked from Marion to Lorien and back again. "I'll just go in the bathroom and change," she said.

"I'm going to look for Jim Conyers," said Marion.

Meanwhile, back at the electric Scout meeting, Jay Omega had succeeded in logging on to a nation-wide computer chat on Delphi, and he established his own conference, devoted to "a discussion of the Lanthanides." He labeled his file MORE FANDANGO, reasoning that the word "Fandango" would be a red flag to anyone who remembered Pat Malone, and that everyone else would give it a miss. This was not entirely true; a few people chimed in wanting to discuss the lambada, an association which eluded the sedentary Omega, and a few college-age chemists tried to get up a discussion of the periodic chart, but after a quarter of an hour, someone from Indiana actually did check in, responding with: IS THIS ABOUT P. B. MALONE? AND, IF SO, WHAT ABOUT HIM? HE'S DEAD. The message purported to be from one J. A. Bristol.

Jay typed back: YES, BUT NOT FOR AS LONG AS YOU THINK, PERHAPS. I NEED TO TALK TO SOMEBODY IN MIS-SISSIPPI ABOUT VERIFYING P.M.'S 1958 DEMISE.

Meanwhile, other people chimed in with their own opinions of Malone's novel, and of *The Last Fandango*. Jay replied: CAN WE TABLE THESE TOPICS? BIOGRAPHICAL DATA URGENTLY NEEDED. IS ANYONE ON FROM CUPERTINO, CA?

Of course there was. Cupertino, which is in

California's Silicon Valley, has more computers
than bathtubs. The response to Jay's request was
almost immediate. "Kenny," another collegian, said:
NEVER HEARD OF THIS MALONE GUY, BUT I LIVE IN
CUPERTINO. SO?

Jay consulted the notes he had scribbled down,
containing everything he could remember about Pat
Malone. PLEASE CHECK PHONE DIRECTORY FOR AN
ETHEL OR A MRS. PAT/PB MALONE, he told Kenny.

Two other conference crashers were ignoring
Jay's line of questioning to pursue an argument of
their own about the symbolism that one of them
saw in *River of Neptune*.

In exasperation, Jay fired at them: HAVE IT ON
GOOD AUTHORITY THAT THE NOVEL PROPHESIES THE
COMING OF NINTENDO. YOU HAVE NOW REACHED EQUI-
LIBRIUM. GO AWAY!—HAS ANYONE OUT THERE EVER
SEEN PAT MALONE? LATELY?

NO, BUT I SAW ELVIS AT PIZZA HUT LAST WEEK.

Jay was beginning to understand why the police
hauled people in for questioning: so that they could
hit them. He ignored this last bit of baiting and
waited for serious replies. What did he need to know
about Malone, anyway? He made notations on one
of his data sheets:

"Malone's hometown?" Get Marion to find out.

"Cupertino, Ca—Ethel Malone—Verify." Beside
that he wrote: Kenny.

"If dead, what happened to his possessions." He
scratched that one out. The book in the dead man's
suitcase had belonged to Curtis Phillips. Malone
had only autographed it. Jay put in a new item:
"Compare handwriting samples."

"Mississippi—Malone's death—Verify."

"Richard Spivey?"

"Malone—Physical description."

"Cause of death."—Marion working on it.

"Elavil." Ditto.

"Washington Med School. Body donated?"

He glanced back at the computer screen. Three messages were waiting for him. One said: MOONFIRE SPEAKING. I THOUGHT PAT MALONE WAS AN IRISH PUNK ROCK GROUP—ALL FEMALE. Another respondent had shot back: NO! HE WAS THE SALMAN RUSHDIE OF FANDOM. The third note was from Kenny: ETHEL IS IN THE PHONE BOOK. NOW WHAT?

It helped that the desk clerk had become convinced that everyone connected with science fiction was crazy. After the barrage of requests she had endured that day (pickle jar cover, corpse removal, indefinite use of a telephone line), Marion's request for a list of all the Lanthanides' room numbers seemed positively reasonable to her. She copied them out on the back of a Sunday Buffet flier and handed it over with a weary sigh. What would they be wanting next? Electric soap? She closed her eyes to check out her headache on the Richter scale. At least she was now psychologically ready for the Tennessee war gamers' convention coming up in September.

Armed with this guide to the other guests' whereabouts, Marion first checked the restaurant to see who was there: nobody she recognized. Either they went to dinner early, or they had called down for room service. As she studied the diners in the restaurant, though, she realized that there was a familiar look about at least a dozen of them. Many of them were bespectacled and heavyset, and they wore T-shirts with slogans on them and hairdos that had never been fashionable. Several of them were reading paperbacks while they ate; the others appeared to be arguing. Fans! Marion backed slowly toward the door before she turned and fled.

"Well," she said to herself as she waited for the elevator, "at least it will give me a pretext for dropping in on people. I can warn them that the fen have arrived." Waving, she caught the attention of the long-suffering desk clerk. "Yoo hoo!" she called as the doors were closing. "Will you please not give out these room numbers to anyone else?"

"Sure," said the desk clerk to the closed elevator doors. "Everybody except *you* is a crank, right?"

Marion tapped gently on the door to the Conyers' room, hoping that they weren't the sort of people who went to bed ridiculously early and were smug about it.

Barbara answered the door, and Marion could see that the room's television was on, tuned to *Star Trek: The Next Generation.* "Hi!" said Marion brightly. "Can I come in? By the way, you want to be careful about opening the door without asking who it is. There's a contingent of fans in the building."

Barbara looked at her husband and smiled. "I'm not used to the idea of Jim having fans."

Marion sighed. "You never get used to it."

Jim Conyers motioned for her to sit down in the armchair by the worktable. "We brought snacks from home," he grinned. "Because Barbara's a skinflint. Want a beer? Diet Coke? Autograph your forehead?"

"Diet Coke," said Marion. "Unless you really need to practice the autograph. Seriously, though, I'm here to talk to you about Pat Malone."

Jim and Barbara looked at each other. "It was a sad business," he said quietly.

"I know," she said. "We also thought it was a very convenient coincidence. Pat Malone shows up, threatening, from what I hear, to do a new *Fandango*, and suddenly he dies."

"I thought of that," said Conyers, scooping ice into a glass and pouring Marion her drink. "But our secrets are pretty small potatoes."

Marion shook her head. "Not with all those reporters hanging around. And the hotel restaurant is full of fans. Any little indiscretion on anybody's part could—just this one week of your lives—easily make the AP, the *Enquirer*, and *Time* magazine. But, of course, that's just idle speculation, until we know how Pat Malone died."

"Presumably we'll find out sooner or later."

"It had better be sooner," said Marion. "Unless you want this to leak to the press. We thought that since you are a local attorney, you might be able to tap some inside sources and find out. We really need to know."

Jim Conyers thought it over carefully. "All right," he said. "I can't see any harm in it. I'll do what I can. I'll call your room when I've found out anything."

Marion gave him a helpless smile. "Could you please call now? Our phone line is kind of tied up."

She sipped her Diet Coke and chatted quietly

with Barbara while Jim Conyers consulted the telephone directory and began to make his calls.

"I think it went rather well today, don't you?"
asked Barbara. "I was awfully afraid they wouldn't
find anything. They weren't terribly organized, you
know."

"They'd never misplace their manuscripts," Marion
assured her.

"Well, I hope the New York editors like what they
read." She lowered her voice to a conspiratorial
whisper. "I want to remodel the kitchen."

Jim Conyers was oblivious of his wife's conversation. "Well, that was fast work, Dennis," he was
saying into the phone. "Guess we're lucky it's the
slow season, huh? Say that again, will you? I need
to write it down. How do you spell that? Oh, just
like it sounds. M.A.O. And what are you calling
it?—Think so, huh?—Okay, Dennis. Keep me
posted. Yeah, if I can help you out, I will. Thanks
again."

The two women looked up at him expectantly.
Conyers set down the phone. His face was grave. He
picked up the note pad and held it at arm's length.
"According to the medical examiner, he died of
having something called an MAO inhibitor mixed
with his medication. And they think it was murder,
so they'll be back in the morning to talk to all of us."
He looked sternly at Marion. "Another thing.
According to them, the deceased was one Richard
Spivey. Now who the hell was Richard Spivey?"

Marion shook her head. "I wish I knew."

CHAPTER 13

BRENDAN SURN WAS quiet now. For nearly an hour Angela Arbroath had sat with him, held his hand, and talked soothingly of times gone by. At last her soft Southern voice had seemed to penetrate his anger, and tears drifted down his cheeks. Now he was sitting on his bed, clutching his silver NASA jacket, and staring off into nothingness.

Angela patted his hand and eased away from him. "I think he'll be all right for now," she told Lorien Williams.

The girl summoned a grateful smile. "Thank you. I've never been able to calm him down as quickly as that. Mostly when he gets into rages at home, I just leave him alone until he tires himself out." She sat huddled on her twin bed, in a black T-shirt and slacks, looking very small and lost. Dark circles shadowed her eyes.

"I suppose this is more than you bargained for when you took this job," said Angela.

Lorien hesitated. "I was such a fan of Mr. Surn," she said at last. "I had read everything he ever

wrote, and all the biographical material I could find
on him. He seemed so grandfatherly, somehow. You
know, like Yoda. And I wasn't very happy with my
parents. They were always hassling me to give up
fandom and get some mundane job, like being a
stockbroker." She made a moue of distaste. "I
thought I'd go and see Brendan Surn. He'd understand me."

Angela sighed. She had heard it all before. Science fiction writers build castles in the air, and the
fans move into them. (And the publishers collect the
rent.) It was easy to find solace in someone else's
storytelling, or in their apparent acceptance of what
you are, and to build a soul for them. Surely, the fan
thinks, he will like me as much as I like him; let me
go and see him. It usually leads to disappointment:
neither faces nor souls are as pretty in real life as
they are on paper.

Angela remembered her own fascination in the
fifties with Miranda Cairncross, a woman writer
who wrote a wonderful tale about a Danish girl
called Gefion who becomes caught up in the Ragnarok, the Norse version of Armageddon. She had
found so much wisdom and lyrical beauty in *Ragnarok* that she read it over and over until she had
nearly memorized it. She couldn't wait to meet the
author, and at a book signing in New Orleans one
Christmas she got her chance. Clutching her tattered copy of *Ragnarok*, she stood in line, half
expecting to be picked out of the crowd as a soul
mate and whisked off to tea with the author. She
had even made a green velvet cloak like the one

Gefion wore in the novel, so that the author would know of her devotion.

But the magic friendship did not happen. Miranda Cairncross turned out to be a gawky, colorless woman who seemed dismayed at the prospect of talking to the crowd of fans hovering around her table. She signed the books with fierce concentration, as though she were shutting out her surroundings, and when she finished each one, she would look up at the purchaser with a taut, forced smile. Angela could not imagine anyone less like the bold and reckless Gefion of *Ragnarok*. When she reached the head of the line, Angela handed over her book and said, "I really love your writing."

Miranda Cairncross peered at her over the pile of books, took in the sight of the plain young girl in a green velvet cloak, and reddened slightly. "I do what I can," she said. Moments later she returned Angela's copy, inscribed "There is no frigate like a book, M. A. Cairncross." Angela recognized the Emily Dickinson quote (another interest she might have shared with the author), but at the time she was disappointed that Miranda Cairncross's dedication had not been more personal.

Years later, after she had run into Brendan Surn at a few conventions and seen him besieged by soul-starved young strangers, she saw things from the other side, and she realized that touching people through their books was the best that most authors could do. Anything else was a letdown. By then she had also realized that the Dickinson quote about books being frigates was meant perhaps as a gentle warning from the author, telling her not to stray too

far from life. She saw Miranda Cairncross years
later, a frail old woman who had been brought to
Worldcon to receive a plaque. Angela decided that
the best way to thank her would be to leave her in
peace.

"Yes," she said to Lorien Williams. "So you went
to see Brendan Surn, thinking that he would be
your friend."

"I guess so." Lorien was close to tears. She
glanced over at the staring figure of Surn and continued, "When I got to his house, the place was a
mess, and he didn't seem to know how to cook or
anything, so I said to myself, I'll just stick around
until his household help comes back. But they never
did! I think his maid must have quit, and he never
got around to advertising for another one."

"So you stayed?"

She nodded. "I didn't know what else to do! I
mean, I couldn't leave him. I guess I could have
later, after I learned how to manage everything. I
could have hired someone, I guess. But he seemed to
need me. And I didn't know what else to do with
myself anyway." Her voice broke. "But it isn't like I
thought it would be! Sometimes, when he's wet the
bed again or burned up another teakettle trying to
boil water, I'll say to myself, This is the man who
wrote *Starwind Rising*. This is a being of greatness.
But he isn't! He's just an ordinary, sick old man.
And I feel trapped."

"Did you become friends?"

Lorien shook her head. "He's never reacted to me
the way he did to you today. I think I'm just a conve-
nience for him, not a person!"

There is no frigate like a book, thought Angela. Aloud she said, "Fans are not friends, dear. It can be dangerous to forget that."

Jay Omega didn't even look up when Marion entered the room. He was staring at the screen of his computer as if it were showing Indiana Jones movies. "Your ferret is reporting in, sir," said Marion, tapping him playfully on the shoulder.

"Shhh!" he said. "I'm talking to somebody."

Marion looked around the otherwise empty room. "Who? Friend of Curtis Phillips?"

He slumped back in his seat and looked up at her. "No. Not a demon. A guy out in California, and one from North Carolina. Whole crowds of people. Look at this." He tapped a block of text on the screen.

Leaning over his shoulder, Marion read aloud: "To J. O. Mega. From Kenny in Cupertino. Called Ethel Malone's number. The woman who answered says Ethel is in a nursing home, and that she's her grandniece. She says her Great-Uncle Pat died in 1958. Thinks they have a death certificate around someplace. Physical description: 6'2" (she thinks); green eyes; black hair; very pale. Says she sometimes gets crank calls from fans. Asks that fans not make pilgrimage to her house, as she barely remembers Great-Uncle Pat. Wants to be left alone. She sounds cute, though. I'm thinking about asking her out.—Kenny."

"Let me type a reply thanking this guy for his trouble," said Jay. "Then you can tell me what you found out, Marion. By the way, have we eaten dinner?"

Marion reached for the room service menu. "I thought you'd never ask."

When she came back from ordering a couple of chicken dinners, Marion turned back to Jay. "So, did he fake his death certificate so that he could get rid of his wife as well as his friends?"

"I don't think so," said Jay. "A guy from Mississippi went down to his local library and found an obituary for Pat Malone in an old newspaper on microfilm." He grinned. "Somebody who called himself Jim Hacker offered to break into the records of the University of Washington medical school, but I declined."

"Good. I'm sure the dean of engineering takes a dim view of professors being wanted by the FBI."

"I also got some interesting reminiscences from some old-timers that didn't quite square with things here. I get the funny feeling that the Lanthanides are still playing 'you and me against the world.' By the way, can you get me a copy of the time-capsule stories?"

Marion looked smug. "I already did," she said. "I asked Geoffrey Duke to make one for me. I thought it might be useful in case I decide to do an article."

"Good. Have you read them yet?"

"Of course not. I've been running errands for a certain engineer with delusions of grandeur."

"Oh. Well, sometime tonight I wish you'd take a look at them."

"Don't you want to see them?"

Jay shook his head. "No. I need you to read them in that sharklike way that English majors read things. Analytically."

"I see," said Marion dryly. "I'll try not to mistake that for a compliment. Anything else?"

"You have read the Lanthanides' published work, haven't you?"

"I just finished teaching the early science fiction course, remember? Of course, I have!"

"I thought so. Good. That ought to wrap it up."

"So what do you think about all this?"

"You first, Marion. Any news?"

Marion nodded. "Angela Arbroath says that Elavil is used to control depression, among other things, and Jim Conyers phoned his friends in law enforcement, and was told that the case is a suspected homicide, and that the investigators will be back sometime tomorrow to question everybody. Something called an MAO inhibitor got added to Malone's medicine. Apparently, a tablet had been crushed and added to his drink."

"MAO inhibitor. I know what that is. My Uncle Ewen . . . Well, anyway, that's interesting. Anything else?"

"The police have the deceased listed as Richard Spivey."

"Good," said Jay. "And do *they* think he was Pat Malone?"

"The Lanthanides? Yes. Angela says he had to have been. He knew stuff that only one of the Lanthanides would know." She ticked off the members' names. "Dugger's dead, Deddingfield's dead, Curtis Phillips is dead, and all the rest of them are here. Besides, if he wasn't Pat Malone, why would any of them kill him?"

"I wondered that," said Jay Omega. "And I don't

know. But I rather think that they do." He looked thoughtful and then embarrassed. "Marion, did you bring my SFWA directory in that rat's nest of bibliographic papers you insisted on packing?"

"Yes. And don't say it was a waste of time, because I still might interview one of the Lanthanides for an analysis of early S-F for one of the journals. Maybe."

"You probably won't, but I'm not complaining about the fact that you brought it. I just need my directory."

Marion retrieved the booklet containing the membership list of the Science Fiction Writers of America and resisted the urge to fling it at him. Jay began to flip through the dog-eared pages. Several entries were marked with comments (e.g. "Sent thank you note") and a few had telephone numbers written after them in pencil. "She's not in here," he muttered.

"What are you up to now?" asked Marion.

Jay continued to thumb through the booklet. "Who is the most famous person I know in science fiction?"

Marion searched her memory. "Well, you shook hands with Arthur C. Clarke once."

"No. I mean the most famous person that I can *impose* upon." He handed her the booklet. "And your choice is limited to the people I have phone numbers for."

Marion began to flip through the pages, going from back to front. "You served on a committee with him once . . . didn't we meet her at a con last spring?" Finally she stopped turning pages, deliberating over one entry.

"Did you find someone?"

She took a deep breath. "John Brunner is an extremely nice person, and he seems to like you," she said carefully. "But since it is about three o'clock in the morning where he lives in Britain, I'd advise against presuming on his benevolence."

"Good point," said Jay. "I suppose I could wait until five A.M. to call him. That would make it ten on a Sunday morning where he is. But I wanted to get this done tonight."

"Get *what* done?"

"Look, if the Lanthanides don't get this solved very quickly, there will be all three rings of a media circus. I think I'd better explain that to them."

"I think they realize it."

"Like hell they do. They're just sitting around playing dumb and hoping it will all go away. But it won't, unless they start cooperating very quickly."

Marion's eyes narrowed. "What does this have to do with John Brunner?"

"Nothing."

"Then why are you going to call him at ten o'clock on a Sunday morning?" she wailed.

"Because I'm hoping that he has Jazzy Holt's phone number, and that he'll give it to me."

"You are going to call Jasmine Holt?" gasped Marion.

"Not unless I have to," said Jay grimly. He looked at his watch and sighed. "I guess we'd better try to settle this thing now. Tomorrow may be too late.

Could you round up the Lanthanides and bring them here?"

"Why would they want to do that?" asked Marion. "Most of them hardly know you."

"Tell them that we will meet here at eleven to resolve this thing. If they don't show up, I will consider that permission to report my findings to the police instead. And then I'll call a press conference."

"You're going to do that? *You?* The person who wouldn't even tell the local paper about your award nomination?"

"This is different," said Jay. "Their sense of priorities is beginning to get on my nerves. And besides, I liked the man who was killed."

Ruben Mistral might have objected strenuously to Jay Omega's proposed meeting, except for the fact that his body was still running on California time, so it still seemed the shank of the evening to him, and he wasn't sleepy. Besides, the threat of adverse publicity appealed to the practical side of Mistral's nature, and he agreed that some sort of discussion would be prudent. Marion persuaded the others to come by ending her summons with the statement: "—And Ruben Mistral is coming." With varying degrees of reluctance, everyone agreed to turn up at Jay Omega's room in one hour's time.

Jay spent the hour before the meeting online with the Fandango grapevine he had created in hopes that he might learn more useful bits of information about Pat Malone. He also made a phone call to Raleigh, North Carolina, to check out a theory of his own. Marion read the time-capsule stories, with occasional snickers or caustic comments which Jay steadfastly ignored. Finally, though, ten minutes before the Lanthanides were due to arrive, he logged out of Delphi, switched off the computer, and turned to Marion. "Well?" he said. "Have you read them all?"

She looked thoughtful. "Oh, yes."

"What do you think?"

In most unscholarly terms, Dr. Marion Farley told him.

At five minutes to eleven the Lanthanides began to arrive. Jim and Barbara Conyers came first, bringing a bottle of wine, as if they were accepting a dinner invitation. Marion seated them on the bed nearest the window, and left Jay to exchange pleasantries with them while she went to answer another knock at the door. George Woodard was there in his pajamas and bathrobe, giving a slumber-party air to the gathering. He was followed by Angela Arbroath, who was arm in arm with a dazed-looking Brendan Surn. Lorien Williams came in after them, appearing more tired than nervous. Finally Erik Giles and Ruben Mistral appeared, bringing along chairs from their own rooms.

"I'm too old to sit on the floor," said Erik. "Met Bunzie in the hall, and he agreed with me. Here we are. What's this all about?"

The Lanthanides turned expectantly to Jay Omega, who reddened a bit under their solemn stares. "I guess you're wondering why I asked you here," he said softly.

Jim Conyers scowled. "I'm wondering why we bothered to come."

"Well," said Jay. "Believe it or not, I mean well. I know that this anthology means a lot to most of you, and that you want the time-capsule retrieval to be remembered as a solemn and meaningful event—and not as the prologue to a sensational murder story."

George Woodard yelped. "Pat Malone was murdered?"

Mistral's response was more pragmatic. "Who knows this?"

"The police. Maybe some reporters by now, but if you're lucky, they haven't made any connection yet between the deceased and the reunion. They will, though, if this thing goes into investigation. Especially if they find out that Pat Malone had come back to life for this reunion."

"He's right," said Ruben Mistral. "We need to talk about damage control. Jim, you're a lawyer. What can we do?"

Jim Conyers shrugged. "Cooperate, I guess. Once the medical examiner ran that tox screen and found a suspicious substance present in the deceased, there was no chance of stopping the investigation. The longer it drags on, the more publicity there's going to be."

Erik Giles interrupted him. "Could I have some of that wine, Jim?"

The others shushed him and went on talking at once, but Barbara Conyers flashed him a sympathetic smile and handed him the bottle and a plastic glass.

"What if we called a press conference and said we had nothing to do with it?" asked Angela Arbroath.

Jim Conyers shook his head. "People might naturally wonder why you saw fit to call a press conference over the demise of a total stranger. And *then* you'd have to tell them it was Pat Malone, and *then*—"

"Was it?" asked Jay Omega.

"What?"

"Was the dead man really Pat Malone? Can anyone swear to that?"

The Lanthanides looked at each other. "Well, after thirty years. . ." said Angela hesitantly.

"He was still pale," George offered. "And six feet tall."

"I thought Pat looked like a frog in the old days," said Barbara Conyers. "Sort of saucer-eyed, you know, and loose-lipped. But we've all changed so much. I wouldn't have known any of you on sight."

"It hardly matters," said Erik Giles, taking a sip of his wine. "He knew things about us that no one else could have known."

"He enjoyed it, too!" said Woodard indignantly. "He was going to make us all look like fools again. Just like he did to everyone in *The Last Fandango!*"

Ruben Mistral looked from Jay Omega to the laptop computer still set up on the table, and back again. "What are you getting at?" he asked.

"I'm trying to help you people settle this, before we all become suspects for the local police," said Jay. "And I think George Woodard made a key point just now. The man who died was going to make fools of you all by telling things that you didn't want made public. I think someone murdered him to prevent that. So, if we knew what the secrets were, it might help us guess who killed him."

Erik Giles smiled gently. "You needn't do all this on my account, Jay," he said. "I know I invited the both of you here, but you needn't feel responsible for me. We're not such old fogies that we can't take care of ourselves."

"It's the man who died that concerns me. One of your little secrets caused it."

Angela Arbroath shook her head. "The least important secret might have been the one he was killed over. How could you tell?"

Jim Conyers looked amused. "You're not suggesting that we confide in *you*, are you? If we didn't trust one of our own, why should we let you hear our secrets? Assuming, of course, that there are any."

"Well," said Jay Omega, shrugging. "I thought you might want to see the murderer punished. Or at least stopped from killing again. Especially since he killed a total stranger."

Angela stared. "What are you saying?"

He spoke slowly and carefully. "That man was no more Pat Malone than I am." He waited for the exclamations of shock and disbelief to subside before he continued. "The man's driver's license said that he was Richard Spivey, from a little town near Raleigh, North Carolina. And I believe that to be true."

"Richard Spivey!" cried George Woodard.

"Do you know him, George?" asked Erik Giles.

"I'd never seen him, but he'd been subscribing to

Alluvial for years. Richard Spivey from North Carolina. He didn't write very often, though. He *never* discussed the Lanthanides, or claimed to be one of us."

"What address was used?"

Woodard shrugged. "A post office box, I think."

"How do you know he wasn't Pat Malone?" Angela demanded.

Jay pointed to the computer. "Because I asked." He told them about the call to Ethel Malone, and about the man in Mississippi who had found the obituary. "I think Pat Malone died a long time ago, and somebody decided to take his place. True, he had information that only one of the Lanthanides would know. Where would he get it? I thought the fact that he was on Elavil was an indication. *And* he was from North Carolina."

"Curtis!" cried George Woodard. "Curtis was in a mental institution in North Carolina."

"And Elavil is a drug used in psychiatric cases," whispered Angela. "Are you saying that this man was only *pretending* to be Pat Malone?"

"I don't know," said Jay sadly. "I think he may have actually believed it by now. He and Curtis Phillips were both patients in a psychiatric facility outside Raleigh. I know, because I called and asked. I'm pretty sure that he had heard Curtis Phillips talk about the Lanthanides for years and years until it actually became real to him. He remembered it as an experience, the way you visualize a movie you have seen, or a particularly vivid novel."

"But he didn't even know us!" Erik Giles protested. "Why would he want to embarrass us?"

"Because that's what Pat Malone would have done," said Marion.

Woodard laughed bitterly. "Another damned fan hoax!"

"It was very convincing," said Jim Conyers. "But I must agree with our host here that we have an obligation both morally and legally to provide any information that we can."

No one spoke. Brendan Surn seemed to have forgotten that they were there. The others glanced at each other nervously.

"If no one wants to confide in us, we could make some guesses," said Jay. "For example, there are sexual goings-on that one might rather forget three decades after the fact." He held up a folded slip of paper. "I have Jasmine Holt's phone number here."

In fact, he had a blank piece of paper, but he counted on the fact that no one would ask to see it, and the bluff worked.

"That business about my wife being promiscuous was totally exaggerated," said Woodard. "We were both believers in free love back then, and I believe she had sexual relations with a good many members of fandom. It was a philosophical statement. I see no reason to be embarrassed by it." Beads of sweat made his skin glow like damp cheese. He pushed a greasy forelock away from his eyes. "Of course, she's not at all like that now."

"Your kids might be less tolerant, though, George," said Jim Conyers. "Mine sure were." He sighed and glanced at his wife. "I guess I'd better tell you about this before you call Jazzy."

"Jim!" said Ruben Mistral warningly.

"The statute of limitations passed long ago, Bunzie," said Jim Conyers. "I checked."

"It was at a con, and we had all had too much to drink," said Mistral. "And we—I wouldn't call it rape, would you, Jim? We didn't know she was underage."

"You guys raped Jasmine Holt?" The question was out of Lorien's mouth before she could think better of it. "Sorry," she muttered, and pretended to read the cable television guide.

The color drained from Barbara Conyers' face. "Oh, Jim," she whispered.

He looked away. "It was before we got engaged," he muttered.

"Come on, no big deal!" said Bunzie jovially. "That was a hundred years ago. By the time she married Curtis we were all pals again. And when she married Peter I gave the bride away."

"I doubt if Pat would have told that story," said Erik. "He was just as involved as we were."

Marion glared at the Lanthanides, looking considerably less sympathetic than she had moments before. "There are some literary secrets here, I think, that might have been worth revealing." She noted with satisfaction that the Lanthanides had begun to look uncomfortable. "Take Dale Dugger's story, for example. It isn't very expertly written, but the atmosphere is wonderful. It's about a Martian soldier coming home from the war to find that he has more in common with the enemy aliens than he does with the people back home. It sounded very familiar."

Lorien Williams blinked in confusion. "But—that

scene you described is famous! It's in Brendan's book *The Galactic Watchfires*. That's the chapter when Tarn-yan returns to Qar."

Mistral shrugged. "So what? We lived in each other's pockets in those days. Who's to say that Dale didn't write the scene after hearing Brendan tell the story?"

"And Curtis Phillips wrote about a mad wizard who has sex with a demon. Both those guys were fairly recognizable, too." Marion looked down at her hands, so as not to look at any of the Lanthanides.

"Curtis was crazy," said Erik Giles.

"Yes," spluttered George Woodard. "But I remember he told me—"

"Shut up, George!" said Mistral.

"And you're going to let them publish this anthology?" Jay marveled.

Mistral shrugged. "For a pile of money. We'll write prefaces to all the stories that will take the sting out. And we may do a little judicious editing."

Still blushing, Marion continued. "Why doesn't Peter Deddingfield have a story in the time capsule?"

The Lanthanides looked at each other, but no one spoke.

"Everybody else is there. Angela, Pat, Dale, Curtis, George, Erik, Reuben Bundshaft, Jim Conyers, and one by C. A. Stormcock. But you always said that you were C. A. Stormcock, Erik!"

He raised his plastic glass to her in a mock toast. "So I was."

"But you aren't, Erik, are you?" she said, looking at the other Lanthanides for confirmation. "Don't bother to lie to me, folks. I read those stories. The Stormcock story is obviously by the guy who wrote *The Golden Gain*, and the story signed 'Erik Giles' is just as obviously written by the person who wrote the *Time Traveler Trilogy*."

Marion looked at the stricken face of her old friend, and then at Jay Omega. "Maybe we shouldn't discuss this in public," she murmured. "Maybe, Erik, you and I could just—"

He finished the contents of his glass and set it down. "It's all right," he said. "These people all know, my dear. They've known for more than thirty years. We just didn't think that it would ever matter much." He turned to the Lanthanides and smiled. "I can't think why I invited them to come with me. I suppose it serves me right for being a coward. I didn't want to face all this alone. Or perhaps subconsciously I was tired of the pretense."

Angela shook her head. "You couldn't know that Pat Malone would show up. And we would never have given you away, Stormy."

"So you're Peter Deddingfield?" said Jay.

"I was once. But I wasn't the important one. The fellow who married Jazzy, and who wrote all those wonderful books later on—I always think that *that* is the real Peter Deddingfield. I gave up the name when we both left the Fan Farm. When I knew that I did not want to become a professional writer."

"Buy why?" asked Marion. "If you had published as Stormcock, and he hadn't published anything. Had he?"

"No," said George Woodard. "People have always wondered why Pete Deddingfield's first published short story was so bad. It's because the 'old' Pete wrote it. Stormy, I mean."

"So Peter Deddingfield—the famous one— was really Erik Giles. Why switch names?" Marion persisted.

"Can't you guess, Dr. Farley?" asked the professor in a gently mocking tone. "Because my old friend had something that I wanted and he no longer valued. Erik Giles had a doctorate in English."

Marion stared. "You don't have a Ph.D.?"

"No. He didn't need one to be a writer of science fiction, which he had both the talent and the desire to be. I, on the other hand, had written one book that other people liked far more than I did. I was tired of it all: the puerile jokes, the posturing, the financial uncertainty. What I wanted more than anything was a nice soft job on a college campus, where I could teach my classes and be left alone with my dignity." He smiled, remembering. "So Erik Giles said to me, 'Take the damned degree. We'll swap names, and we'll both be happy. Swear the Lanthanides to secrecy, and who'll ever know?' "

"But you taught all those classes!" Marion protested. "You went to conferences!"

"I didn't write very many journal articles," he reminded her. "Tenure was easier twenty years ago. As for the rest of it, impersonating an English professor isn't very difficult. I have a knack for being pretentious."

"But you could have got a degree of your own," said Marion.

"Yes, but by the time I could afford to, I was already employed as Erik Giles, and there seemed little likelihood of ever being caught. By then, I couldn't risk being exposed as a fraud. No university would have hired me after that, regardless of my credentials."

"What about your families?" asked Jay.

"Mine died when I was in my teens, and Erik's mother passed away while we were living in Wall Hollow. It was easy to lose touch with old friends back in Richmond. And as time went on, there were fewer and fewer people who might have known."

"Except Pat Malone," said Jay.

"Yes. When he came back, I knew that he wouldn't keep the old secret. He would revel in exposing the deception. It wouldn't have mattered for my old friend, who died rich and famous. But I enjoy my job at the university, and I wanted my pension in a few years' time."

Angela Arbroath clasped her arms against her body as if she were suddenly very cold. "Oh, Stormy," she whispered. "Did you kill him just for that?"

He considered the question. "I'm not sure," he said at last. "It seemed the most pressing reason at the time. But I think the real reason was that I was so damned disappointed that he wasn't dead I couldn't stand it! I went to his room to reason with him, but I took the medicine with me, so perhaps even then I knew. . . . Anyhow, it's a better world without Pat Malone in it." He looked at Jay Omega. "I suppose the autopsy gave it away?"

"The MAO inhibitor," said Jay. "I knew that it's prescribed for hypertension. If you mix it with Malone's—er, Spivey's—Elavil, it lowers the blood pressure too much, and causes a coma, and then death."

"Yes, I suppose I was lucky that he was taking his own medication, and that he was old. Otherwise he might have survived to enjoy my disgrace. He'd have liked that."

Jim Conyers interrupted. "You don't have to say anything else, Stormy! You need an attorney. I'll be happy to represent you. When the police get here—"

The once and future Erik Giles waved him away. "It doesn't matter, Jim," he said quietly. "The other thing you must not do with an MAO inhibitor is take alcohol. And I've just about finished that whole bottle of wine by myself. I'll be dead by morning." He swayed slightly as he stood up and tottered toward the door. "Now, if you'll excuse me, I will go gently into that good night."

He could see himself
in six months, afloat on the refilled Watauga
where the drowned swim forever. . . .

—DON JOHNSON
Watauga Drawdown

CHAPTER 14

JAY OMEGA WATCHED the sun rise over the brown
wasteland of Breedlove Lake. Beside him in equal
silence sat Marion Farley.

Erik Giles (they still thought of him that way)
had not gone particularly gently into that good
night, as he had wished. The roomful of witnesses to
his prospective suicide had been impelled to call the
police, or, attorney Jim Conyers warned, they might
be considered accessories, since suicide is still a
crime. By the time a rescue squad arrived from New
Wall Hollow, it was too late. The combination of
alcohol and medication had done its work irre-
versibly, and if Erik Giles had not gone peacefully
and with dignity, he had nonetheless gone, despite
the application of respirators, injections, and the
defibrillator.

When it was over, Jim Conyers talked to the offi-
cers in charge of the case and convinced them that
there was no point in wasting county money on a
murder case when the perpetrator was already
dead. They agreed that for official purposes, their
report would read that both Richard Spivey and
Erik Giles had died of heart conditions in unrelated

265

circumstances. The press would not be told otherwise. No mention of Pat Malone was contained in
any summary of the weekend's events.

"I said I'd defend Stormy, and I did," Conyers told
the others. "There will be no scandal attached to his
death. It was the only defense he wanted."

Marion leafed through the time-capsule manuscripts for the hundredth time. "Did you know it
was Erik all along?" she asked Jay.

"No. After we learned that an MAO inhibitor had
been used, I knew that the killer would be on medication, but that didn't exclude any of them, really. I
thought it might be Brendan Surn because he is a
bit unbalanced."

Marion gave him a faint smile. "Pretending to be
somebody else," she mused. "The mental illness of
fandom. I did it myself once, you know."

Jay looked startled. "Did you?"

She nodded dreamily. "Just for one night. It was
back when I was in college. I got a blind date with
some guy whose parents were stationed in the
Philippines with Voice of America. All he could do
was moan about how homesick he was. So to make
him happy, I pretended to be Petrice Jones. She was
my best friend in high school, and she had lived in
the Philippines until her sophomore year. After
three years of listening to Petrice, I knew all her
classmates by name, her old teachers—everything!
The guy had a wonderful evening talking about old
times with 'Petrice.' And I took care never to see
him again."

"You meant well. I'm not sure Richard Spivey
did."

"No. But I think Pat Malone would have been pleased. I can imagine him in some smoke-filled hereafter enjoying the sensation of his unscheduled return. It almost makes me believe in demonic possession."

"Are you going to tell the university about Erik's impersonation?"

Marion sighed. "I've been going over it in my mind for hours. But I always come to the same conclusion: no. It seems to me that it doesn't matter what name Erik used during his adolescence. He was the professor everyone liked and respected, and he wouldn't want to lose that in death. Most of our colleagues have never heard of an S-F writer named Deddingfield, anyway. Why spoil his memory? He was a good teacher."

"That's what I thought," said Jay. "Let him be remembered as the professor. He wanted out of fandom badly enough to kill for it. What's one more secret among the Lanthanides?"

The literary auction for the Lanthanides time capsule took place as scheduled at ten o'clock Sunday morning in the Holiday Inn in Johnson City. Sarah Ashley accepted the sealed bids and promised to reconvene the group at eleven to announce the winner to the press.

Enzio O'Malley was having brunch with Lily Warren on his company's American Express card. "Well," said Lily, toying with her eggs Benedict. "Do you think you got the anthology?"

O'Malley shrugged. "I doubt it," he said, stifling a yawn. "How about you?"

Lily shook her head. "Fifty K was as high as I could go without making a phone call. After reading the manuscripts, I decided not to make it."

"It'll go high. Those maniacs on Fifth Avenue would pay two grand for a cheeseburger. There's no telling what they'll bid to get this."

"Too bad," said Lily. "Since your company has Surn's back list, I know how much you wanted to acquire this."

"I got a budget," said O'Malley. "If I paid a million for this wad, and it bombed, I'd find myself editing role-playing games in Wisconsin."

"I thought you said that if they publicized this well, it would sell automatically."

"Theoretically, yes," said O'Malley. "But I wouldn't want to bet my career on it. I'm a schemer, not a gambler."

"And are you planning any schemes right now?" asked Lily, smiling.

"It's already done." He yawned again. "That's why I'm so tired. I got up at six A.M. this morning to call London. And I got my book deal." He grinned as he speared another pancake. "So while some checkbook publishers spend a mint publicizing the Lanthanides to sell their crummy anthology, my company brings out a kiss-and-tell book by the celebrated S-F critic—"

"Jasmine Holt!" cried Lily. "My God! She was married to two or three of them, wasn't she?"

"Yep. And she hasn't mellowed any with age, either," said O'Malley cheerfully. "Dirty laundry! That's what people want to read. Who cares what a bunch of postadolescent nerds actually wrote, for chrissake?"

"But they're writers," said Lily. "I thought they had fans."

O'Malley looked at her. "Would you want to bet a million dollars and your job title that there are enough S-F fans out there to buy fifty thousand copies of the over-the-hill gang's juvenilia in hardcover?"

"I guess not," murmured Lily.

"Exactly. I got the Holt memoir for twenty-five K. And we won't have to pay that much to the person who really writes it, either." He flashed her a feral smile. "Literary judgment, Lily! That's what it's all about."

Ruben Mistral was smiling as he put down the phone. The Lanthanides had gathered in the conference room for a catered brunch while they waited for Sarah Ashley to report the results of the auction. "It's over," he announced to the others. "The anthology is sold."

"What's the deal?" asked Woodard eagerly.

"One point two million dollars. It's a hard/soft deal, world rights, fifty/fifty on screen rights."

"What does that mean exactly?" asked Angela.

"And how soon do we get it?" Woodard again.

Mistral smiled at their eagerness. "Sarah will explain the business angles to anyone who is interested. As for the money, you'll get some of it in a few weeks, but don't go on a spending spree. You won't believe the tax bite!"

Jim Conyers stood up. "I guess that's it, then. The reunion has accomplished its goal. We're all free to go, by the way. There will be no further investigation on the two deaths."

"Understood," said Mistral. "And we're all sworn to secrecy. Right, guys?"

"It doesn't feel right to leave it like this," said Angela.

"Not to worry," said Mistral. "We'll do a tribute to Stormy in the anthology. First-class stuff."

Brendan Surn spoke up. "It reminds me of our trip to Worldcon all those years ago. Remember then? We all worked and planned, and we didn't make it out of this valley. Finally, though, one by one, each of us did make it out. Some of us became famous and well off, but we always missed what we had here. Never quite found that anywhere else. And now we all come back for the big reunion and we find that we can't get back in. Not really." He looked out at the red clay scar between wooded hills. "We couldn't get back."

"Yeah, sure, Brendan," said Ruben Mistral. "Can't go home again, right? Well, people, I got a plane to catch." He shook hands with Conyers, hugged Angela, and headed for the door.

George Woodard hurried to catch up with him. "Listen, can I talk to you for a minute?"

Mistral tried to glance at his watch without being too obvious about it. "Sure, George," he said. "Another business question?"

"No. I have a favor to ask," said George, looking nervously about. "You see, in western Maryland we have a little science fiction convention every September. It's called Mason/Dixiecon. We have a few panel discussions, a little art show. We show old movies. You'd really like it, Bunzie. And I was wondering . . ." He took a deep breath. "Would you consider being our guest of honor this year?"

Ruben Mistral winced at the thought of spending an entire weekend in a dreary burg in Maryland, signing autographs and telling high school kids how to make it in Hollywood. But before he could plead a prior commitment, his mouth opened, and he could hear Bunzie saying, "Sure, George. I'd like that. Count me in."

They walked out together, with Woodard prattling happily about *Star Trek* blooper reels and Fifties starlets.

Lorien Williams was packing Brendan's belongings in his old leather suitcase while he stood at the window looking out on the barren shore.

"I heard the drawdown is ending today," she said to him. "The hotel clerk said that the dam is repaired, so next week they'll be letting the lake fill up again."

He did not seem to have heard her. After a moment, she shrugged and went on packing. He was much better today; more alert and in good spirits. She wondered if the time change had bothered him. It was a pity to put him through it again so quickly, but at least she'd know what to expect when they got back to California. She'd have to field all the phone calls until Thursday at least. She looked longingly at the new Bob Cameron paperbacks she had bought to read on the trip. She still hadn't got around to them. Too bad. Bob Cameron was a really great author. She loved his futuristic stories. Lorien sighed and looked back at Brendan.

Someone knocked at the door. Lorien waited a moment to see if Brendan would respond, but he seemed not to have heard. She decided to answer it.

"I'm getting ready to go," said Angela Arbroath, setting her suitcase inside the door. "I thought I'd just stop in and say goodbye." She was dressed in a shapeless brown dress for traveling, and her hair was pulled into an unattractive bun: the invisible woman.

Brendan Surn turned away from the window. "Hello, Beanpole!" he called out. "Good to see you!"

Angela smiled at the look of surprise on Lorien's face. "He means me, all right," she told the girl. "You should have seen me back in '54."

"You're better today, aren't you?" she said to Brendan Surn. She sat down on the bed beside him, reaching up to brush a lock of silver hair away from his face. "You look better this morning."

He sighed. "It comes and goes, Angie. It's like a sea mist. Sometimes my mind can't see a foot ahead in any direction, and at other times it's as clear as it ever was. I just take my pills and hope."

Angela took a deep breath. "Listen, Brendan," she said briskly. "I hear you've got a big fancy house in California, and I have to tell you, I have no interest in even visiting anyplace like that. But I tell you what: I do have the prettiest little white cottage in Mississippi that you ever saw. I have a herb garden, and cats, and the warmest, sunniest kitchen in the world. And I have a guest room."

He nodded, beginning a smile.

"Brendan, nobody's promising anything right now, but would you like to come and stay with me for a while, and see if you like it? I think maybe Lorien has places of her own to go."

Brendan Surn looked down at her with his wisest, gentlest smile. "Yes, Angela," he said. "I'd like to sit in a garden now. I've seen what there is in the sea. Can I come today?"

Angela motioned for Lorien to come over. "Let's talk it over, Brendan," she said. "All three of us. We have all the time there is."

Jay and Marion were carrying their bags out of the lodge when they met Jim Conyers. He slung a suitcase into the back of his station wagon and followed them to their car.

"Is it over?" asked Marion. Her face was still strained and swollen-eyed.

"Yes," said Conyers. "The police are calling off the investigation on both deaths, and the auction went as planned. A little over a million, Bunzie said."

"I'm sorry about the way it turned out," said Jay Omega. "I was trying to help."

The lawyer nodded. "You were right. A murder investigation wouldn't have made things any better. And I think that when Stormy had found out that it wasn't Pat, it would have ended just the way it did."

"Brendan Surn was the only one who didn't tell lies," mused Marion. "Remember, he kept saying that Pete wasn't dead. We thought he was just senile."

"I wish it could have been a better reunion for you," said Jay.

Jim Conyers looked out at the dead lake. "It was the right reunion," he said at last. "Bickering, posturing, arrogance, and occasional lapses of genuine affection. They were my best friends, God help me." He smiled. "They were the best friends I ever had."

In the office of a small print shop in Cato, Mississippi, an elderly man was reading *People* magazine. He was sitting with his feet propped up on the old oak desk, a few inches away from a computer screen glowing green in the shadows beyond his reading lamp. His black-framed glasses slipped down on his sloping nose, revealing bulging eyes that made him faintly resemble a frog. The top of his head was a hairless dome, but the fringe that remained encircling his ears was still jet black, emphasizing the pallor of his wrinkled skin. He was six feet tall, hollow-cheeked and gaunt, and he possessed an expression of clever malevolence. He was reading about the retrieval of a time capsule in Wall Hollow, Tennessee.

Turning to the photograph of the assembled Lanthanides, mugging for posterity with a mud-caked pickle jar, the old man burst out laughing. "What a bunch of fuggheads!" he snorted, and turned to an article about a New Orleans jazz festival.

The message on the computer screen read: "THANK YOU FOR HELPING ME VERIFY THE DEATH OF PAT MALONE BY FINDING THAT OLD OBITUARY COLUMN IN THE LIBRARY. JAY OMEGA."

He glanced at it and laughed again. "Fuggheads."

Don't miss the first in the acclaimed Ballad series by

SHARYN McCRUMB

IF EVER I RETURN, PRETTY PEGGY-O

A *NEW YORK TIMES* NOTABLE BOOK

Long-gone friends and the casualties of war haunt Peggy Muryan, a folksinger hiding from her past. A threatening postcard and a mysterious disappearance force Peggy to turn to Sheriff Spencer Arrowood, who has skeletons in his own closet. Arrowood must come to terms with his own past as he tries to prevent Peggy from being murdered by hers.

IF EVER I RETURN, PRETTY PEGGY-O
by Sharyn McCrumb
Published by Ballantine Books.
Available in bookstores everywhere.

SICK OF SHADOWS

The very wealthy and eccentric Eileen Chandler is set to be married, but someone is willing to resort to murder to halt the impending nuptials. Eileen's beloved cousin, Elizabeth MacPherson, is on hand for the ceremony, and Elizabeth is not amused. No one in the wedding party is above suspicion when Elizabeth sets out to unmask the culprit.

LOVELY IN HER BONES

When the leader of her archaeological dig is murdered, forensic anthropologist Elizabeth MacPherson finds herself on the case. It takes a second mysterious death to start a cauldron of ideas bubbling in her head. And when she mixes a little modern know-how with some old-fashioned suspicions, Elizabeth comes up with a batch of answers that surprises even the experts.

HIGHLAND LADDIE GONE

Elizabeth MacPherson is having a rollicking good time at an annual Scottish festival when the loathed Colin Campbell is found murdered. Then a second murder silences everyone's bagpipes for good. Enter Elizabeth, who will use her insatiable curiosity to find the killer and let justice prevail.

PAYING THE PIPER

Elizabeth MacPherson is on an archaeological dig on a remote Scottish isle when several members of the team die under mysterious circumstances. Is the excavation cursed by the ancient dead, or is something—or someone—more modern responsible? With her own life on the line, Elizabeth is determined to unearth the answer.

THE WINDSOR KNOT

Elizabeth MacPherson has a rather hectic summer in front of her. Between finishing her doctoral thesis and planning her impending wedding, she must solve the case of a man who has died twice. And if she can accomplish all this, she might just get to have tea with Her Majesty the Queen!

MISSING SUSAN

The unsinkable Elizabeth MacPherson is on a tour of England's most famous murder sites with the cantankerous Rowan Rover, the tour guide who has been paid to murder an unsuspecting woman. No would-be assassin needs Elizabeth on his tail. And she'll be there until the end of the tour or the completion of Rowan's mission, whichever comes first.

MacPherson's Lament

The chilling legacy of the Civil War shocks Elizabeth MacPherson when she ventures south to Danville, Virginia. Her brother Bill has gotten himself mixed up with some daughters of Confederate veterans—old ladies who'd asked him to sell an antebellum mansion but had something more sinister planned. To help him, Elizabeth has to uncover a Civil War secret that may be the key to the ugly truth.

And from Fawcett Books:

IF I'D KILLED HIM WHEN I MET HIM . . .

When forensic anthropologist Elizabeth MacPherson becomes the official P.I. for her brother Bill's fledgling law firm, she quickly takes on two complex cases. A perfect lawyer's wife for twenty years has shot her ex-husband and his beautiful late-model wife in cold blood. And Donna Jean Morgan is implicated in the death of her Bible-thumping bigamist husband. Elizabeth's expertise, including her special knowledge of poisons, leads her to the most challenging case of her career.

SHARYN McCRUMB